Mystic Thunder

A Mystic Waters Novel

JC Wardon

Cavanaugh Sisters Trilogy, Book One

Mystic Waters Books, JC Wardon
Tennessee, USA

MYSTIC THUNDER
Copyright © 2016, JC Wardon
Trade Paperback ISBN: 978-1-944454-93-7

Editing by S.R. Paulsen, Kim Jacobs
Copyedit by Gilly Wright
Cover Design by Calliope-Designs.com

Original Digital Release, January 2014
Original Trade Paperback release March 2016

MYSTIC THUNDER

Three identical sisters...
Three individual mystical gifts...
And Three Thousand Years of warnings to never fall in love....

Millennia of tempestuous ancestral history forewarn Rayne Cavanaugh to hide her ability to communicate with ghosts. But—

When the nephew of the man she just can't resist goes missing in the mountains of Mystic Waters, West Virginia, she must decide between self-preservation and love.

PROLOGUE

Blood chilled his veins as his mother's screams of terror and agony ripped the air. Sweat poured from his hairline, a stream that ran along his temple and down his face, his neck, his chest and back. His armpits were drenched, as were his boxers and jeans, but they were wet with pee and he feared more, something that would have embarrassed him under any other circumstances.

Witnessing the murder of his father when the peppering of bullets shattered the large dining room window only moments before had thrown a family celebration into chaos and his otherwise normal life into horror. Too much soda—a rare occurrence given his health conscious mother—and the full bladder that resulted, had Gavin trotting toward the bathroom right before it had all started. Those few seconds away from the dining room table were the only things that kept him from being injured or dead from the spray of bullets, too.

He'd never made it to the bathroom but had pivoted around when his mom's screams pierced his eardrums. Gavin saw her half drag her lower body as she attempted to crawl from her overturned chair to his dad's side where she tried desperately to revive him. Her terrified eyes turned to him only once to tell him to hide.

He froze at first and then ran forward to try to help, but she'd slapped him hard and told him to get out before he got shot too and that they had to hide quickly because someone was trying to break in the front door.

Fear had propelled him into his room and into his closet, with the expectation that his mother would follow.

But the crash of wood splintering and his mother's more terrified screams had put that hope to rest, and now indecision warred with self-preservation and had for so long he felt ashamed.

The house was sweltering as the fireplace had been running wide open in his dad's attempt to keep the electric bill down, which made the closet stuffy to the point of smothering, though that might have been caused by his hyperventilating breaths.

When he couldn't stand the screams any longer, Gavin threw open the door with the intention of making a quick dash to help her. But his legs failed to work right, so he lumbered across his room and through his door just in time to see a man pull the trigger of a gun held only inches from his mother's head. As skull and brain-matter sprayed out the other side of her skull he fell to his knees hard to stare at her prone body as blood poured onto the floor.

Disbelief and revulsion slapped him backwards drawing the attention of his parent's killer. Vomit spouted from his mouth as the heavyset man turned toward him and raised the gun. The evil gleam in the monster's lifeless eyes loosened his bowels again.

A shout from outside and glaring blue and red lights coming through the broken window accompanied by blaring sirens that deafened his own screams did nothing to deter the advance of the killer. Gavin couldn't move, could do nothing but wait for the impact of a bullet ripping through his body. But those now rushing the house apparently spooked the assassin as he lowered the gun, spouted a threat, and fled through the back door.

The chaos that followed did nothing to alleviate the shock, the overwhelming grief, the surreal funeral, and finally relocation to his uncle's cabin after he refused to stay with anyone else. It had all been accomplished with him drowning in a dreamlike state that kept him going. He'd been questioned, he'd been hospitalized, he'd been medicated, and he'd been sent back to school after they all thought it would be best for him to try to resume a normal life.

But they hadn't known, and he'd dared not tell, normal was over for him. The very man they were looking for had made it clear to open his mouth would be a death warrant and worse.

The greasy-haired fat man was a monster who came back night after night, in nightmares so real Gavin knew he would never escape them. And he feared, not death, because it would have ended his nightmares, but the threat being carried out while he was awake.

Chapter One

The continuous glare, the blinding flashes of a dozen or more cameras, and the multiple questions being shouted at her, magnified the pain of Rayne Cavanaugh's ever-increasing migraine. She backed away hoping to escape the media circus, but those who were there to capture the news as it was happening were clearly not about to let her slip away.

She looked to her left, and then to her right, as the reporters flanked her on every side. She tried getting the attention of one of the many police officers present, hoping someone would come to her rescue, but they were too busy talking to each other and the child's mother, to look her way. She finally accepted she had no choice but to make a statement, though it was the last thing she wanted to do.

Rayne held up her hands, and the reporters immediately quieted, though the accompanying cameramen were still too close for comfort. She swallowed what felt like a shell-encased boiled egg before opening her mouth to speak. "Please. This isn't about me. This is about a tragic end to a child's life."

"How did you know where the body was?"

"Do the police call you often to help solve cases like this?"

"Why haven't we heard of you before now?"

More questions were thrown at her as the mass of reporters held their mics in her face. Rayne caught the gaze of a man she'd seen on the local news channel, and wondered why she had ever thought him a good reporter, as he jostled with another for the position closest to her.

Though she wanted to lie, there was no way around telling the truth, as the mother of the victim had already told everyone Rayne talked with her dead child, who'd revealed not only the killer, but the location of his decaying body as well. Once the police followed up on the mother's information and found it completely accurate, right down to the type of bag he was incased in, they contacted her and asked that she meet them at the site. As they hadn't given her any other choice, she'd done just that, not knowing the media had been called too.

"I—" Her heart pounding painfully. Rayne couldn't make herself say the words. The reporters' hungry eyes made her feel as if she was about to be consumed by a pack of wild dogs. She could almost see them drooling with anticipation, as they moved in closer. She took a step back and bumped into a solid form so she spun around, only to find the man she'd been dating for the past seven months glaring at her.

"Yeah, Rayne, just how *did* you know where the body was?" Jamison Fray demanded, his cheeks flushed, his eyes angry.

Desperation had her reaching out to him, but Jamison shuffled back quickly as if she'd suddenly developed the plague. Hurt, but not surprised, Rayne ignored them all and pushed past the reporter and cameraman to her left, heading toward her car. As far as she was concerned, she was finished with this ordeal, but an officer whose help she would have welcomed seconds before broke from the group talking to the mother of the victim and hurried to intercept her. When he blocked her from moving forward, she stopped and balled her fists.

"I'm sorry Ms. Cavanaugh, but we still need more information from you."

Rayne took several cleansing breaths as the throng of reporters encircled them. She ignored everyone except the officer. "You have my number," she said as quietly as possible. "You can contact me. I have an appointment right now."

The officer looked at her and then those around them, as he slowly nodded. "Of course. I'll be in touch this afternoon."

Relieved, Rayne watched as he commanded the reporters to let her pass. Grateful, she quickly made her way to the car without looking back to see if anyone followed. Once inside she started the engine and threw the car into drive, only looking then to see if Jamison was concerned enough to follow. Since he was nowhere in sight she lifted her foot from the brake pedal and began moving forward at a snail's pace. Peripheral vision alerted her that the reporters were no longer restrained and were once again approaching quickly, but she ignored them, hoping she didn't have to run anyone down to escape.

Her head pounding, Rayne slowly maneuvered around police cruisers, unmarked police cars, television news vans, and the other emergency service vehicles whose owners had come to be a part of the fray. Concentrating on her exodus, it took a moment for her to realize moisture was running from her nose. She reached up and touched the area between her nose and upper lip and then looked down at blood-covered fingers before reaching for the box of tissues she always kept on hand both in her car and at home.

As she pinched her nose and breathed through her mouth, Rayne broke free of the tangle of cars and sped up to head toward the highway and home. Tears formed from both the pain in her skull and the realization that she was forever trapped by genetics that had finally exposed her to the world, and, not unexpectedly, ended what she'd hoped was a promising relationship.

Rayne wanted to scream out her anger and frustration. She wanted to crash into something and shatter it to smithereens. After years of extreme caution, one persistent child ghost succeeded in making her break the first and most important rule her family lived by. She had failed to keep the secret that safeguarded them all. And she had to hurry home to let them know before they heard about it from someone else or saw it on the news.

Her sisters would be even more disappointed in her

now than they had been before. It was irritating to realize their opinions mattered as much as they did, though she'd never let on that she noticed. Of course, Haven was too kind to say anything. But Destiny had made it clear time and again she thought very little of Rayne's years of post-graduate studies into ancient languages and civilizations. She also felt it was a mammoth waste of time for Rayne to translate and chronicle their family's long history and, even more so, to catalogue their vast possessions both here and abroad.

The exit ramp leading to the highway was as congested as it always was this time of day, so Rayne ignored that route and kept on driving, ending up in the lower income side of the city few tourists ever saw. Los Angeles, the city of Angels, was not so angelic here.

Disreputable business establishments gave way to weathered homes with shabby yards, some with garbage littering streets and lawns, and many with rusting cars sitting atop concrete blocks. It wasn't a part of the city she knew well, so she kept on driving and continued wiping at her nose until the leather seat on the other side of the console was filled with bloody tissues.

Rayne kept her speed down and her eyes on the residential road as she reached for another tissue, only to feel the box was empty. She pinched her nose with her finger and thumb, and was nearly gasping for breath as she glanced over to see if there was a used one that wasn't too saturated. When she looked back up her breath hitched as an image jumped in front of the car.

Slamming on the breaks flung the used tissues, the empty box, and her purse from the passenger seat onto the floorboard. Her heart beating wildly, Rayne stared at the large ghost before her as its glittering essence mingling with the heat vapors radiating from the hood of her car. Panic turned to anger and finally to despair as she recognized the pesky ghost who made a habit of harassing her.

Having reached her limit, tears of fury poured from Rayne's eyes while blood backed up behind her finger and thumb. She released her nostrils and gave up trying to save the blouse and slacks she'd purchased the day before. As both forms of liquid mingled and dripped from her face, she threw the car into gear and drove straight through Mr. Watson's ghost, hoping if she'd insulted him enough he would leave her alone.

Because she'd been forced to take the scenic route, it was almost an hour and a half later before she made it to their massive home. The boxy, mostly glass and steel modern structure owned by her family was a welcome sight, and Rayne couldn't wait to get to the top floor occupied by her and her sisters.

Since her mother and her mother's identical sisters had purchased the entire property from a well-known movie star, the current generation needed only the four thousand square feet of rooms they routinely occupied. The three lower floors were used for storage, to house the aunts whenever they decided to take a break from their travels around the world, and to park a museum-worthy collection of expensive cars.

Though she had been deep into categorizing the family treasures when the policeman first called her to meet them at the recovery scene, she knew she wouldn't be able to return to the third floor today to continue the job. Nausea built as did the headache, and all she wanted was some pain medication and a long nap between the cool sheets covering her bed.

As she pulled into the parking garage, Rayne noticed that only one other car was missing. She groaned, knowing Destiny would be the one home, as Haven was at work.

Her oldest sister was the last person she wanted to confess to about anything. Destiny had neither Haven's positive attitude nor her even temper. Resigned to dealing with anger and criticism, Rayne left the car and rode the elevator to the top floor. As the doors opened she took a step inside and stopped when Destiny rose from the couch to look in her direction.

"Oh my God! What have you done?"

Rayne winced at her sister's raised voice and then realized Destiny was looking at her with horror rather than anger. She glanced down and understood why when she saw the red stains covering a good portion of the new blouse. Her face probably looked as bad.

"I have to tell you. But I need to sit down. And I need my medication. Please."

Rayne crossed the room and fell onto the large faux leather couch her sister Haven had insisted...no, *relentlessly insisted,* she buy, laid her head back against the cold, butter soft cushions she was grudgingly coming to love, and closed her eyes.

"Here, take these."

Rayne opened her eyes at the sound of Destiny's whisper. She looked up at her physically identical sister and nodded, then struggled to sit up. She took the migraine medication, popped it into her mouth, and then chased it with the bottled water Destiny deemed clean enough to drink.

Destiny made a habit of *deeming* a lot of things.

Calling her sister a *little* pushy was an understatement. Destiny treated her as if she couldn't think for herself; offering suggestions when none were needed, giving gentle, oh-so-ladylike nudges, or sometimes not-so-subtle nudges, to steer Rayne in certain directions when she was fully capable of forging her own path. She was less pushy with Haven, but that was only because Haven smiled at her then ignored her.

It was tiresome to be treated like a baby when in fact they were all the same age. She couldn't help that she was the youngest of the three by seven, and four minutes respectively. Just like she couldn't help that the dead wanted to communicate with the living and used her to get their messages across. No matter what it cost her in physical pain.

"It's getting worse, isn't it?"

Rayne nodded, knowing the day's disastrous situation, on top of the horrendous headache, was causing her to have ungrateful thoughts. The truth was she loved both her sisters, and though Destiny did try to interfere in her life, she knew it was because she loved her, too.

As she waited for the pill to take effect, Rayne watched her sibling slide onto an overly large round chair. Destiny moved with the grace of a butterfly landing gently on a rosebud, whereas she had always been closer to a bull in a china shop—with cleats.

"Your nose is bleeding, again." Stark concern put tiny lines at the corners of Destiny's eyes as she reached for the tissue box at her side.

Reflexively, Rayne's fingers moved to just above her lip, then she pulled them away to take the tissues. "I'm a mess."

"I've never seen you bleed this much. You need to tell Haven."

Rayne pulled the tissue away and shook her head. She knew it was only concern on her sister's part, but *really*, she didn't need all this mothering. Besides.... "She can't help. You know that. Telling her it's happening this much will only make her feel worse than she already does for not being able to heal me."

A frown flattened Destiny's full lips. "It isn't fair. We can help others. But we can't help each other. I've never understood that."

Rayne nodded. The three sisters had never been able to use their hereditary gifts on each other. It had always been that way as far as they knew. According to the Cavanaugh diaries, once known as the Royal Books of Kavanaugh and passed down for thousands of years, the gifted women in the family could only use their gifts on those without a blood connection.

Her own ability to contact the deceased was an aggravating burden she'd handled and hidden for so long. But now the secret was out, it would be worse. She closed her eyes, hoping the medication would kick in quickly, knowing she couldn't stand the confrontation to come while in so much pain. The ringing of her cell phone startled her and kicked her pain up a notch.

"Here, let me get that for you."

As sluggish as the medication was making her, Rayne was unable to move fast enough to stop Destiny from reaching over to grab her phone. Rayne wanted to protest, afraid it might be the police officer she'd talked to earlier, but Destiny had the phone to her ear before Rayne could form the word *stop*.

"Hey Sis.

"Yes, you did call her. But she's having a migraine.

"Oh. No. I haven't. Wait."

With her headache easing as her brain floated on a cloud of medication, Rayne watched with dread as Destiny lifted the television's remote and pointed it at the screen. She switched it from the movie she'd been watching to the local news channel, and Rayne's stomach thudded in dread.

There she stood, surrounded by the reporters, looking as terrified as she'd felt at the time. She relived the questions that had been shot at her, and her own trembling responses. But what was most captivating was that she now saw Jamison's face as it had been before she'd turned around.

He hated her. The mouth that had once worshiped her with words and kisses was twisted. Eyes that had once looked at her adoringly, glared at the back of her head. When she backed into him and then turned around, everyone watching saw his revulsion. Tears filled her eyes as she watched herself flee, only to be stopped by the cop.

She knew Destiny was looking at her now, but she didn't have the strength or the guts to look back. Rayne waited for the words that would skin her alive, but Destiny surprised her by moving to her side.

Rayne's tears increased when her sister pulled her close and held her in a gentle hug. "I'm sorry. I never meant that to happen."

"I know. I'm sorry, too. That man is nothing more than a little boy wearing men's clothes. I can't believe he treated you like that. What was he doing there anyway?"

That Destiny hadn't asked what Rayne was doing there was the kindest thing her sister had ever done. She shrugged and pulled away, afraid she would get blood on Destiny's clothing too. "I don't know. He comes that way on his commute. Maybe he saw the circus and was being nosy. Or maybe he saw the car."

Destiny smiled gently. "It does stand out."

Rayne felt herself smile, too. "Yeah. But anyway, I'm sorry about this being a media event. I've never had anyone out me before. I make them promise. I always make them promise before I tell them anything."

Destiny nodded. "I know that, too. But people sometimes don't keep promises. And maybe this woman was so overcome she forgot. Regardless, what are you planning to do about it?"

Rayne shrugged, her eyes getting heavier by the minute. "I'm going to have to sleep because I can't think right now. But afterwards, I'll think of something." She struggled to rise then allowed Destiny to help her, all the way to her room. She didn't even protest, as she normally would have, when Destiny told her to undress while she turned down the bed. Seconds later she was between her cool sheets and drifting off. But before she let her mind go completely she opened her eyes and smiled at her sister. "Thank you."

Destiny tilted her head. "For what?"

Rayne sighed. "For not yelling at me about the news or about Jamison. I should have known better than to fall for him, but I had hoped the curse we live under wasn't really true. Maybe I have to accept, that even after three thousand years, nothing has changed for us Cavanaugh women. Just like the stories, we'll never find lasting love."

****.

Destiny left the room and quietly closed Rayne's door. She walked the long hallway back to the living room lost in thought. It bothered her that Rayne had expected her to be angry, though Destiny had to acknowledge she probably would have been if it hadn't been so obvious what an ordeal Rayne had endured.

The sound of the elevator's arrival had her hurrying the remaining distance to the living room and she arrived as Haven stepped from the platform. "That was fast."

Haven looked around. "I know. I was on my way when I called. Where is she?"

"Just put her to bed. She bled all over herself. Worse than I've ever seen. And she's a mess emotionally."

Haven sighed. "I bet she is. I couldn't believe it. I was in the break room on our floor and another nurse told me to look at the flat screen because she thought it was something that had been taped earlier, and she thought it was me. I couldn't even correct her. I was so shocked. And the look on Rayne's face.... I was afraid she was going to have a stroke."

"Her equivalent. She had to have lost at least a pint of blood. Her clothes are ruined. She got the bleeding to stop before she fell asleep, but it's dried all over her face and neck. I didn't have the heart to tell her how bad she looked and was afraid to wash it off once she was out. She needs to sleep this off before facing the consequences."

Haven walked around the island that separated the kitchen area from the open concept living space. "I need a drink. What about you?"

Since none of them drank alcohol on a regular basis, Destiny knew she was being offered bottled water. "Yes. Definitely.

"So how did you get out of work so quickly?"

Haven handed the bottle to Destiny before settling on the couch. "I told them I had a family emergency, and I guess I must have looked as panicked as I was, because my supervisor didn't even question me but told me to go. So I got my purse from my locker and hurried out of there."

"I'm glad you did. We have to figure out what to do. This thing could really get out of hand."

Haven looked at her for several seconds before speaking. "I think we have to let Rayne handle it."

Destiny shook her head. "I know you, and *she,* think I

boss you around too much. I don't mean to. But I feel like in this case we're all at risk. Even that nurse thinks you're the one who talks to ghosts. And I could have the same issue when one of my patients comes in for therapy. What do we do then? Tell them *no*, it's our identical sister who's the quack? Have you ever told anyone you work with that we're identical triplets? I haven't told anyone who comes to me."

Haven shrugged. "No. And I don't know what I'll say, but I'll have to say something. Every busybody at the hospital will be curious since this will spread like wildfire, but I still think Rayne has to choose how to handle this. It isn't our decision to make."

"I don't agree. This needs to be contained. And she isn't in shape to handle anything right now."

The ringing of Rayne's cell phone stopped them both as they turned to look where Destiny had laid it on the table. Destiny lifted it and looked at the screen. "It says LAPD."

"Don't answer it."

Destiny hesitated a second longer then pushed the touch screen twice; once to open the line, and once to put it on speaker. She ignored Haven's glare as she turned her attention to the caller. "Hello."

"Ms. Cavanaugh?"

Destiny hesitated again. "Yes?"

"This is Officer Brooks, we spoke earlier?"

"Yes."

"I needed to get additional information from you. I can come to your place, or you can come to the station. Which would be better?"

Haven violently shook her head and mouthed, *"No!"*

"I can come to you. It will take me about an hour. Is that okay?"

"That will be fine. I'll be here. Thank you."

"Bye." Destiny hit the red bar, closing the call.

"Are you out of your mind? Rayne will be furious!"

"No she won't, because she won't know. I'll handle

this and make it go away. Did you see her face when those reporters were questioning her? There is no way she can handle a police interrogation."

Though Haven opened her mouth to continue her protest, she shut it immediate. "You're right. Damn. She hates when you tell her what to do. She'll have a fit if this ever gets back to her."

Destiny tried to ignore the thrill of victory. It reminded her of the mean streak she hadn't ever understood, but couldn't deny existed within her. "Then we have to make sure it never does."

Haven sighed. "So what is your plan?"

Destiny smiled. "I'm going to read this officer and find out what I need to say to divert his attention, then, I'm going to feed him information that will put a stop to his questions."

"But what about the media? They already have the bone and will likely chew it to death."

Destiny nodded, more concerned about them than the officer. "I'll ask him to make a statement, if possible. Or I'll make one of my own. Either way, this has to die today."

Haven shook her head. "I don't know how you can make this go away that easily. You need to rethink this."

Destiny downed her water and rose to take the bottle to the recycling bin as she pondered her options. With a smile she returned to stand in front of Haven. "I'll tell him the woman misunderstood. That I, meaning Rayne, hadn't actually talked to her son, but that I'd overheard a conversation in a crowded bus, and brought the information to her just in case it meant something. After all, the case and that woman have been news for the past week."

"And when he asks you for a description of the men talking?"

"I'll tell them I couldn't see them, that there were too many people between me and them."

Haven shook her head again. "This is stupid. They won't buy that. You act like you can wave a magic wand

and make this go away. Life isn't that simple anymore. None of us inherited Mom's *gift*."

Destiny walked to the large wall of glass facing the Pacific Ocean. She looked out past the city below and watched the movements of the sparkling water and foaming waves, as was her habit when she needed to work out a problem. She turned back, forced to acknowledge Haven's concerns. "If only these damned *gifts* would be of use to *us*.

"Don't get me wrong. I know I'm the luckiest of the three of us. Unless I told, no one would be aware that I'm an *Intuit*. People can't tell that I can see what they think and feel, or that I read their auras all day long, but that doesn't mean it's easy on me. If I could turn it off and on at will, that would be one thing. But I can't. And it isn't easy walking around and seeing colors and knowing others' thoughts all the time. Sometimes I get sickened by how evil people are. The only peace I get is when I'm here. So it's a blessing that I can't read you and Rayne, or the aunts.

"But for you and Rayne, it's like you're always one second away from disaster. Like today. This was going to happen eventually because Rayne can't get ghosts to leave her alone until she does what they want. And you…. You can't touch anyone casually. You have to wear those awful gloves all day at work… I frankly don't know how you deal with it.

"As far as the police, I don't have any better ideas. Rayne isn't going to be able to handle this. Do *you* have a better idea?"

Haven joined her at the window, concern and sadness in her emerald eyes. She looked down at her hands. "No. But I'm going along with this with reservations. Rayne deserves a chance to clean this mess up, but *I know* it will cost her more than she can afford. If she doesn't find a way to get those migraines and nose bleeds under control, I'm afraid…I'm afraid for her. It makes me so angry that I can't touch anyone else without my hands healing them, but then I'm useless to her!"

"That's exactly what I'm talking about. It would be better if we were all just normal. At least then it wouldn't matter if we couldn't help her."

"Is that why you're always so angry?"

Destiny looked over at her sister, hurt by the words, but knowing they were justified. "I don't mean to be. And I don't know why I am. But I'm sorry I come across that way.

"Rayne was afraid I was going to yell at her because of what happened today."

Haven nodded. "So was I."

Destiny closed her eyes and had to tamp down the stirring of irritation that met with Haven's words. Sometimes she felt like neither sister liked her and their closeness left her standing on the outside. But she knew they didn't mean to exclude her, just as she knew their distrust of her mood swings was justified.

Haven wrapped her fingers around Destiny's wrist, causing her to open her eyes. "I'm sorry. I should have said something more supportive."

She looked torn, then released Destiny's arm before stepping back.

"There is something I have to tell you, too. Something that happened yesterday at the hospital.

"I wasn't going to because I thought you'd get angry at me, and yell, and I was already so upset I just couldn't stand having you angry at me...I was already so angry at myself. But I feel bad now, not saying anything."

Destiny took a deep breath, wondering how often her sisters kept things from her out of fear of her reaction. She had to make an effort to stop being so hard on them, and she promised herself that she would. "I'm sorry you felt you had to keep it from me. Please, tell me. Is it something else we need to handle?"

Haven shook her head. "No. It's handled. But I almost cost a man his job yesterday, and it scared me to death.

"You know I never take off the latex gloves unless I'm putting on a new pair, or my shift is over. It's a joke among the doctor's and other nurses, but I usually just laugh it off and tell them I'm such a germaphobe that I can't help it.

"But there was this little kid that broke his arm and the technician was taking X-rays. I wasn't even supposed to be there, but I was delivering a request for Doctor McMichael's on my way out of the hospital because my shift was over. When I stepped into the room, the kid was getting off the table before he was supposed to. The technician was behind the glass looking at the computer-generated picture of the X-ray he'd just taken. He glanced up to take the folder from me and saw that the kid was about to fall and yelled for me catch him. I reacted without thinking and ran to grab the little boy and put him back on the table."

Destiny's eyes filled. "My hands heated immediately and I knew what was happening. But I couldn't say anything so I ran out of there as quickly as possible. But when I went back to work this morning I'd heard that the technician was suspended pending the outcome of an investigation."

Destiny frowned. "Why?"

"Because he took more pictures after I left, and since the ones after I touched the kid were unlike the ones before I touched him, the technician kept taking more and more, until finally he'd used up thousands of dollars worth of resources, both in electricity, and the materials used to print out the pictures. Since the hospital can't justify charging the insurance company for such a large amount, it falls back on the technician. And the hospital is up in arms because the original pictures showed one thing and the later ones something different, and they can't explain that either."

Destiny grinned. "But the kid's arm is healed, right? That should mean something."

Haven sighed. "But it isn't. At least not like it should be. I don't know what happened, but instead of healing like it should have, it healed wrong. And they had to re-break it to set it right. But the worst thing is I think they are going to find a way to blame the technician for all of this."

Destiny studied her sister. "Your gift failed?"

Haven nodded. "I'm just sick about it. Maybe I should have held him longer once I touched him instead of running like I did. But it's never taken more than a touch for such a small wound before. I don't know what to think."

Destiny turned back to the vista that was often the only comfort she had in her lonely world. "That is scary. I've never known your gift to fail."

"It never has before. But I've hidden it and made sure I didn't use it for so long, maybe it's…rusty?"

A muffled clap of thunder drew their gazes to the sky. The floor to ceiling window of the large steel and glass home still displayed the city of Los Angeles and the ocean beyond for all it was worth, but the view that had been all they'd known since their first memory made Destiny feel unsettled now. As did the oddly colored, churning clouds building outside of the window. She turned to Haven to see if she noticed, but Haven was frowning down at her hands.

"I want to leave Los Angeles…."

Destiny and Haven turned at the same time. Rayne stood at the end of the hallway just inside of the living room looking as rumpled and disheveled as she ever had. The bottom half of her face was still streaked with dried blood and tears.

Though nearly imperceptible, Haven's sharp intake of breath was audible. "Sister…."

Destiny bit her bottom lip, and nodded. "I saw this coming." She held up her hand when Rayne's gaze flew to her face. But before she could speak, Destiny sighed heavily. "No, I didn't *see* it coming. I meant I can tell you aren't happy. I'm not sure any of us are. Things just feel wrong to me…I don't know how to explain it."

"An imbalance," Haven offered tentatively.

There was nothing to explain as far as Destiny was concerned. Her sister had hit the nail squarely on the head.

"Yes," Rayne said, advancing on them. "I haven't been happy, even before today. Being badgered by ghosts was bad enough. Approaching the people they wanted me to convey their message to was worse, but I've felt obligated to, as much as was safe. Now, after all this, and Jamison's reaction, I've decided I can't keep pretending doing this is okay. I want to go away for a while.

"If nothing else, I need a long break from my life."

Destiny's insides quivered at the thought of the three of them being separated, but one look at Rayne was enough to make her put her own feelings aside. "Take a vacation."

Haven nodded. "Yeah! Somewhere clean. Somewhere fresh. Somewhere where no one knows anything about you."

Though there was still pain bracketing her eyes, Rayne smiled at them both. "I want to, but... Go with me? Both of you."

"If only," Destiny sighed out the words wearily. "I've got three new bookings left this week on top of my regulars over the next month. Then I've got a pap that took months to get, though I'd throw that one out the window in a minute if I could." She blew out a long breath, wishing she were as free as Rayne. "But you go. Find somewhere with lots of trees, untouched soil, and pristine waters. The mid-south maybe?"

Destiny threw Rayne a startled glance, her brows pulled together in confusion. "This sounds crazy, because we both know I can't read you, but I *feel* you should look at a map and find something, like we used to do with our mother when she would swing her necklace in that game, remember? When we pretended we were going to go on a mystery trip?

"How did her saying go?" Destiny bit her bottom lip, frowning as she always did when thinking of their mother. "I know! Swing it high and swing it low and off to fairyland we go. Crystals and dragons, waters and trees, take us on the midnight breeze."

"That gives me chills! But you're right. I haven't thought of Momma's game for a long time," Rayne said, the excitement in her eyes melting the last evidence of her migraine.

"Me either," Haven added. "Do you think it will work without Momma holding the necklace?"

Rayne looked from one to the other, her smile as bright as it'd been for a very long time. "There's only one way to find out!"

Destiny and Haven followed Rayne to the floor-to-ceiling marble fireplace they'd never used. Across the mantle sat several items that were only moved for one or the other of them to dust, depending on whose turn it was to clean their shared space.

Rayne gingerly lifted the rectangular wooden box that took up a good portion of the center of the mantel. The rough wooden lid opened with a squeak as the centuries old metalwork hinges made of hammered silver, blackened with age, screamed in protest. Her breath caught audibly as their mother's special scent filled the air around them.

Bypassing the family photos, the elementary school pottery she and her sisters had made, and their loving mother had treasured, and the mortar and pestle that their mother had used to grind herbs, Destiny watched as Rayne ran a finger over the glass-incased ring that held their family crest. Then she set it aside to open the lid of a long, thin, silk-lined box and lifted the necklace out.

Her heart hurting, Destiny bit her bottom lip as Rayne lifted the necklace that was nothing more than a roughly hammered silver crescent moon pendant. Set within the copper star at its tip was their mother's power enhancer, known to the family as a Celestial Divinity Crystal. The diamond was neither cut nor polished, yet it sparkled as if both.

The large medallion was as old as time her mother once said, and Destiny and her sisters had always been fascinated by the charm. The long black leather that held it had graced Celestia Cavanaugh's slim neck until the day she'd been laid to rest.

A smile reached Rayne's lips and a tear slid down her cheek as she placed the metal between her hands and closed her eyes, just as their mother always did before the game started. It took everything Destiny had to keep from grabbing the charm, as she'd always felt she was the closest to their mother. But Rayne's need for its power overrode her own feelings of selfishness, so she resisted the strong and embarrassing urge to demand it be handed over.

"Its warmth is amazing." Rayne said, smiling at Haven, before lifting it to hold against her lips.

Jealousy sparked when she saw the smiles that passed between her sisters, but Destiny pushed it back again and was glad she did when Rayne's emerald eyes sparkled with delight as Rayne turned her way. "Get the map, please, Dee. Mommy will tell me where to go."

Chapter Two

"So you're ready?"

Rayne nodded to her sister as she glanced back over her bedroom one last time. "Yes. That's everything I'm taking."

Destiny looked over the complete six-piece set of matched luggage, the carry-on bag, and then at Rayne. "Are you ever planning to come back?"

The question gave Rayne a moment's pause because she'd been asking herself the same question since allowing her mother's pendent to decide her destination. "I'm planning to, yes," was the best she could offer.

Destiny stared at her for long seconds. "Planning...but not sure?"

Rayne lifted the suit bag and strapped it over her shoulder before reaching for the two smaller bags. "I don't know. Right now all I know is that I need to go."

The torn expression on Destiny's face gave Rayne a sinking feeling that hit her stomach hard.

"You need to really think about this. Haven and I talked about it. What will change by you leaving? Really? You can't run from who you are." Her lips twisted. "Who *we* are."

Rayne lowered her bags to the floor and advanced on her sister who let hers fall as well. Pulling Destiny into a gentle hug, Rayne closed her eyes. She knew her sisters had no problem with her going away on a short vacation. But, the thought of the three of them being separated for the first time for any length of time, scared them. It scared her, too.

She had no choice if she wanted to keep her sanity. Staying wasn't an option, now at least, until the furor died down. Although she'd surprised her sisters by agreeing to let Destiny handle the police, none of them had been prepared for the fallout as it ended up being ten times worse than expected.

The news hadn't gone national, as far as Rayne knew, but Los Angeles television and radio stations were either seeking her or mocking her, and she'd had all she could stand.

Thankfully her sisters seemed to be handling it better than she was. Both Haven and Destiny told those they worked with that they had a twin, and not to believe everything they saw on television. And since neither would say any more about it, they were sure people would move on soon enough. Rayne hoped so. She felt incredibly guilty for putting her sisters in such a horrible situation.

"I won't stay away forever. No matter what I'll be back. Either to stay, or to visit often. You know I will."

Wiping at her wet cheeks Destiny pulled away. "Okay. I'm being foolish. We are grown women. There is no reason to act like a baby."

Rayne felt her own eyes fill but she refused to let this turn into a weepfest. "You aren't acting like a baby. We are all we have. A part of me doesn't want to go."

Destiny retrieved the bags and sniffed. "But you must. Let's get you to the airport. Haven will meet us there to see you off. She'll be getting off work now."

Rayne gathered up her things quickly, before all the sorrow she felt at leaving her sisters made her change her mind. It surprised her to realize that saying goodbye to both sisters was going to be the hardest thing she had ever done. She'd always wanted a chance to be on her own. But she'd always wanted to be normal, too. Finding out that one of them was actually attainable was completely different than fantasizing about it.

Because somehow, she knew, she would never come back for good, even if this town called Mystic Waters was just a temporary stop to somewhere else.

The simple fact was, LA no longer felt like home, but

because of Haven and Destiny, it was where her heart would remain.

An hour and fifteen minutes later, after fighting the freeway traffic, Rayne couldn't help but smile. It wasn't often she and her sisters walked together, side-by-side. But when they did, as they did now while rolling her bags into the airport, people stopped in their tracks and stared.

Identical in every way except personality, their long dark auburn hair swinging with each long-legged step, their emerald eyes assessing, and their highly receptive senses absorbing every nuance of the air around them, she knew they made quite a sight. They always had. As they approached the check-in counter and kiosk, even the airline attendants stopped what they were doing to stare.

Pretending they didn't notice, the sisters set the luggage down and turned to each other. Destiny and Haven pulled Rayne in for a tight hug, causing a tug in her chest. They stood there as others watched, still in silence, and held on for several seconds before Rayne pulled back. She swallowed the knot in her throat and struggled to restrain the tears threatening to flood her eyes. "I'll call as soon as I land in Nashville. Then again when I land at the Gatlinburg-Pigeon Forge Airport. My layover is probably just long enough to touch base, but I will. And then I'll have a bit of a road trip. Not sure about cell service in the mountain areas. I'll just have to see."

Both Haven and Destiny nodded, as they too struggled with the good-byes. Finally Destiny cleared her throat, "I guess we should go, and let you go, since we seem to be holding up the airport's flight schedule."

Her words carried enough so that those behind the counters and in front of them suddenly seemed to realize they'd been rude and were staring. As others started loading their bags on the scales, Rayne sat her largest one on the stainless topped scale before her, too, then she turned to her sisters. "I love you guys."

They hugged again quickly before Haven and Destiny turned to leave. Rayne bit her bottom lip and turned back to the attendant, sitting her next suitcase on the scale. "I'm going to West Virginia."

She wasn't certain, but she could have sworn the man muttered under his breath, "Lucky West Virginia."

Following the departure of her sisters, Rayne had a moment to relax, which was a mistake. As she awaited the boarding of her airplane, the number of souls in the lounge quadrupled. Those still of the Earth were never a problem because she wasn't exactly psychic in the sense she could read living people, but their relatives who had already passed into the next realm gathered around their living loved ones in shadowy bundles, vying for her attention. The spirits always recognized a medium and wanted to relay whatever message they had to share. Given the rarity of her abilities, they made it clear they weren't passing up this chance.

Being in such a large crowd of people was something she tried to avoid. Within minutes the assault on her senses condensed into a ball of pain lodged at the base of her skull as one spirit after another tried to come forward. Rayne closed her eyes and mentally envisioned a door closing, effectively shutting them all out. It was a technique her mother had shared shortly before her death once Rayne's gift had solidified. The instant relief was like a glass of cold water after hours in the wilderness. She took a cleansing breath and relaxed again, until they called that her flight was boarding.

Rayne maintained her distance throughout the long flight and layover. Once she was able to board the plane she'd chartered for the next leg of her journey, Rayne was more than ready to hear nothing but the hum of the airplane's engines as it made quick work of the short flight from Nashville to the Gatlinburg-Pigeon Forge Airport.

Landing at the small county airport with its one landing strip was an enjoyable experience, Rayne decided, liking how quickly she disembarked and gathered her bags. She stood chatting with the pilot on the tarmac as a woman drove a golf cart toward them. Compared to the complications and impersonal feel often experienced at larger airports, this one seemed almost cozy. The smiling woman who greeted her waited while the pilot loaded her luggage on the back of the golf cart, before he turned back to his plane.

"Welcome! I hope you had a good flight."

Rayne grinned, liking the country twang of cart driver's voice and the feeling of welcome in general. Her excitement grew as they approached the circular center of the small building that was obviously either new or well maintained. Its brown and tan, stone and stucco exterior blended well with the cleanliness of its surroundings and the barely greening, still mostly brown and black mountains in the distance. Though the center of the building had two stories, the wings on either side were singles, and she guessed that's where she'd find the rental car company she'd called.

"So, where are you headed?"

Not used to strangers asking personal questions, Rayne had to take a second to remember she was in the southeast where people were reported to be overly friendly, so she relaxed back into her seat. "Mystic Waters, West Virginia."

"Oh, I've always wanted to go there. I've heard so many folktales and legends about that place since I was a kid. They say the lake holds magic. Can you imagine how cool that would be?"

Rayne grinned as the woman laughed. She had read as much, but she wasn't about to say so. The woman seemed so excited to be the one to relay the titillating information and her excitement was contagious. "Really? That's interesting."

"You'll have to tell me all about it on your return trip if you're coming back this way. Not that it's any of my business, but why didn't you just fly straight to West Virginia?"

Rayne shrugged. "I looked at the flight schedules, and saw that I'd have a longer layover going through Nashville to that airport, than if I chartered a plane and came here, then drove the rest of the way in."

"I don't blame you. And we're glad you did. It'll be a beautiful drive."

As she came to a stop, an elderly overweight man wearing a flannel shirt and overalls immediately exited the building with a stainless steel trolley, and waddled his way toward them. "Jake will take your bags. I've already told the rental car clerk that you landed. We only have the one— rental car company that is. Lisa is the woman who took care of everything for you."

Surprised and delighted, Rayne exited the golf cart and shook the woman's hand. "Thank you so much."

As she turned to follow Jake she looked back to see the golf cart and its perky driver were headed back to get the next group disembarking from a slightly larger plane than the one she'd arrived in. Upon entering the building the few people mingling around greeted her with such a friendly, strongly accented welcome that she almost felt she'd stepped onto another planet.

That it wasn't an international airport was plain to see. Not only was it extremely small compared to the other airports she'd traveled through, there were no escalators or human conveyor belts, or even a hint of a security screening. And since commercial flights couldn't land on the small runway, luggage was unloaded with its owner so there was no need for a baggage claim area either. Rayne looked around at the simple lounge, with its water fountain converted fireplace, and smiled at the quaintness of it all as she was led to the front desk.

"Welcome! And thank you for coming. If you'd like to see a great view of the mountains take the elevator on up to the second floor. But if you're in a hurry, your car is ready. Just head on out front and Lisa will be there waiting with the paperwork she needs you to sign. Jake is already heading there with your bags."

Though she was tempted to go see the view, Rayne was ready to get the final leg of her journey underway. Since she'd be living on a mountain, she figured she'd have plenty of time to enjoy mountain views later.

As she walked across the blackened concrete floor toward the airport's entrance a diverse group of early twenty-something's came in chatting to each other. Each one greeted Rayne with a nod or a friendly hello even though they were just passing by. She grinned back and responded in kind, something she had never done before when traveling, and the feeling she had made the right decision in leaving LA, and coming to a place that seemed so much simpler, was solidified even more.

The rental car paperwork was handled quickly and though not particularly sporty, the car was clean and well maintained and it didn't cost her the arm and leg it would have back home. She glanced at the map she'd had Destiny pull up and print out and delighted in the fact her mother's pendent decided Mystic Waters, West Virginia, was her destination.

The thought of the area having magic was probably just as the woman said, legends and folktales, but it never hurt for an area to attract tourists, and people used whatever means they had to bring capital to their cities and towns.

According to the map's route planner, Mystic Waters was less than a hundred miles away, and from what she could tell, a good part of the trip was through the countryside and over the mountainous terrain.

Which suited Rayne just fine.

A couple of hours of alone time were exactly what she needed after all those hours surrounded by so many people. Even though she had shut out the ghosts, the day had been filled with too much sensory overload. Between the crying baby and the complaints and grumbles of those traveling the first leg of the trip, which made that flight nearly unbearable, she'd been at her wits end by the time they'd disembarked in Nashville. The short hop and skip between the two Tennessee airports had been much more pleasant, but enough was enough.

Thank goodness that part of the trip was over.

After the initial awkwardness of driving a different

type of car than she was accustomed to, the trip was a pleasure. She traveled two lane roads through the Tennessee countryside with only a few cars meeting her here and there. It was so different from the bumper-to-bumper rides she was happy to leave behind in Los Angeles, as was the scenery.

Never had she seen so many trees or mountains as she traveled south and west from the Gatlinburg area until she reached the winding road that took her east on a rollercoaster ride up and over the Blue Ridge Mountains, then back down the other side. The car trip was over too quickly as far as Rayne was concerned. It had really been a pleasure to drive the mountain and take in the magnificent views of heavily wooded lands with their varying shades of gray, blue and green sometimes broken by small patches of cleared land for either a firebreak or mountainside farm.

Mystic Waters was at the eastern foot of the Great Smoky Mountains, separated, she'd read, only by the lake famous for being fed by hot mineral springs. As the woman at the airport said, folklore claimed the lake's *mystic* waters healed the downtrodden spirit, mended broken hearts, as well as lured those with magical powers to its shores. It felt right arriving in a place whose name honored magic and, though she figured it was just her good mood, Rayne felt as if the chilled air welcomed her when she turned off the heat and opened her windows.

At the base of the mountain, she headed south, immediately entering the town's city limits. Large yet quaint older houses lined the streets, each having manicured lawns displaying very large trees and the indication of well-maintained gardens. They were the types of homes that had housed generations of large families at a time before people were concerned with overpopulation.

She turned onto a narrow street between a massive church and a funeral parlor that looked like it too had once been a stately home. Smiling at what she saw, Rayne passed three smaller streets with similar houses on the northern side of the street, and what were both new and older business buildings on the southern side.

The Internet map had Rayne remaining on Third Street until she reached Mystic Lake Road, but she needed supplies and the keys and maybe even to set up a post office box. She thought about it for a moment and then decided to hold off. She'd noticed on her trip down the mountain several people got their mail at home, as the road department made little areas for the postal employees to pull into, to get them out of the faster moving traffic.

Mystic Waters was everything the real estate Internet site and the woman on the phone said it was. Quaint, homey, a little bit mysterious, and very neat and clean. Rayne reached North Main Street and turned right then laughed with joy at reaching such a lovely destination.

The woman at the Chamber of Commerce she'd spoken with, when planning her trip, directed her to contact a man named Tom Whitehawk, as he owned several rental log cabins up on the mountain. She'd gotten his father instead when she'd made the call, and Frank Whitehawk informed her he handled acquiring renters for his son, and if she had any problems once she was there one or both of them would take care of anything she needed.

He'd been so friendly and had sounded so old Rayne couldn't help but wonder what it was like to have a father or even a grandfather in one's life to handle anything. But that wasn't the way it worked for the Cavanaugh women; never had been, and she guessed it never would be either.

Once she met with Mr. Whitehawk and had the keys, she got the supplies she felt she'd need for a few days and then made the short trip up to the cabin. She didn't want to have to turn around and come back to town for any reason. After the endless days of travel preparation and the travel itself, all she wanted was to settle in. And vegetate.

At least for a day...*or three.*

It was only after Rayne turned onto North Main that she realized how still everything was. Though there were a few people, or small groups of families or teenagers milling about, she marveled at the differences between a large city and a small town. There was little foot traffic, and she'd only met a couple of cars, three trucks—two of which pulled flatbed trailers with large rolls of hay stacked atop them—and she hadn't seen even one cab.

As Rayne approached what she figured was the main hub of the town, she could see pansies dancing in large barrel-type planters that lined concrete sidewalks. These fronted shopping establishments that had gleaming plate glass windows and doors that were nearly identical on either side of the two-lane street. Budding, uniformly spaced trees that had obviously been planted years before were nestled in concrete and brick squares within the sidewalk, too. As she had passed through other such settlements on the western side of the mountains, Rayne figured the south liked uniformity in their little towns.

Rayne read each establishment's sign until she spotted the one Frank Whitehawk had indicated was his. Thrilled to finally have a chance to move her body, Rayne stepped from the car and stretched her legs until she felt most of the kinks were taken care of.

She grabbed her purse and hit the remote to lock the car before turning to enter Whitehawk's Wares. Rayne smiled as she approached a beautiful young woman who clearly had Native American blood. "Hi. I'm Rayne Cavanaugh. Is Mr. Whitehawk in?"

The woman looked at her for a moment as if assessing her, and Rayne had to fight to retain her grin. Slowly the woman nodded, seeming satisfied with whatever it was she was looking for.

"I'm Rachel Whitehawk. Uncle Frank isn't here right now. He's down a couple of doors at The Fried Pickle."

Rayne couldn't help but smile at the name. "Is that a restaurant by any chance? I'm starved."

Rachel nodded. "It is. You aren't from around here, are you?"

Rayne had to remind herself that people would be curious and she didn't need to fear their questions. It wasn't like anyone would ask if she'd talked to a ghost today. At least she hoped not. "No. I'm not." She started to turn away. "Thank you for the information. I'll go see your uncle."

Rayne felt bad about being so abrupt, but she really had no intention of letting anyone know where she was from. Unless someone had posted that fiasco in Los Angeles on the Internet, they would be out of luck, but she wasn't going to give anyone a way to look her up, just in case.

She didn't bother to glance up at the sign names as she walked in the direction Rachel Whitehawk indicated. It was clear where the smell of food was coming from, and whatever it was they served had her stomach lurching to attention. She stepped through the open double glass doors and smiled at the scene before her.

Though the establishment was as narrow as Frank Whitehawk's had been, this one was quite deep and filled with little square tables that went down the center, with the same tables either standing alone or pushed together, only leaving enough room along the walls for someone to scoot across the seemingly endless red benches to sit and face an opposing chair across the tables.

"Dammit! I will not believe that. Those things do not happen in Mystic Waters!"

"Those things happen everywhere. We have to be realistic. It's not like in our day."

"Are *you* going to be the one to tell Garrison that Gavin is probably dead? After all that boy's been through? *I'm not.* I'll come out here every Saturday for the rest of the year and beyond if that's what it takes."

"Well, you do that. Your arthritis will allow it. I'm sure. Besides, I think we're wasting our time!"

Rayne approached two elderly men who were engaged in the argument, hoping neither was the man she was looking for. "Excuse me. I'm sorry to bother you," she stated, only to have them turn on her quickly, anger radiating off both. She took a moment to give them time to compose themselves before speaking. "I'm Rayne Cavanaugh. I was wondering if you could point me in the direction of Frank Whitehawk."

Both elderly men seemed to deflate at once. The larger of the two by a good fifty pounds tapped the rubber tip of his cane that he'd slid off his forearm into his hand. "Well, there, Ms. Cavanaugh, welcome. Sorry 'bout giving such a pretty lady a bad impression. Frank's over yonder," he said, pointing deeper into the café, "sitting with Captain Grammar."

Rayne smiled at him and nodded her thanks before moving forward. As she was used to men staring at her, she ignored the other patrons as she made her way to the table indicated. Both the police captain and the man who was undoubtedly Frank Whitehawk stood at her approach. They smiled at her, and she wondered if anyone in the south ever frowned.

"Hi there. You must be the Ms. Cavanaugh, Frank was telling me about."

Rayne nodded, thinking the sheriff a handsome man. Remarkably symmetrical features offset deep blue eyes and were framed by a thick head of well-groomed black hair accented with silver at his temples. He was taller than her five-feet-nine by a good six inches and held his solid form erect in a way that made the uniform look like it had been designed with his physique in mind. Though she figured him old enough to be her father, there wasn't an ounce of fat or sagging skin to mar what were clearly superior genetics. She felt herself grin. "Hi. Yes, I am."

"Nice to meet you. I'm John Grammar, and this is Frank Whitehawk," he said, indicating the man with the kindest eyes she'd ever seen.

Rayne decided then and there these two older gentlemen had taken advantage of the magic waters of Mystic Waters Lake. As attractive as John Grammar was in his way, Frank Whitehawk had to have once been a sight to see. As tall as the police captain, but with skin the color of worn copper and waist length hair as white as snow, Frank

Whitehawk radiated a silent power and proud bearing that pulled Rayne in. She felt drawn to him and couldn't look away as he looked deeply into her eyes. Slowly he smiled, and Rayne was able to take a breath.

"Welcome, Rayne Cavanaugh. You have finally come."

Not sure what to make of his statement, she smiled, liking that though he had wrinkles deeply etched into his features, the mischief in his sky blue eyes gave him the look of youth and the tilt of his wide mouth bespoke a sense of humor she was sure she would enjoy should they get a chance to become friends.

Rayne's smile faltered. Given his obvious heritage she thought it very strange that his eyes were blue, but as soon as the thought solidified Frank Whitehawk's irises were so brown they were nearly black. Startled, realizing that the long day was finally catching up with her, Rayne rubbed her own eyes and hoped the men didn't notice that she hadn't responded immediately, or that she was suddenly weak in the knees. "Uh, yes, I have. Thank you so much for letting me rent the cabin. I really appreciate it. I wanted so badly to be on the mountain."

"It was meant to be used by you." He reached into the pocket of his jeans and pulled out a simple ring holding two keys. "These are yours. But you will not need them long."

Uncertain how to read his meaning she nodded and took the keys and couldn't help but notice the very large turquoise stone topping a hammered silver ring. She tore her gaze from the enchanting ring to look back at Frank's smiling face, and for only a second she was certain his eyes changed colors again.

Chapter Three

"Uncle Garrison! Catch me!"

Garrison laughed as he took off at a run but tempered his gait to give his nephew time to get across his parents' patio before catching the little guy up and throwing him in the air. "I've got you!"

He lowered Gavin and cradled him in his arms before lifting his shirt and blowing a raspberry on his little belly. Gavin squealed as he yelled, "Fart, fart!" giggling so hard he eventually peed in his pants. Garrison laughed as well as he turned his nephew over and lowered him to his feet, careful to keep the five-year-old positioned so he wouldn't end up smelling like urine as well. "Go tell your daddy you need clean clothes."

Garrison smiled as he watched his nephew run back into his parents' house, before turning to let the sun warm his face. The smell of roasting pork came from the pit he and his brothers dug the summer before, when Garrison was home on a short leave. He couldn't wait for the taste of succulent pig to compliment the side dishes his mother, sister, and sister-in-law spent the last couple of days putting together.

They were celebrating his homecoming again, only this time it was for real. His decision to leave the military had been hard made. But his father and mother weren't getting any younger, and his brother had asked him to consider coming back for good, rather than re-upping for another six. He'd thought it over and decided it was what he wanted as well, especially since his nephew was nearly five, and if he did another stint, he'd have to delay his dream.

"Hey, butthead. Thanks for sending me the kid with the pee pants. He hasn't pissed his pants in almost three years!"

Garrison turned and smiled at Grey. "Your kid. Your problem."

Grey nodded. "Just wait until you have one. Speaking of which, you plan on looking Ava Sheppard up now that you're home for good?"

Garrison shook his head, grinning. "Nope."

Grey knocked into him. "Thought you liked her."

Garrison glanced over, still grinning. "Like her just fine."

"Got somebody else in mind?"

"Nope."

Grey shook his head. "They say if you don't use it, you lose it."

Chuckling, Garrison turned to his oldest sibling. "Who said I wasn't using it?"

"Mom thinks you're gay."

Garrison burst out laughing and grabbed his older brother by the head, spun him around, and attempted to get him in a headlock. But Grey's years of training as well as his regular workouts at the police station's gym didn't make him any easy pansy. They wrestled for position until a loud clearing of the throat had them pulling apart.

Garrison Sr. looked at them both with a grin. "Good to have you both here. But those pigs aren't going to turn over on their own, and your momma doesn't like her meat burned. Figure it's time to flip them."

"Yes, sir," Garrison and Grey said together, before grinning and pushing at each other some more. Their father rolled his eyes heavenward, before turning to go back into the house.

"Got you some gloves, sissy-boy?"

Garrison pulled his from the back pocket of his jeans. "Got mine. You got yours, Lucy?

Grey shook his head. "That's low. I'm going to tell Mom."

They both laughed as they headed toward the barn, the long walk giving Garrison time to appreciate the scene he'd been blessed to grow up with. The wooded acreage in the distance was heavy with the leaves of mid-summer, the air toasty and a tad humid. The grass showed a slight case of stress which made sense as he'd been told it hadn't rained for almost two weeks, and the summer sun had added a hint of yellowish-brown edge to the thin green blades. Both the barns and white triple rail fences looked freshly painted though, and the pasture was mowed as cleanly as any golf course.

Garrison was glad to be in a position to help his dad out now with some of the chores, wondering if Grey and Gary still came over, or if his father hired the work out or did it all himself. He swatted at a buzzing insect then bumped into Grey just for the hell of it.

Grey made a fist and held it out toward him. "We get behind that barn and pigs aren't all I'm going to flip."

"You and what army?"

Grey surprised him by charging into him and they ended up on the ground wrestling, and throwing punches, both laughing hard.

"See what silly boys Daddy and Uncle Garrison are?"

Gavin raced toward them and Garrison rolled out of the way just in time for Grey to catch his leaping son. They both laughed as Grey locked his arms, holding Gavin up away from him, but the child's kicking legs connected with his brother's crotch, and Garrison winced as he was certain he'd also felt pain.

Grey's arms buckled and Gavin landed on his chest. With little grace he set the child away from him and curled into a sitting position. Garrison slid a glance to his sister-in-law only to find Joy with both her upper and lower lips clamed between her teeth. The merriment in her eyes belied her attempt to look at her husband with sympathy.

Garrison rolled to his feet and held out his hand to help his brother up, but Grey shook his head and blew out several windy breaths. When Gavin approached his father again, Grey made a heroic effort to smile at his son, but the tears in his eyes told their own story.

"Hey, kiddo. Can you and Mommy go get me and Uncle Garrison something to drink?"

"Sure, Daddy!" He turned quickly and ran to grab Joy's hand, pulling her back in the direction of the house with the energy of a little bull.

She sent one last look at her husband, then Garrison, shaking her head. "We'll be back shortly."

Both men nodded as she allowed herself to be pulled along. Garrison held out his hand again. This time Grey took it and slowly rose to his feet.

"Have to give you credit. I'd have been screaming like a little girl."

Still slightly bent, Grey winced and laughed at the same time. "Oh, I was…on the inside. Son-of-a-crocodile that hurts!"

"Guessing I'll be flipping those pigs by myself."

Grey attempted to stand and breathed his way through the process. "Just give me a minute."

Garrison nodded and looked away. He knew he shouldn't think his brother's pain was funny, but he couldn't help the smile that kept pulling at his lips. When he had himself back under control, he turned back to find Grey looking at him with mock disgust.

"Go ahead and laugh. I'd be rolling on the grass hooting right now if it had been you instead of me."

Though he didn't laugh, Garrison freed his smile. "Well, Lucy, let's head toward that pit. With or without your help, Pops was right…those pigs aren't going to turn over all by themselves.

"Garrison."

He shook his head, thinking his brother hurt worse than he'd known. His voice was suddenly much higher.

"Garrison!"

The image of his brother mouthing his name faded away, yet his voice got even higher.

"Garrison! Wake up!"

Opening his eyes, it took several seconds for the clutter to clear Garrison's mind so he could get his bearings. When he realized he'd fallen asleep in the woods of the family farm, and Kate was standing over him looking down at him with real concern, realization hit hard and he roared out in anger.

His brother wasn't really here anymore. His sister-in-law either. The dream had seemed so real because it's exactly what had happened all those years ago. But they were both gone now, and his nephew was still missing. The weight of losing them all over again brought tears that were instantaneous and unstoppable, turning his sister's compassionate features into a funhouse reflection.

****

Garrison dragged himself up the steep gravel driveway from the flat spot he'd had graded to park his truck and trailer. The pickup looked as beaten and banged up as he felt. Only it had the benefit of being inanimate. Without feeling. Without this draining, renewed sense of loss. The trailer looked a little better, but it hadn't moved for weeks now. There had been nothing to deliver since he hadn't been able to work. His furniture was becoming quite popular not only in Mystic Waters but all over the country thanks to the Internet. But his heart hadn't been in cutting, shaping and sanding.

All he'd done for endless weeks was traipse wooded mountain terrain, both on his own property and the surrounding properties. His neighbors had and still were helping, but so much time had passed that they were starting to ease away, going on with their own lives. And he would have to, too…if only to keep from going crazy with worry and grief and to pay the bills that came no matter what kind of tragedy life threw at you.

Tears filled his eyes again, reminding him of the mess of an impression he'd left with Kate. He was sure she ran straight to their mother, concerned for him, when she needn't bother the lovely woman who had made his upbringing as wonderful as any kid could ask for. Mary White had enough to deal with, as did the rest of his family.

That he'd held it together this long was something, Garrison guessed, but he had to buck up and not cause his family more worry than they already carried. Sucking in both the overwhelming despair and the threat of additional tears took effort, but he'd been trained as a Marine and he had been trained well.

Unfortunately all that training, which had seen him through three tours of duty in godforsaken countries, through the deaths of men who had become brothers, through the shock and disbelief of the unexpected violent loss of his real brother and sister-in-law, didn't seem to come to his aide now as another tear escaped to run down his cheek.

He felt broken inside.

He had let everyone down.

Garrison wiped the liquid away with the sleeve of his flannel shirt as he thought of Grey and Joy as he'd so clearly remembered them in his dream. The love he'd felt for them, and the trust they'd put in him was tearing him up inside. They had planned well, making out a will with no expectation of it ever being needed, naming him their child's protector, and he failed them.

Where are you?

How could a sixteen-year-old boy just disappear? How could he have missed that Gavin wasn't handling the death of his parents as well as Garrison had believed? Was it even remotely possible the kid had been kidnapped as some were suggesting?

The questions were driving him crazy. The fear was driving every other part of him.

The state police first thought the grieving Gavin had simply run away, then they were making noises that Garrison had been involved in Gavin's disappearance...foul play they'd called it. A person of interest, they'd called him. The local police had been quick to correct that train of thought, thank God. He hadn't needed that distraction taking him away from looking for his nephew.

That was one of the best things about living in the same town your entire life. His family had grown up with the families of those now running the town. The mayor was a third cousin twice removed or something. The current police captain was a distant relative and friend, the sheriff one of his brother's best friends from high school on. They'd grown up together, had careers together, and even their children were the same ages and close friends. The local real estate owner was also a distant cousin somehow, as was the high school football coach, several of the storeowners, and so on, and so on.

They gave to children's charities, to the police fund, and several of his cousins were volunteer firefighters. His parents had even gone through the PATH training so they could take in kids when the local Department of Children's Services needed someone to foster them. And, he knew once this thing with Gavin was concluded, they planned to take some on long term.

In essence, generations of his family had proven themselves, as had he, giving their hearts and hands in service not only to the growth and quality of the community but to the country as well.

He'd come from good people and he had never desired to be anything but good people. Which was true of just about everyone he knew in Mystic Waters. Garrison was proud of his town, and until he'd somehow lost his nephew, he'd felt he had deserved their pride in him.

Reaching the steps of the cabin was a relief. He was tired to the bone. Hungry too, which was something given he'd not had an appetite for weeks. He resisted the urge to settle his behind on the bottom lacquered upside-down split-in-half logs that made up the steps and pulled himself up five more using the hand carved rail.

Even the pride and pleasure he'd taken in building his log cabin with his own two hands had lost its luster, as had his shop of half-filled orders for the furniture he made. Having Gavin missing, not knowing if he was okay or not, not knowing if he was alive or not, was taking every ounce of his energy. He had to find the boy. Or die trying.

After entering the hand carved front door made by his friend, Tom Whitehawk, Garrison made his way across the small living area and headed to the back where he'd transformed his office into a room for Gavin. His own room was up the open-backed stairs in the loft, but he didn't have the energy to make the climb yet.

In the last few weeks, he'd lost considerable weight. He'd gone from being a stocky ex-marine to almost skinny. Not that he cared, but the loss of weight had taken a great deal of his energy as well, and it was something he knew he would have to correct. Not taking time to eat, and not eating simply because he didn't feel hunger, was taking a toll he couldn't afford. He needed his strength. Gavin needed his strength.

The boy's room hadn't been touched since the day the police came and looked it over. And he'd only allowed them to look through things in the hopes of finding the kid. Once they'd left he put the few things they moved back where Gavin had them, with the expectation his nephew would be returned immediately.

That hadn't happened.

Now the room was covered in a light layer of dust. Nothing earth shattering, but dusty in a way he never normally allowed. Being raised by very neat parents and having a career in the military had instilled a sense of cleanliness and order in him his mother had once joked would drive a woman crazy—if he'd ever take the time to find one.

Gavin had been raised the same way. Even in his grief, in his loss, the boy had kept his new room clean and neat. He'd washed his own dishes after a meal. He washed, dried, and put away his clothes without having to be asked, or told.

The only problems they'd had was Gavin having to go back to school a couple of weeks after the murder of his parents. He hadn't been able to deal with his friends, his teachers, anyone really, who wanted to offer sympathy over his loss. He wouldn't participate in sports anymore. Didn't get up and get ready so they could go to church. Had even begged out of going to see his grandparents, aunt, and cousins, even though he had always enjoyed spending time with them all and it had always been the way of things for the White family. They had been raised close-knit, having gatherings at every opportunity.

What Garrison feared now was he should have seen all that as a red flag. Maybe he should have gotten the boy some therapy beyond what his brief stint in the hospital offered. But folks in Mystic Waters didn't see therapists as far as he knew, and it had never occurred to him.

He'd believed time and care would take care of the loss for both of them. He'd given Gavin odd jobs helping in the shop to keep his hands busy and his mind focused on something other than his loss. He'd done his best to help with homework, though the kid took classes Garrison knew he'd never have been able to pass, even though he'd always done pretty well in school. The kid was a *brainiac* who had taken so many college prep classes he'd put Garrison to shame.

He'd always been so proud of his nephew, as had his brother and sister-in-law. *God rest their souls.*

Since the tragic day of Grey and Joy's murders, and up until the point of his disappearance, Gavin's grades had taken a dive. On top of that there had been a rare drug search at the high school and though Gavin hadn't been implicated after an investigation, he'd endured the embarrassment of being accused by another student. Turned out the kid had made it up to get the attention of a girl who liked Gavin more, but the added damage to an already damaged soul had taken its toll.

It hadn't mattered to Gavin that Garrison had believed in him from the get-go—*no* questions asked. Nothing had mattered to him after that, it seemed. But Garrison had still hoped time would take care of everything.

How stupid he'd been.

Why had his brother and sister-in-law believed him competent enough to care for their child? He wasn't. And Gavin, wherever he was, was paying for it.

Where are you?

The plaguing thought, the fear of not knowing the answer, was breaking his heart. He didn't know what to do. Searching all day every day, until his legs were aching like they never had in all the years traipsing over desert landscapes in both Iraq and Afghanistan, was making no difference. Having all his friends, neighbors, and even strangers from town giving their time and talents hadn't made any difference either. There was no sign of the kid. No hint of foul play. No nothing.

Just nothing.

Tears filled his eyes again and Garrison allowed them to fall. He was too tired to fight them anymore. Too tired to pretend he could handle what was happening. The steady stream turned into a gully-washer that took his breath and tore sounds from his throat that were a mixture of anguish, anger, and despair. His legs gave and he landed on the wood flooring in a heap then pulled his legs up and lowered his head on his knees.

Nothing in his life, not even the loss of his beloved brother, had prepared him for the depth of hopelessness tearing into his soul.

Chapter Four

Spring was a chill in the air topped by baby blue skies. And the view from the back balcony of Rayne's rental cabin, overlooking Mystic Waters Lake, was like nothing she'd ever seen. How had she lived all these years and never known of such a peaceful place?

Carrying her hot cinnamon tea back inside, Rayne took her time looking around. The cabin was as cute as it could be. Nothing fancy. Very rustic. But clean and functional with the most wonderful handmade decorations and hand-embroidered linens. The quilt on the feather bed and the spectacular hand-carved bed would go for a fortune in LA. The hand-carved furniture in the living area wasn't huge and chunky, like she'd expected, but was high quality, almost delicate with its lovely designs, and had an air of antiquity. Rugs were braided rags and ranged from feet-wiping size inside the front door to a good ten feet of oval covering the wood flooring in the lounge area.

The layout of the cabin was wonderful. Rayne loved that the bedroom was up ladder-like stairs that led to a loft that ran halfway across the back of the cabin. She could stand at the railing and see straight down into the living room where a rock fireplace and floor-to-ceiling chimney cradled such a warm fire that she hadn't needed to change from her light cotton off-the-shoulder cropped nightshirt and matching short-shorts.

Something she would have to do as soon as possible though was find some winter pajamas since this early spring meant cold weather in the mountains of West Virginia. *Nope... I'm not in California anymore.*

From front door to back balcony was the living area, kitchen area, and bathroom lit by massive un-curtained windows. The cabin had a long driveway and sat so far back into the woods there was apparently no need for curtains, though Rayne knew she would have to get used to that. The night before she had gone to bed early just to get away from those exposed windows and then had felt foolish as the only thing likely to see her was a deer or raccoon.

The rustic front porch held equally rustic furniture and ran the entire length of the house. Where the balcony at the back overlooked the lake and town of Mystic Waters, the front porch overlooked a short clearing of yard that ended in a wall of thick trees, broken only by the driveway, and a tree here and there that had apparently been left behind when the land had been cleared.

On her second trip around the main floor, Rayne took a minute to admire an extremely large Aloe Vera plant someone had placed at the picturesque window. She was glad there was something else alive in the cabin besides her. It was truly strange to be living all alone first time since conception.

She shook off the melancholy threatening to ruin her first full day in Mystic Waters and grabbed the brochures she'd snagged off the check-in desk at the airport, before topping off her teacup. She smiled at the whimsical teapot that matched her cup and saucer as she poured the steaming liquid. After tucking the advertisements under her arm and balancing the china, she headed to the front porch. If she was taking a vacation, she was going to do it right. With so much to see and do in the area, she needed to map out plans, and the brochures were sure to help.

Rayne started to push open the wood framed screen door to step onto the porch but she stopped herself just in time. On the other side of the screen, about three hundred yards away from the porch, a man kneeled down, seeming to inspect the grass. She took a quick step back as her heart kicked up a notch, hoping the dark interior of the cabin kept her from his view, while she kept him in hers.

He ran his hands just over the recently mowed growth as if allowing the grass blades to tickle his palm. After shaking his head he slowly unfolded his body until his tall thin length nearly blended in with the trees trunks in the distance.

Rayne hurried to set her cup and the pamphlets on the closest surface and then went back to close the front door. She bit her lower lip, hoping against hope the hinges didn't squeak, and sighed in relief when it silently swung closed. She quickly threw the deadbolt and turned the lock on the knob.

Thankful to be locked in, she held her breath, while making her way to the edge of the grand front window. There was no way for her to cover the window now, though she promised herself she'd ask Frank Whitehawk what he'd recommend as soon as possible. Having a heart pounding in fear, and feeling dangerously exposed, was not what she'd had in mind when looking for a place to reside. If she'd wanted those things, she could have stayed in Los Angeles.

Rayne glanced back into the living room to see if she'd laid her cell phone close by, but she'd already learned when trying to call her sisters the night before the service was basically nonexistent. She didn't see the phone lying around the room anyway, which meant she'd probably left it in her purse up in the loft, with a dead battery, as she hadn't thought to plug it into the charger.

Frustrated, she turned back to the front of the room…and screamed. The man with his face pressed against the window jumped back and his look of shock would have made her laugh under any other circumstance.

"I'm sorry!"

The muffled words did nothing to slow her heart so she turned and ran to the stairs to crawl up them as quickly as she could. Her purse was on the bedside table so she grabbed it and dumped the contents onto the bed. But the phone wasn't there. She searched frantically through the open suitcase lying on a cedar chest at the foot of the bed, but it wasn't there either. She found it atop a tall dresser but the baseball bat resting against it looked like a better option.

Silently thanking whoever had left it there, she grasped its neck and ran to look down over the railing into the living room below.

Her hands shook and her chest rattled with each shaky breath, but seeing that the front door was still closed gave her a minute to settle. Gathering her wits, Rayne went back and grabbed the phone. Although the yellow light indicated it was close to dying, it hadn't yet. She slid the ring on the screen to wake it up, but as she'd suspected she had no signal.

Disheartened, she dropped the phone on the bed and returned to the top of the stairs. Her senses on high alert, Rayne started a slow descent, holding the bat in front of her. Arriving on the main floor, Rayne lifted the bat in a ready to swing position before moving forward. She glanced in every direction, pivoting sharply once to check to make sure he wasn't behind her. Feeling like she was trapped in a horror movie she blew out sharp breaths as she made her way back to look out the big window.

He wasn't where she'd left him, so Rayne allowed her shaking arms a reprieve, but she only lowered the bat to a more comfortable position. She stepped to the right and looked to the left, and sure enough he was there.

Since he wasn't casing the house, or trying to break down the front door, but only sitting on the top step of the porch facing the field, she relaxed her arms even more as she studied him.

His sandy hair barely curled around the edges of a billed cap. His broad back was covered in a hip length beige jacket that matched the cap, and exposed only a couple of inches of his blue jean clad bottom, which looked so solid it didn't even flatten on the wooden board. Rayne felt a flash of annoyance that she'd even noticed *that*. When she looked back up, her breath caught and her cheeks heated. He'd turned his head and was angling his body before lifting his hand in a quick wave.

So many impressions hit at once Rayne didn't know which to follow. His tanned face was arresting: angular chiseled cheekbones, a square, slightly whiskered jaw, wide lips that were only full enough to fit his face to perfection. His looked weary, yet his chocolate eyes studied her patiently, as if waiting to see if she would accept or reject him. For some reason that made her smile. His lips lifted slightly in response, and she felt herself sigh.

Hoping she wasn't making a foolish mistake, Rayne went to the front door and turned the deadbolt. She bit her bottom lip and blew breath out of her nostrils before turning the lock on the knob. Pasting a shaky smile on her lips, she opened the door and was surprised to see he was no longer sitting on the porch but was back down on the ground in front of it, looking up at her. Appreciating that he'd moved away, as it eased her anxiety further, Rayne relaxed even more.

"Hi. I'm Rayne. And you are?"

"Terribly sorry. I saw the strange car, and I knew Tom kept this cabin unoccupied. He's never rented it out before." A frown crossed his features bringing his brows closer. "I'm sorry to intrude. Are you a friend of Tom's?"

At the mention of her landlord, Rayne opened the screen door and stepped out. Cold air hit her bare legs and blew through the thin cotton of her pajamas, reminding her how scantily dressed she was. She sat the bat beside the door's frame and crossed her arms over her chest in an attempt at modesty.

"Actually I haven't met him yet. His dad rented the cabin to me. I wanted a place on the mountain and practically begged to get it." As her teeth started chattering, Rayne hugged herself tighter.

His lips lifted at that. "Frank's a good judge of character, so I'm sure he gave in only because he was comfortable doing so. I'm Garrison. Garrison White. I live on the next property over about a half mile hike in that direction." He pointed in the direction parallel to the road. "I'm really sorry I scared you."

Hugging herself tighter as her knees started to knock, Rayne gazed in the direction he indicated before looking back at him. "So what brings you out here?"

His broad shoulders fell and some of the light left his eyes before he answered.

"My nephew, Gavin, is missing. He has been for close to two months now. I walk by here every morning and try to check out new areas each time, so it gets later each day before I head back to my cabin. I'll circle back away from your cabin as much as I can from now on, if it bothers you."

Rayne shook her head. "No. It's fine. I'm sorry about your nephew."

A slight lifting of his lips didn't match the stark concern and fatigue in his eyes. "Thank you." He shook silent a moment as he assessed her. "You look about to freeze. Please go on inside. I need to get home and get to work."

Rayne nodded but couldn't stop studying him. Garrison looked so tired, even more than that, a little lost, and she found herself wanting him to stay. "Would you like to come in for some hot tea before you head back?"

Garrison shook his head. "I've already intruded. But thank you."

He started to turn away and Rayne hurried to the edge of the porch. "Wait."

Garrison turned back, his head tilted inquisitively. "Yes?"

Rayne wondered if the cold air caused steam to lift from her cheeks as they heated with embarrassment. After all, what could she say? That she liked listening to his deep southern accent? That she was suddenly aware of how alone she was and it was starting to unnerve her a little bit? That he looked so tired that the nurturer in her was demanding she help in some way?

None of those things justified her delaying him if he wanted to go. "I just wanted to say that you aren't intruding."

He looked from her to the direction he was going in and then at her again. "A cup of hot tea sounds good, if you're sure."

Rayne took a deep breath and shrugged. "You don't look *too* dangerous." She glanced back where she'd left the bat resting against the doorframe. "And I'm armed." She retrieved the bat and struck a hitting pose, grinning.

Garrison stared at her as his lips slowly lifted again, only this time the smile didn't stop before it solidified. His first real smile took Rayne's breath, and her arms slowly lowered until the tip of the bat rested on the wood plank of the porch. She turned toward the door but hesitated before entering. With a quick look back she smiled. "Could you give me just a couple of minutes to get dressed?"

Garrison's smile slipped slightly as he nodded. "Absolutely."

Having no idea why she felt so relieved, Rayne entered the house with a, "Thanks."

Twenty minutes later Rayne had her sweat pant covered legs curled against her body as she sat on the couch watching Garrison. He'd carried in, and was now stacking, the fifth armload of wood he'd insisted she needed handy. He straightened and wiped his hands on his jeans before lifting his second cup of tea. She could tell it wasn't his drink of choice as his nose wrinkled a little each time he took a drink, but she was impressed he was too polite to say so. Even after she'd poured him a second cup.

"Thank you. I could have done that myself, though. And you don't have to drink the tea if you don't like it. Not everyone does."

He lifted his head and swallowed, his Adam's apple bouncing with the effort. He grinned then and set the cup back down. "That obvious huh?"

Rayne laughed. "Yes. I'm sorry I didn't pick up on it with the first cup, but you downed it so quickly all I thought about was how it must be scalding your throat."

Garrison took the rocking chair she'd offered him earlier and stretched out his long legs. "I prefer coffee, but I appreciate the offer. I'm going to have to start carrying more than one bottle of water if I'm going to be out so long."

Rayne hoped he didn't see her sigh. It wasn't that she was actually swooning, but looking at him really was a treat. Thankfully she'd learned her lesson with Jamison, or she might be tempted to do something stupid like ask to join him on his walks. Since she *had* learned how disastrous spending a lot of time with a man was, Rayne promised herself she wasn't going to get interested in anything with him beyond neighborly friendship.

Not that he was asking.

Garrison looked from her to his hands and back again before standing. "I'd better get home. I'm way behind on my work. But thank you so much for the rest…and the tea."

Rayne rose as well and followed him to the door. When he turned and held out his hand, she took it to shake, ready to thank him again for bringing in and stacking the wood. But the contact sent a little jolt through her system and all she could do was stare at him.

His eyes sharpened before he relaxed his fingers and let go. "Thanks again, Rayne. And welcome to Mystic Waters." With that, he backed out of the screen door then turned to walk down the porch steps.

Rayne watched as he walked away, until he was out of sight. She stepped out onto the porch. The morning was turning to early afternoon so she took a seat and rested against the back, wondering about that spark of connection she'd felt when touching his hand.

He seemed so nice, so kind, but mostly so weary with the weight of his worry. Even though she knew there could never be anything romantic between them she couldn't help but wonder.

If nothing else, Rayne knew she would have to try to help him in some way. And the only way she knew was to open the gift she'd closed so tightly when traveling. Promising herself she would only try this once, she closed her eyes and took the time to mentally unlock the series of locks before picturing the door swinging open. When she opened her eyes, she allowed them time to focus in the increasing bright day.

Dew still clung to the grass and budding leaves in patches. The air glistened with remnants of the fog that still hung low in some spots. Birds chirped and flew here and there, but there was nothing else.

No spirits waited to meet her.

Rayne swallowed, knowing she had to try harder. She had never *summoned* a spirit. They always found her and made themselves known when there was a relative in distress. They usually only did this when their loved ones were present, but occasionally, like the child who badgered her into public exposure, they sought her when she was only aware of a situation. And then there were the others: the unconventional lone spirits who sought her help without a connection to anyone still living. Those cases were the hardest to handle because, in her experience, they were older unsolved deaths or jailhouse executions where someone was falsely accused of a crime, and the ghosts couldn't find peace until their name was cleared. The only way for her to help them was to nose her way into their history without revealing why she wanted to be there.

She had only done so twice under the name of research and had no desire to ever do it again, as both times she'd been forced to visit the prisons where they'd been executed, and the drain on her own spirit had taken too hard a toll.

She blew out a breath and glanced over to make sure her neighbor was completely out of sight, and more importantly, out of earshot.

Satisfied she was all alone, Rayne opened her hands, palms up, and bowed her head to channel the teenager. She envisioned the uncle, and took slow even breaths, allowing his haunted brown eyes to stir her soul. "Gavin White?"

She waited and then repeated his name again. But nothing happened. She tried one last time and something in the air around her stirred, but still, there was nothing to indicate his spirit, or any other, was in her presence.

Rayne opened her eyes and leaned forward to look around, curious by the strange stirring of energy. It was completely different than what she normally felt from a person who had once walked the earth, but now hovered in the realm her family called the *Etherworld,* and it was a little unnerving.

Either the kid was still alive, or he wasn't willing to meet her. Frustrated, Rayne tried again. "Gavin? It's okay. If you can hear me, I'm here. I won't hurt you. I'm trying to help you."

Still there was nothing but that strange energy. She tried to ignore it since it didn't feel threatening, but it didn't feel friendly either.

Rayne resettled herself and tried again, waited for several more minutes without results, then decided she wouldn't get upset with her failure. If she wasn't able to summon Gavin to her, there was a chance he was still alive. The problem was there was no way to give even that small sliver of hope to the uncle, as death wasn't the only tragedy that could befall a child.

As much as she wanted to help Garrison, Rayne knew she could never reveal who and what she was. Even with solid proof of something that could help recover Gavin White, *that* was out of the question.

****

Garrison trudged over rocks and broken branches, moss and pine needles, and paid no attention at all to where he was going. All he could think about was the vision of loveliness he had just escaped as fast as his tired body had allowed.

He wasn't exactly sure why he'd felt the need to get away so quickly, other than the fact her beauty had distracted him from what had to remain his only focus. He wanted to blame the distraction on being dizzy with fatigue, but the truth was, meeting her threw him off balance and gave him something *lovely* to think about for the first time since Gavin went missing.

She was quite possibly the most beautiful woman he'd

ever seen, which was saying something. Healthy living, the great country air, and the mountain mist had bred a lot of beautiful ladies in Mystic Waters. His sister, their friends, even his own mother, who looked nothing close to her age, could rival the prettiest women on TV and in the movies.

Rayne Cavanaugh. Just the name rolled through him in waves, crashing on rocks he hadn't thought about for some time, swelling in places he had no right to think about for more than one reason.

But he had thought, *a lot!*

Garrison had wanted to run his rough fingers through her long auburn hair all the way down to where it cupped the curve of her tight little bottom. He'd wanted to drown in emerald irises then kiss the corners of eyes that tilted up as exotically as a feline's. He'd wanted to count how many times her long dark lashes rested against her skin when she blinked, then touch the arch of her brow when she focused on him.

Her breasts were small and high, and he was certain she'd been mortified by his seeing her with such thin attire as she'd attempted to cover her breasts by crossing arms. He was glad she didn't realize that all she'd managed to do was push them together a little. The short-shorts sleep set she'd worn had clearly revealed she didn't sleep with underclothing and wasn't used to the coolness of a West Virginia morning.

He had to give his parents credit for his upbringing. As soon as his mind registered the initial flash of flesh when she'd stepped out of the door, he'd either kept his eyes on hers or kept them off her all together, and he was pretty certain his response to her hadn't shown.

So much about her attracted him as a man, but it was even more than that. She seemed to have a gentle nature, a reserve that was friendly yet careful. There was no flirtatiousness, no strutting her stuff, which she was more than justified in doing with that slim yet curvy body and those mile long legs.

Given how they'd met, and with the degree of the

cabin's seclusion, it was no wonder she had shown signs of fear at first. She gotten over it quickly though, obviously a woman who trusted her instincts, and he admired that. The thing, though, that kept buzzing in his mind on the walk back, was that second's touch between them.

His whole body had gone on alert. His heart had raced. His tired vision had cleared. Even the hairs on his arms had risen as if reaching out to hold on to her. He'd never before experienced that flare of heat from simply touching a woman. Of course it could have just been static electricity.

That's hogwash, and you know it.

Garrison shook his head, bemused. The woman had really gotten under his skin.

Though he knew he was alone, Garrison looked around before adjusting himself so he could keep on walking comfortably. Well, as comfortably as he could, given the fact he couldn't get her and her gorgeous face, hard nipples, and those short-shorts that matched her barely there nightshirt, out of his mind.

He hadn't meant to look, but when she'd turned to go inside to change her clothes, he'd unintentionally gotten a peek at the rise of her perfectly rounded butt cheeks where they met those long legs. And he'd been thankful for the few minutes of still chilly air before she'd returned to invite him to join her.

Of course he'd made up the excuse of needing to get her some firewood inside, and he felt a little guilty that, while she'd been thinking him chivalrous, he'd really only been working out some jittery demons and buying time to wrestle them into submission.

Rayne Cavanaugh....

Garrison huffed out a half-laugh at his sudden obsession as he continued walking, somehow able to maneuver over and around branches and rocks he paid no attention to.

What was it about her that had him so captivated? So enthralled? So awestruck....

Gorgeous?

Yes, she was, but he had known beautiful women.

Kind?

Yes, but that was something he expected from people. The rule. Not the exception.

Sexy?

Yes! And, hell yes!

But those were things that didn't usually matter on such short acquaintance. He knew nothing about her; where she came from, if she was just visiting or was looking to move to Mystic Waters permanently, or if she was married...or involved.

Another heavy exhale and Garrison realized he was standing at the door of his cabin. He looked back with a frown, wondering how he had gotten there. He swung his head from side to side, amazed something besides his sorrows had held his attention for the long hike back, and even more amazed he felt physically great. Energetic! Revved up! And, after taking a vigorous breath, he had to blow another one out. Because he was *still* completely hard.

He entered his cabin and headed to the shower, determined to shake her from his system so he could focus on what he needed to accomplish for the next several hours. Or, if that wasn't possible, allow thoughts of her to satisfy his need to expel the jittery energy that had his heart and mind speeding like a runaway train.

He didn't have time to think about a woman, gorgeous or not. He had to put in time at his shop.

Folks had been nice, waiting on orders well beyond their expected delivery dates. But he couldn't put off his work any longer. Not only had he built a reputation as a quality furniture maker since he had returned home all those years ago, he had a reputation for dependability in filling orders when his customers expected them. Then there were the bills starting to pile up on the kitchen table, and he had never been late paying a bill in his life, until recently, when he simply forgot.

Looking for Gavin had consumed him for so long everything else had gone to hell. Not that he really cared. If there were a way for him to look for his nephew every day all day, he'd do it until he dropped dead. But life didn't work that way. Even in death. Even in tragedy. Life kept going. It didn't feel fair. But it was what it was.

Reputation and bills would never stop him from looking, though. Every morning he'd get up even earlier and try to look a little farther than the day before. Every night, after he finished working he'd continue to check in with law enforcement, see what they were doing to find his nephew, and let them know if he felt they weren't doing enough.

His head was starting to tell him it was useless, but his heart wouldn't allow him to stop, even though he wasn't sure he still held hope.

Chapter Five

The blare of Eric Church coming from the speakers surrounding the large metal shop nearly overpowered the buzz of the sander. Garrison belted out the songs matching the tone and twang of the singer while taking the sharp edges off a leg that would soon complete a kitchen table. He allowed his body to move and his foot to tap, while keeping his mind focused and his hands steady.

The relief of working again, of getting lost in the work, was cathartic. It didn't solve anything other than to fulfill the customer's order, but it did give him a measure of peace to be working with his hands and to have his mind uncluttered and focused, since anything other than complete concentration could cost him a finger, a hand, or more.

The CD changed to another disc, and Reba's grab-you-by-the-heart-and-twist-until-it-screamed voice sang of having to share her man with another woman. Garrison sighed, wishing the worst thing happening in his life was women problems. That led him back to Rayne Cavanaugh, which was another distraction he'd been trying to avoid the last three days by working so diligently after each morning's search. He glanced at the large round clock he kept on one of the support beams and realized he should have stopped and made lunch hours before. He pulled back and flipped off the lathe before releasing the leg and inspecting it.

Mrs. Winch would be pleased with the intricate design he'd carved into the legs as well as the inlays he'd placed into the tabletop. The backs of the chairs had the same inlay and their legs the same carvings. Of course none of these pieces were exactly like the other, as each piece was hand carved. But they were all close enough that a layperson would have to look hard to see the differences.

"That's nice work."

Garrison nearly dropped the leg as he swung toward the door. He'd left it open for ventilation even though it was still cool, as was typical in early spring. What wasn't typical, any time of year, was a beautiful woman standing in his shop looking somewhere between pleased with herself and unsure, perhaps about being welcome.

Like any man would not welcome her....

"Sorry. I would have knocked, but you were singing, and the music was loud, and the whine of the...*lathe, is it*...was earsplitting. I don't know how you stand it."

After having convinced himself his reaction to her had only been a result of exhaustion the other morning, Garrison now had to acknowledge the truth, and there was no way to stop the smile that pulled at his lips. "Yeah, it's a lathe. So how long have you been standing there?"

A mischievous grin caused dimples to appear at each side of Rayne's lips. "Long enough to hear you crooning. And to see you can't dance."

"Ouch! Guess you wouldn't be interested in getting a bite to eat with me then?"

Although it had only been an innocent question, Garrison couldn't believe the words came out of his mouth, or that his breath was actually lodged in his lungs while he awaited her answer. He hadn't made a carefree comment, or had any type of conversation that didn't involve his nephew, for so long he couldn't even remember when.

A flash of unease, or maybe distrust, flashed across Rayne's pretty green eyes. Then she smiled and shrugged.

"Depends... Dinner at a real restaurant? Or hunt and kill something in the woods to cook on a spit?"

It took only a few seconds before he realized she was joking. Then she laughed at her joke, or his reaction, and regardless, his heart kicked against his chest. Her eyes still twinkled with mirth, as dimples formed deep craters in her cheeks.

"You do know I'm joking. Right?"

Garrison nodded and forced his mind to disengage from the hold she had on the rest of his body. "I was hoping so. Or I'd have to believe you have a very limited view of us poor country folk."

Rayne's grin held as she advanced farther into the shop, slowly pulling her gaze from him to look around. Her slow perusal and the approval in her catlike eyes had his chest swelling. When she captured his gaze again, she shook her head as if in wonder.

"This is really something. Did you make all this furniture yourself? I see some that would match what's in my cabin. It's magnificent."

Garrison nodded, his chest now about to burst from her praise, feeling like a five-year-old who had won a stay-in-the-lines coloring contest. But he loved creating something new that looked like it was centuries old. And he loved when people appreciated his art. "Yes, with my nephew's assistance here and there, when he was here."

Rayne looked at him hard when he mentioned Gavin, as if to see how he was. It was perhaps the first time he'd been able to talk about his nephew without getting choked up in a very long time. Garrison cleared his throat. "I miss him. And I'm afraid that I'm never going to see him again...this side of Heaven."

There. He'd finally said it out loud. And though it still scared the shirt off his back, there was a degree of acceptance, which scared him more than anything.

Rayne placed her hand on the machine he used to turn the appendages of his furniture as if testing to see if it was still hot. She kept her gaze on him, searching his eyes. He could tell she was thinking deeply by the mixture of expressions flashing across her face, and he wondered if the mention of his missing nephew made her uncomfortable or frightened her so she couldn't figure out what to say.

"I believe he's alive."

Her solemn words held conviction. And he wanted so badly to believe them. But there was no basis for her assurances. He sighed heavily. "I want to believe that, too. I'm just not sure I do anymore." He shook his head against the sudden rise of despair, knowing the choking in his throat would lead to another breakdown if he let it. He felt blindsided by her words, after he had just congratulated himself on getting past that hump.

"Garrison. I really think…um, I think you have to hold on to hope."

Garrison frowned, uncertain why her talking about his nephew was making him angry. It wasn't anything more than he'd told himself and his family for weeks. He looked at her, wondering if her sudden appearance should concern him more than intrigue him. "Do you know anything about this? His disappearance, I mean?"

Rayne shook her head. "No. I'm sorry. I…I'm sorry. Please forgive me."

She turned away, heading back toward to door, but something inside of him was primed for a fight, and she had invited herself into it. "Wait!"

Rayne turned back, and the look of regret on her face almost stopped him, but his mouth seemed to have a mind of its own. "What are you trying to do? I'm dying over this. I don't need someone who knows nothing about any of it, someone who doesn't even know Gavin, to stick their nose where it doesn't belong."

Instead of reacting with the shock and anger he needed from her, Rayne shook her head before softly apologizing again. Even knowing she'd meant to be kind, even knowing his growing agitation was illogical and over the top, Garrison could no longer contain weeks' worth of pressurized fury that had built inside until he could barely breathe. Something inside of him shattered and more horrible words barked from his mouth. "You need to take your intrusive little butt and get out of here. Now! I'm busy. I have orders to fill, and I don't have time for this."

His chest heaved as she hesitated and then nodded slightly, the hurt in her eyes clearly for him instead of herself. He wanted to take back the words, but more than that he wanted to pile on many more. Garrison locked his lips together and struggled with the angry demons that had him by the throat, knowing to open his mouth now would only add insult to injury.

"Okay. I was…I'm…really sorry." Rayne didn't move for a second longer.

Her look was one that said there was more she wanted to say, but with a shake of her head, she turned and left, her unspoken words hanging in the air to shame him. Garrison stood frozen for several seconds before realizing he still held the table's leg. He inhaled a furious breath before slinging it against the metal wall where it splintered, bounced, and showered down on furniture and the concrete floor.

I'm an idiot.

A stupid idiot who had taken weeks of suppressed frustrations out on a woman who didn't deserve it. Garrison cursed, knowing he'd made a complete ass of himself, knowing his reaction to her kindness resulted from months of hurt and fear that had started with his brother and sister-in-law's murders, but also because she represented escape from it all, if only temporarily. He'd tried, but failed, to put her out of his mind so his focus could stay where it belonged: on finding Gavin, on disappointing his family, on failing his brother. Thoughts of her, of holding her, of touching her offered the hope of escape. Thoughts of her holding him in her long slim arms, of touching him with her full raspberry lips, had made him crave the comfort a beautiful woman could provide, if only for a moment's reprieve. And it shamed him to no end.

Guilt was a bitch.

He forced himself to retrieve the shattered pieces of wood instead of following after Rayne to apologize for his behavior. If he did that right now, he was afraid he'd tell her how much he liked her. How attractive he found her. How desperately he needed to escape his life and wanted to do so with her wrapped within his arms and him trapped within her body.

Garrison snorted on a half laugh, knowing what an ass he really was at the moment. What woman wanted to be used? And since when had he ever thought to use one for his own selfish purposes? *Never.* That's when. Which meant he needed to keep his distance from her.

Which meant he needed to forget she existed.

Like that was even a possibility.

****

Rayne took her time walking back across the property that separated their cabins. She hadn't meant to go to his place. She'd just needed the exercise after nearly two days of sleeping off and on as she tried to recover her strength.

From the moment she'd decided to leave her old life to travel across the country to try out a new one, she'd busted her behind tying up loose ends as quickly as possible; the biggest was to finish cataloging their local assets and finally properly storing the family diaries.

The huge fireproof safe she'd purchased and had installed was now bolted into the hidden concrete closet she had constructed on the garage level floor of their LA home. Although it bothered Rayne for them to be so far away, she'd made them as safe and secure as she could, as the storm shelter contractor had promised the room she wanted would withstand hurricane and tornado and was sealed against fire and flood. In essence, he said, she was insured against everything except the apocalypse, though he'd had no idea that the contents that now filled the structure were too valuable to insure, because they could never be replaced.

She'd left the combination with both Destiny and Haven, knowing neither sister would ever bother to look at the books or her notes. Once she was certain where she would reside permanently, she planned to ask if they cared if she took possession of them once again so she could continue to study and chronicle the information for herself, her sisters if they ever became interested, and future generations.

Her mind returned to Garrison. She certainly hadn't

meant to say what she'd said. He was angry now. She'd heard the crash from whatever it was he threw at the wall of his shop. And she heard his bellow afterwards. But angry was better than broken. And that's what she saw in his eyes when he spoke of never seeing his nephew again.

If only she could help without revealing too much.

Not that she had any reason to believe she *could* help...or that he'd ever speak to her again. No spirits had come to her. When she'd been with him, she thought for sure some would come forward, as she hadn't closed the door she'd opened following their first meeting. But nothing. *Nada.* It was a little disconcerting to realize she was disappointed she couldn't contact a spirit when the only thing she had wanted in coming on this little escape was to avoid them.

Rayne tripped over a rotting branch and caught herself before falling. As she leveled out a cool breeze blew across her cheek and she felt that she was alone, yet not alone. She turned slowly, uncertain, but there was no one there.

"Hello?"

Another cool breeze tickled her nose as mist formed only a few feet away. Rayne waited a beat as she considered what might be happening. "Who are you?"

There was no answer and after a moment Rayne decided she was imagining things. After all, what were the chances spirits would come to her just because she was thinking about the fact they hadn't?

Her mind flooded with the vision of a young black bear cub running beneath a silver cloud that hung so low it touched a mountaintop. But there was no *voice,* as she had come to think of the words that formed in her head and usually accompanied the images she saw.

Her curiosity piqued, Rayne processed the image. "You are native to this land?"

As soon as the image solidified, it shifted like a writhing snake giving her the impression of a young man with long dark hair. He stood as if bracing against the wind, with only a small square flap of deerskin covering his loins.

Nothing else shielded his still wavering, lithe body.

His facial features were not clear, as each head movement caused wave after wave of action, making it seem as if a snapshot was taken every nanosecond and his face was trailing paces behind.

It was a little nauseating to watch.

His agitation was clear in the movements, but being unsure of the reason for his agitation Rayne held her ground and waited. Though the brave's image was different than any she had experienced before, the inability to define the facial features was not unusual at all. Unless there was a purpose for it, faces were rarely clear to her.

"Who are you? What are you called?"

The image faded slightly and Rayne held her breath. She knew better than to push. As the young man solidified again, he hesitantly pointed to the ground. She followed his lead and looked down, but saw nothing but twigs and dried leaves on the ground. When she looked up his image contorted and again she saw a black bear cub.

"What are you telling me? Your name? Does it have something to do with the dirt and a bear cub?

A sharp gust of frigid air chilled her face and lifted her hair. She froze, not sure if he was angry she couldn't figure out what it was he wanted her to understand. But she had never played charades with a spirit before and she wasn't sure what to do next.

"Okay. Is it Cub?"

A blast of cold air.

"I'm guessing that is a *no*. Is it Bear?"

This time the wind was warm then cool, then warm again.

"Well, darn it! What am I supposed to figure out from that? Help me out here!"

The wind around her rose suddenly and dried leaves swirled around her feet, climbing to her knees, then her waist. She raised her hands, palms out, and mentally yelled *Stop* and the wind died down immediately. "Do that again and I will not listen to you!"

A sense of overwhelming sadness weighed Rayne down, making tears smart her eyes. Her irritation dissolved. The sadness she was feeling was obviously his. "I'm sorry. Let's start over. I'm Rayne Cavanaugh. I don't understand you. And I don't know why I can't."

The image of the young brave pointedly moved his arms as if he were jogging.

"Running?"

Warmth immediately replaced the chill she'd been feeling.

Rayne smiled. Now they were getting somewhere. She watched as he pointed to the ground and became the bear cub.

"Running Bear?"

A feeling of delight lifted her spirit. "Okay...."

Instead of one of the reactions she expected, his image solidified and settled. She watched as his fingertips touched each other, and then when he pulled his hands apart, there were letters that held only a few seconds before dissolving like falling glitter.

She frowned. "Can you do that again?"

He repeated his actions, and more prepared now, she quickly made a mental note of each letter.

"Qaqeemasq?"

And there it was. That feeling she was right.

"Qaqeemasq or Running Bear, which should I call you?"

He wavered, but just hung there, and she figured either or both was fine. "Qaqeemasq, why have you come to me? Do you know about the missing boy?"

She held her tongue and took the time to look around as she waited for a response. The spirit of the young Indian was hesitant, and she wondered whether it was because she was new to the area, or if it was simply because she was white. There had been many tears shed in the area when the white man invaded the native's lands and time did not heal all wounds. Not even for those who had passed over.

She knew that thought was from him as well, which led

to her next question. "You came to me. And I mean no harm. What do you want me to know?"

He turned away from her and pointed to the west where there was nothing but the budding trees, greenish-brown brush, and last fall's leaves. Rayne frowned. "I don't understand.

"Does this have to do with the missing boy?"

He kept pointing, standing so still he seemed a statue.

"Is he over there somewhere? Is he hurt?"

Rayne's frantic questions went unanswered as the young Indian continued to point. Frustrated fury had her advancing on the image she saw before she realized she was going toward nothing. He wasn't there anymore, if he actually ever had been. She exhaled heavily then forced herself to calm down. Had she completely imagined him in a desperate attempt to help Garrison?

No. She hadn't. Not that she really understood what she saw, or *imagined,* when dealing with ghosts, but he was, or at least had been real, of that she was certain. Still, she had no idea what he wanted but that didn't mean she could ignore a possible lead on the missing teenager. So she headed in the direction he'd pointed.

For a quarter of an hour she kept walking. In an effort to make sure she could find her way back she broke small branches along the way. Doubt, followed by aggravation, settled in as time went on and she found nothing. It was more than a little creepy walking for so long in the strange woods all alone.

Having had enough, and feeling maybe she *had* imagined the young Indian, Rayne turned back, then stopped with a gasp.

There, captured on a loosened piece of tree bark, was a scrap of cloth.

There wasn't much to it, only a ragged inch of blue and green flannel at best. But it was something she couldn't ignore. A chill ran up her arms as she pulled it from the tree. She was tempted to rub the material between her thumb and forefinger but resisted because she was afraid it might deteriorate in her hands. Or worse, if there was some way to take a DNA sample from it, her touch might compromise the sample.

Rayne held onto the cloth by pinching a tiny corner as she searched the immediate area several times. But there was nothing else. No footprints. No more scraps of cloth. No teenage boy. It was disappointing.

Rayne was honest enough to admit, even if just to herself, that her motivations weren't entirely selfless. For some reason, she wanted to make him smile at her again.

Shaking her head at her foolishness, Rayne took another moment to look around. She didn't even know the man. Why in the world he suddenly seemed so important was not only a mystery, it was ridiculous. The last thing she needed was to become one of those women who needed to make other people...okay, *a man*...happy in order to be happy herself. Her sisters would laugh their heads off if they knew she was even thinking such a thing, and her ancestors would ask why she hadn't learned from their mistakes after reading diary after diary about the disastrous relationships they'd all suffered.

Knowing the absurdity of even having deep thoughts about Garrison White, Rayne located the closest broken branch and headed back the way she'd come, picking up the pace once she reached the area where she first saw the native son.

She felt certain now she hadn't imagined the Indian. And she knew she had to hurry back to Garrison's place in spite of his feelings toward her and her own fears of wanting to be liked by him. If there was any chance this tiny piece of cloth was a clue to what had happened to his nephew, personal feelings didn't matter, and there was no time to waste.

Chapter Six

The sight of Garrison's home and shop was welcome. Rayne was breathless and her heart was near to bursting from the speed with which she'd moved across the forested mountainside. As she slowed and attempted to catch her breath, the picturesque view of the smoke twirling from the log cabin's chimney, the scent of wood-smoke filling the air, and the big long jawed, long eared brown dog on the porch was so blissfully picture perfect reason returned...and with it doubt.

After all, what had changed? She still didn't know anything significant and she couldn't explain how she had come by the scrap of cloth. If she dared tell him how she found it, he would think she was a nutcase, as many people did. And that had been in LA where nutcases were a dime a dozen.

She came to a stop, indecision weighing like an iron anchor. The truth was there was nothing she could say to him. Nothing she could do for him. Anything she did would only add to the anger he already felt toward her and the devastation he experienced on an ongoing basis.

She couldn't do it. She couldn't add to his misery with something that most likely was nothing. She turned to head back to her cabin, wishing she had done so initially.

"I'm sorry."

Rayne froze then slowly turned. Garrison was standing at the open door of his shop. The stress of his life weighed heavily on him, reflected by the dark circles under his eyes and the days old stubble on his jaw. She opened her mouth to tell him she was the one who was sorry, but he didn't give her a chance.

"I can't believe I talked to you like that. That isn't who

I am. I'm just…." He raked fingers through his hair then he ran his hand over his eyes. "Tired. I'm so damned tired."

Compassion swamped Rayne, and before she realized what she was doing, she was standing before him.

"I'm the one who's sorry. I just wanted you to keep hope alive. And you look about to drop. Do you have a bagel? Fruit? Juice?"

A startled expression raised Garrison's brows before he burst out laughing. "A bagel? Fruit? What are you? A California girl?" He shook his head while the laughter settled into a smile. "I have bacon and eggs and probably a can or two of biscuits. Are you offering to cook?"

Rayne hadn't put pork in her system in…she couldn't even remember, because she *was* a California girl, but more than that she was a Cavanaugh and was raised to avoid unhealthy foods. "Busted. I'm into egg whites, fresh fruits, and whole grains, though a little honey wouldn't go uneaten. And, if full disclosure is a must, I occasionally, though rarely, have sweets of the chocolate variety."

Garrison tilted his head. "I think biscuits and gravy and grits sound better. I do have honey though. Local. Friend of mine keeps bees down in the valley."

"Heart attack food."

Garrison looked her over then smiled as his gaze settled on her eyes. "Only if you eat in excess. And I haven't had anything much lately. A *hearty*, pun intended, breakfast sounds amazing."

Rayne didn't allow herself to think of what she was going to do to her body, she was just so happy he was in a better mood. If the man needed hardy, then she would suck it up and give him hardy. *If* she could figure out how she was supposed to cook it. "So what are grits?"

Grits turned out to be *sort of* like oatmeal, if you ignored the fact there were no oats. It was corn, she was certain, as it smelled like corn. But how they made it into the gritty food it was named after she had no idea. She glanced across the cabin where Garrison was choosing from a rack of CDs as she slowly stirred it on his gas burner.

A pop of grease hit her arm, causing her to turn her attention back to the other pans on the stove. The thickest bacon she had ever seen was sizzling and spitting at her from one iron skillet while the yolks of four eggs stared at her from another. Garrison liked his bacon thick as ham and his eggs sunny side up, and since she had never had either she was willing, this once, to try them.

The oven's buzzer sounded indicating the biscuits were done. Rayne turned off the burners on the stove then peeked in the oven as she shut off its alarm. The large golden-brown layered biscuits looked delicious and would be heavenly with honey. Her hips and thighs would just have to look the other way, but it was definitely a good thing she had to walk all the way back to her cabin after this feast was over.

"It smells great."

Rayne smiled as soft instrumental music filled the room. It was nothing like the loud music he played in his shop, thank goodness. She would have had a major headache. The soothing sounds filled the cabin complementing the sun-filled room and the aroma of bacon. He was right. It did smell great. "Everything is about ready. Not sure about the grits, but I did what you said."

Garrison advanced into the tiny kitchen area, instantly taking up all the space. She raised a brow at him as he came to stand inches from her. "What are you doing?"

A curious smile lifted his lips. "I'm checking out what you've done. Never had a California lady in my kitchen before. Wasn't sure you'd know what was what."

Rayne didn't take offense, because she really didn't know a lot about cooking. Still, he was being just a little too smug. "I have talents you wouldn't believe."

She smiled at her own private joke and ignored the flare in his eyes before filling the two plates that he handed her. They took the plates to his small table where he had already placed utensils and two tall glasses of milk. Rayne had to bite her lip to keep from telling him that she really didn't drink milk or eat bacon or anything fried...and certainly not biscuits that came from a can.

She came from a long line of women who had spent their lives learning what healed, harmed, and killed the body, and they'd all been taught never to put processed foods in their mouths unless absolutely necessary. The fact that she came from a place where people were concerned for their figures played only a small part in her family's diet.

He waited for Rayne to sit down before he took the seat across from her. "Do you pray?"

Rayne was surprised by the question, as no one had ever asked it of her before. "I do. Sometimes."

Garrison smiled then clasped his hands before lowering his head. The smile slid from his face as he continued in silence, frowned, then he settled back and looked up at her. "I do. All the time. I have to believe in something greater than myself. I have to believe God is looking out for my nephew."

Rayne wasn't sure what to say. She had her deep beliefs, too. And was certain that there was an afterlife, as she knew those who abided in the next realm and some who had gone on into the eternal one, she just hadn't met anyone besides her sisters who talked about religion.

"I'm glad it gives you comfort."

Garrison shrugged, though she knew it wasn't because he didn't care. It said he just didn't know what else to say about the subject, which, sadly, told her he really was beginning to believe that his nephew was gone forever.

Rayne tried to ignore the insistent voice telling her to tell him about the scrap of cloth. About the Indian who set her path to finding it. After all, Garrison wouldn't believe her. Not in a million years. This was middle-America. God's country. The Bible belt, of all things. But still…. "I have to tell you something."

Garrison chewed his first mouthful, swallowed, took a drink from his glass, swallowed, and glanced at her untouched plate. "Let me guess…you don't eat real food."

Rayne exhaled. She wasn't ready to confess and he had given her an out. She knew she was being chicken, but she couldn't open up that can of worms. At least not yet. "No. Actually I wanted to tell you that you have a milk mustache."

Garrison laughed and wiped his upper lip with the back of his hand, caught her look of surprise then had the grace to look abashed. He picked up his paper napkin and wiped off the back of his hand, though she was certain he would have just used his denim covered leg if she hadn't been watching.

"I promise, my mom did teach me better." He looked pained. "And about earlier, I'm really sorry. I could lie and say I don't know what got into me, but I do."

Rayne couldn't help but send him a sympathetic smile. "I just bet she did. And don't think anything about it. In your place... I don't even know how you hold it together. So if you sometimes don't, it's understandable." There was awkwardness in the pause that followed and she knew it was her fault. "Actually, I...."

The Irish music coming from her cell phone indicated which sister was calling. Rayne cleared her throat and stood. She pulled the phone from her back pants pocket while apologizing to Garrison in a way she hoped he would understand. "Family."

He nodded and resumed eating as she excused herself and stepped away from the table.

"What are you involvchchch in? Are chchchch danger?"

Rayne inhaled sharply then glanced at her phone. She had only one signal strength bar and it was yellow.

But she understood enough to realize Destiny was picking up something. But from all the way across the country? That was *amazing*, Rayne decided, given that they couldn't even read each other when they were in the same room. "I'm not in danger, but how did you know I'm involved in something?" she asked as quietly as she could, moving closer and closer to the front door.

"What chchchch talking about?"

Rayne frowned. "What are *you* talking about?"

The exasperated sigh came through the airwaves loud and clear, and Rayne realized she was telling more than she needed to at this point. Even from across a nation her sister was acting true to form. She was treating Rayne like a child again. "Okay, why exactly have you called? And why are you up so early?"

Destiny's voice held that older sister tone Rayne hated. "Becauschchch you haven't called!

"Haven and I have been chchchch for news. How you like it there. What you chchchch doing. But what are you chchchch talking about? What have you gotten into that you can't even chchchch time to call home?"

Oh geez! Great! Now her sisters would be on her all the time. Better to curtail it now. "Not much really. Just learning to cook different foods and walk the land. Great exercise. Food's still a question. Town's cool." Since everything she said was true she could indulge in a saucy smile.

"Chchchch more. What aren't chchchch telling me?" Destiny insisted.

"Sorry to interrupt, but your breakfast is getting cold."

Rayne froze, realizing Garrison was right behind her. His innocent smile did nothing to alleviate the sick feeling in the pit of her stomach. She didn't need to be a psychic to know what was coming.

"You are with a man? Having breakfast *with a man!* What the hell is going on? You only just got there! Haven! Come here!"

Well, that came through loud and clear. Rayne knew Garrison could hear Destiny's rant because she was so loud Rayne had to hold the phone away from her ear and he had an *'oops!* smile on his lips and laughter lighting his eyes. Sure, he thought it was funny, but she knew she would have a lot of explaining to do or her sisters would go all Amazon warriors on her and come to a rescue she didn't need.

"No! Don't call Haven! Don't wake her up! Stop it!" Rayne spoke quickly, hoping to get Destiny's attention because she was still yelling for their sister. She glanced back at Garrison to tell him she was leaving, but his expression had changed to one of confusion as he advanced on her. He reached toward her butt, touched it, which would have had her reprimanding him if she hadn't seen that he held the scrap of cloth that had apparently slipped into view when she pulled her cell phone out.

She couldn't say a word, not to him or to Haven, who was now on the phone asking in a sleep-groggy broken voice what the hell was going on?

"Where did you find this?" Garrison demanded tightly.

Rayne could only stare at him. Nothing would come to her. How to explain what it was or where she got it or why she hadn't showed it to him already in case it meant something. Nothing at all came to her as she listened to her sister's voices.

"Where the *hell* did you get this?"

Garrison's voice was loud and harsh and woke her from the stupor she'd fallen into. She knew she had to get this situation under control or an airplane wouldn't beat her sisters across the country. She turned her back on him and spoke quickly into the phone. "I'm fine. I'm in the middle of something and can't talk now. But I'll call you later today."

Hoping they understood her better than she could understand them, with all the static and broken connections, Rayne hung up and turned back to Garrison. She took a deep breath then turned her attention to the scrap of cloth. "I found it this morning while walking. And I thought it might mean something. Then when I got here I thought what if it didn't and I only upset you. So I was waiting for the right time to bring it up." Another deep breath and audible exhale was all that was heard for several seconds.

Garrison rubbed the material between his finger and thumb. "It means something. Gavin has a shirt that matches this. It has to be torn from that shirt." He looked at her with hurt disbelief. "How could you not tell me right away?"

Rayne knew nothing she said would justify her actions. And he was right. She should have said something immediately. "I'm sorry."

He shook his head and expelled a heavy sigh. "Okay. As I've been an ass all morning, I understand your hesitancy. Would you show me where you found it?"

Rayne nodded knowing he had forgotten about the fact that he was the only one who had eaten and she was basically starving at this point, but there was no way she was going to bring it up. "Okay." She turned and walked out the front door without another word and didn't speak when he called the bloodhound to follow.

"Is he yours?"

Garrison shook his head. "No. He belongs to a neighbor, but he spends as much time on my porch as he does at home. I don't feed him though, since he needs to remember to go home. His name is Blue. Whenever he's here he likes to walk with me, and he's good company."

After sniffing all the way around her, *Blue*, for all his floppy, lazy ways was quick on his feet and followed them at the lightning pace Rayne set. They passed her cabin and continued on in silence. She didn't know what more to say to Garrison and she was afraid her hesitancy in showing him the cloth had put her on bad footing with him again. He didn't seem to have anything so say either as he trailed behind.

"It looks new and looks like it's been cleaned. And we've had rains, lots of rain and snow since he's been missing."

Rayne slowed her pace to allow him to catch up with her, glad to hear his voice was more thoughtful than irritated. She glanced at the cloth. He was right. It was only a scrap, but it looked clean. And newish, as the plaid wasn't faded at all. Which meant it might not be his nephew's.

"So maybe it isn't his?"

Garrison bit his bottom lip as he stared at it. His brows furrowed, making deep grooves between them. "It is. I think. I don't know. But it could be. I bought him new clothes when he first came to live with me and this color was one he really liked." Garrison shook his head, obviously hopeful but unsure as he glanced up at her. "I need to see the tree where you found this. Maybe there are more clues."

Rayne nodded and dodged a large fallen branch he stepped over. She rejoined him, doubting they would find anything more but hopeful he would see something she had missed. Garrison stopped suddenly and pulled his cell phone from his hip pocket. Rayne stopped too, and looked around hoping, but not expecting, to see further signs that his nephew had been in the area recently.

"Hey this is Garrison White. Get Burt for me, please." He paused for a minute or so then his voice carried urgency. "Burt. There might be a new lead. I'm checking it out now but may need assistance later. I'll get back to you." He turned to Rayne. "I got his voice mail, but that's okay. He checks it often and it will give us a little time to investigate."

Rayne nodded. "Okay. This way. It isn't far now."

Chapter Seven

Burt Thompson listened to the message with mixed emotions. He had been hoping for a lead on the brat but didn't want that damned Boy Scout finding the kid before he did. If the kid talked then Burt was gonna be wading in shit up to his neck.

He should have *offed* the kid when he'd done the parents, but he hadn't been able to pull the trigger a third time. Not because he had a problem killing the little bastard, but because sirens and yelling had surrounded the house and he'd had to hightail it out of there before getting caught red-handed.

All he'd had time to do was warn the kid not to talk or he and the rest of the extended family were dead, too. Apparently the warning had worked as the kid kept his flap shut. But then he up and ran away just when Burt was about to nab him a second time, and that complicated things. Now people were looking for the teenager and suspecting whoever murdered the kid's parents had him.

If only!

Burt blew out a breath as he watched the other officers in their small station mingle around the office. They answered phone calls, joked about one thing or another, and stood at the large, freestanding cork board where the week's crimes and criminals were laid out for inspection and dissection so plans of action could be formed.

Of course the murders of a police officer and his wife, and the subsequent disappearance of their only child, had people working a little harder than usual, but even that furor had died down since there hadn't been anything much to go on in either case.

Burt smiled as pride puffed up his chest. He was a

damn good cop and knew what to do to keep from leaving evidence behind.

He rose from his chair and adjusted his tight grey slacks, pulling them up under the belly he'd somehow grown over the years. He knew he'd have to talk to Martha, certain she must be using hot water and high drying temperatures again when doing his laundry. He'd already had this discussion with her once, and damned if he wouldn't have to take his belt to her again if she didn't stop shrinking his clothes. Wife or not, she needed to straighten up and fly right or he'd teach her just who was boss.

Burt sucked air between the gaps in his front teeth, satisfied with the thought of taking a little hide off the woman he'd married seven years earlier. He resisted adjusting the growing bulge in his pants as he glanced over at the officer sitting at the desk that faced his own. "Got to check something out. Getting some lunch at home, too. Tell the Captain I'll be back by two."

Jason Hill glanced up from his computer screen and nodded, then turned his attention back to his work. Burt didn't hesitate to head to the door. There was no telling what would delay him if he didn't hightail it out of there quickly. The captain had gotten in the habit of using him for a gopher since Grey White's death, and it irritated the shit out of him. He'd been on the force as long as the Captain, but the guy treated him like a rookie or worse most of the time. Burt knew any day he might be fired, just because the guys didn't like him.

Life was never fair.

****

Thirty minutes, a busted lip, a black eye, and rug-burned knees, later, Martha Thompson agreed. Life was nothing short of a nightmare when her husband was in one of his moods, and they seemed to come on him more and more lately, especially after he woke from one of those nightmares he refused to talk about.

She picked herself up off the broken linoleum flooring and pushed her dress back down. There was no chance of retrieving her panties as Burt had torn them when he'd forced himself on her within seconds of entering their home. She stood still once she regained her balance awaiting his instructions. To do anything else would only bring more punishment for whatever it was she'd done this time.

"Go clean yourself up and fix me a sandwich. And don't skimp on the meat."

Martha nodded and headed to the tiny bathroom off the kitchen. She snagged a washcloth and ran it under the cold water before looking up at her reflection. The medicine cabinet mirror was so old it was speckled and it had a crack that ran diagonally from top left to bottom right. The crack was a constant reminder that Burt had slammed her face into it three years earlier. The reminder was more for him, than her, as she never wanted him to forget that he'd once gone too far.

Martha gingerly wiped at the scrapes and bruises on her cheek and arms then re-wet the cloth before lifting her dress and wiping his semen from her vaginal area and inner thighs. She rinsed the cloth out before wiping herself again then held the cloth against her crotch for as long as she dared, hoping to soothe what felt like ripped tissue. It wouldn't be a first.

"What the hell is taking you so long?"

Startled, Martha jumped, and pulled the soothing cloth away before pitching it into the hamper. "I'm coming!" She quickly glanced back into the mirror wishing she had time to freshen her makeup as Burt didn't like it when she was a mess, even when he'd been the one to make her one. She smoothed down the wrinkles in the dress he had chosen for her that morning, hoping he didn't notice where it was wet. The last thing she needed was a spanking when she was already so sore.

Martha left the bathroom and went directly to the refrigerator. The huge container of sliced ham and the thick sliced Swiss cheese package was quickly placed next to four slices of bread. Mayonnaise and mustard were evenly spread before she put the two sandwiches together and placed them neatly on the plate. Three pickles and two handfuls of chips were added just as he liked. She carefully placed the meal and a very large glass of milk on the table for him as he settled his wide bottom onto the creaking kitchen chair.

Before she could move he captured her leg and slid his hand up to her bare bottom. A sinking feeling settled in the pit of her stomach as a tiny thrill tightened her nipples.

"You been drying my clothes too hot again?"

Martha hesitated answering. Either answer would be the wrong. "I tried to do them right."

Burt huffed. "Well you didn't." He pushed his chair back and pulled out the belt he'd left dangling from this uniform slacks when he'd pulled them back up. "Pull up your dress and bend over the table."

Martha looked from the belt to the table where the full glass of milk sat. She swallowed. "May I put your drink on the counter first?"

A chuckle came from deep in his throat. "You're not as dumb as you look. Yes, you may."

Martha quickly moved the milk, relieved he was allowing her to eliminate another reason for punishment as she was really sore and he was messing up her plans for the day. If it spilled it would be her fault, of course. She returned to the table and lifted her dress to her waist before leaning across the wood surface.

She waited, not knowing if she would feel the belt or his hand, ashamed of how the fearful expectation already had her throbbing with need. He made her wait in silence for what felt like forever, knowing he knew the anticipation would be more terrifying than the act itself, and therefore heighten the pleasure for them both. The longer she waited the more excited she got until her legs were trembling so badly she was afraid they wouldn't hold her much longer.

The first sting of the belt threw her pelvis into the table's edge causing an explosion of pain and a riotous orgasm that rode the rest of her spanking. Tears poured from her eyes as the slaps of leather continued, but she only allowed muffled sobs to escape as to cry out would infuriate him and prolong things. When it was over she pushed herself up from the table with shaking hands and lowered her dress.

Her bottom throbbed and was numb at the same time. Her sex was wet again, only this time it was her own juices running down her legs. She waited, as she always did, for his words of love to complement the punishments she knew she needed and to reciprocate the overwhelming affection she felt for him when he gave her what she deserved. But all he did was call her a cunt before plopping back in his chair, farting, and then taking a bite of his sandwich.

Martha retrieved his milk and placed it in its proper place, wondering if she would get another spanking before he went back to work. She glanced at the old, browning, rooster shaped clock on the kitchen wall to calculate the time she still needed to take care of her own business before he returned from work for the day.

She knew better than to be gone when he got home.

Chapter Eight

How could I have been so inept?

That was the thought that kept running through Rayne's head as she made her way back to her own cabin. The search had been completely futile, as she'd expected, which made Garrison agitated again, though she knew that this time his irritation was caused by disappointment, and not her. He'd tried to contact Burt Thompson again, who she learned was the police officer who had volunteered to spearhead the searches, but he had left for lunch and wasn't expected back for a couple of hours.

Garrison had ended the call then turned to her with frustration lining the edges of his mouth. He told her she might as well get on home, which had been his polite way of telling her to get lost, she was sure, and she hadn't wasted any time taking him up on it because she felt everything she said was the wrong thing.

It was a relief to make it back to her place. For the first time she noticed the chirping of the birds, the warmth of the sun, and the absolute peace for which she had first come to Mystic Waters. The song that suddenly sounded from her cell phone made her sigh. *So much for peace.*

Now she had to soothe her sister's ruffled feathers. Rayne was surprised they hadn't tried again earlier, or if they had, maybe the poor signal showing on her phone now had been nonexistent for a while.

"Hey, Sis."

Destiny's voice sounded but the words were so broken Rayne couldn't tell what she was saying. After walking around in circles over much of the yard, Rayne gave up trying to tell Destiny that she couldn't understand her. Finally she found a spot where she could hear her sister's words loud and clear.

"…and you better tell us what is going on right now or we are heading there as soon as we can book the flight."

Rayne exhaled, deciding she wasn't going to ask what all her sister had said. She got the gist of it. "Everything is fine. At least with me. My neighbor is in distress. His nephew is missing."

"Well, why didn't you just say that to begin with? And why haven't you called? We've tried several times! We thought you'd been kidnapped or something. And why were you having breakfast with that man? Why isn't he looking for the kid?"

Closing her eyes, knowing there was no way to cut this short, Rayne decided to keep giving the abridged version. "I stopped in. He was eating and offered me breakfast. I accepted. Then he got information that might be about his nephew. Things got a little crazy. Then I came back to my cabin. And now it's lunchtime and I'm going in to eat because I'm starved. Walking these mountain trails builds an appetite.

"I have really bad signal here so you might have trouble getting through to me. I just wanted you to know so you won't worry. And tell Haven I say, 'Hi.' I guess she's at work by now."

There was a long pause and Rayne waited. There was a chance her sisters would leave her alone a little if she gave up time now.

"Oh, okay. Yes, she's working. But be sure to call as often as you can. Otherwise we'll worry. And you know how Haven gets when she's worried."

"I do," Rayne agreed, wondering if Destiny had any idea that she was worse.

"Well then, tell me all about Mystic Waters. Are the people nice? Met any cute guys? Does everyone talk like we expected?"

The next fifteen minutes covered everything from dialects, a description of the town, the layout of the cabin, and Destiny revealing that she may have met someone who could be important, but there was something about him that bothered her. When the conversation ended Rayne made her way back to the cabin with a growling belly and a pounding headache.

Peaches and cottage cheese, an ice cold glass of homemade lemonade decorated with mint, and the remaining few frozen M&Ms—from a bag she kept on hand for emergencies—later, Rayne settled into the padded porch swing with a novel she'd wanted to read for months. But three pages in she felt her eyes drifting closed.

She fought the sinking sensation but nothing she could do would break the sleep-spell overtaking her. Finally she slid down across the seat and relaxed. As the book fell to the wood slats of the porch, her last thoughts filled with the slight chill edging the warming breeze, the music of chirping birds as they called to each other, and the face of a man who probably hadn't given her another thought once they'd parted. She wished she could so easily dismiss him from her mind.

****

She was a sleeping beauty with her long auburn hair hanging from the slatted seat to sweep the wooden porch deck below. Those long lashes he'd noticed before fanned out to touch the tops of slightly reddened cheeks, and he couldn't help but wonder if she'd gotten a slight case of windburn when they'd been out walking earlier. The rise and fall of her chest was slow and even, and he had to pull his gaze away when he realized he was staring at the curves of her breasts.

Garrison smiled as he studied her, gratified Whitehawk had asked him to build the six foot long swing which nearly took up the entire width of the porch. If Tom had only commissioned a standard length swing, Rayne's long legs would have hung over the end, possibly smacking a support beam as the wind picked up and the swing blew back slightly, before her weight brought it back forward. Once the swinging began, it picked up just a bit each time until her hair folded over itself then stretched out to sweep the porch, before folding back over itself again.

Stunning, was the one and only thought Garrison would allow as he forced himself to look away. As often happened in early spring the temperatures rose and fell rapidly, as did the wind, and if he wasn't mistaken there was rain headed their way. He glanced back at Rayne wondering if he should wake and warn her, or if he should sneak in and find a blanket to cover her instead. But neither seemed doable as she looked so serene and the last thing he wanted was for her to wake to him prowling around inside her cabin.

He'd already made himself look bad enough. And it was time to stop.

Garrison settled himself across the porch in one of the two chairs he'd also built, and thought about how idiotic he'd been around her. It was hard to believe they'd only met a few days before; she'd filled his thoughts so much it seemed much longer. He was embarrassed by his earlier behavior. And only grateful that she seemed to understand what a mess he was and pardoned him, but it was time he started acting like he had some sense where she was concerned, and face the reality that he was attracted to her, for better or worse, no matter that the timing sucked.

It shouldn't have taken almost four hours of self-debate before he gave in and hiked over to ask forgiveness again, as well as to see if he could look at her and feel nothing. But, he'd wrestled with guilt, and as hard to admit, maybe even a little fear. Now he knew why. Apologizing, he was happy to do. Trying to fight all the things about her that attracted him was clearly beyond his control.

Garrison leaned back. Settling into the seat, he closed his eyes. As long as she was napping he would, too. There was no way he was walking all the way back to his cabin only to have to come back again, hat in hand.

The lady was going to hear him out and accept his apology and, then he was going to see if she wanted to explore spending a little time together, here and there. It had been a really long time since he'd courted a woman. Dated, yes. Had sex with, yes. But not courted.

The idea appealed to him. As bad as the timing was, as illogical as the notion was given the mess his life was right now....

Garrison shook himself and opened his eyes only to find those cat eyes watching him, drawing him in, and he was done fighting it.

"Hi."

"Hi," Garrison said, glad that she didn't wake up mad at finding him resting on her porch. He pulled himself upright as she did and they sat there looking at each other. Finally he couldn't help but grin. "I owe you an apology."

Rayne returned his grin with one of her own, and it took everything he had not to cross the porch and kiss her mouth. Since she merely waited for him to continue, he did. "About earlier, I was upset."

"And rightly so."

"I acted like an ass."

"You acted like a man who had all he could take and I was there handing you more. I'm sorry about that."

Garrison shook his head. "You were only trying to help."

Her smile dimmed a little before she shrugged.

"I made a mess of it. I can see you need to be left alone to deal with all this, and I won't bother you anymore."

"You don't bother me. Well, actually you do, but not in a bad way. I'd like to make my bad behavior up to you, if you'll let me.

"I cheated you out of the breakfast you cooked, and it's getting close to dinner time. I was wondering if you'd let me take you out to dinner."

Rayne hesitated as she stared at him and Garrison was afraid she would refuse, which was exactly what he deserved. Although he wanted to press his case, he waited, knowing he'd already been pushing it by coming over uninvited.

"I could eat."

Garrison exhaled, unaware he hadn't for more than a

few moments. "Good."

Rayne raised her brows. "Where?"

A second try at his place at this point seemed a little forward. "In town. We have a nice diner. Great food. Meat optional."

Rayne laughed at that and he felt his libido kick. He kicked back. Though she was certainly gorgeous he wasn't into rushing women, and he'd already blundered with her so much he was treading more carefully from here on out.

"I eat meat. Just not often. And not fried."

"Good information to have."

"I need to get ready." She glanced down and her lips were pulled together when she looked back up at him. "I'll have to wash my hair, too. It's full of dirt."

Garrison grinned. "I think it was sweeping the porch while you slept."

Her brows arched again. "Just how long have you been here?"

Garrison knew that question would eventually come, but he didn't skirt it. "About fifteen minutes or so, I think. I'm sorry. I didn't mean to watch you while you were unaware, but you looked so peaceful I didn't want to wake you either."

She rose and moved to the center of the porch and he followed suit. "I'll give you all the time you need. I'll just hang out here and enjoy the breeze."

Rayne shivered, then looked at him like he was crazy. "It's getting cold. It wasn't this chilly when I fell asleep. Would you like to come in and wait while I get ready? I'll only take about thirty minutes... fifty, tops."

Her smile was suddenly so big it looked like she was posing for a camera he knew she was testing him. *Playfully.* Garrison smiled back. She was such a breath of fresh air in a world that had been dark and dank for what seemed like forever.

"Take your time. But I'll just hang out here. I'm used to the weather, and I can always admire the beautiful view to keep me occupied." Though he knew the view inside would be equally arresting.

Rayne surprised him when she returned to the porch twenty minutes later with a small bag hanging from her shoulder. She had changed from the jeans and shirt to a dress that was both casual and sexy. Or maybe the sexy had to do with the body it showcased.

Garrison followed her to her car reminding himself he had more groveling to do before he could approach the subject of his attraction, and test the strength of hers, if there was any to begin with. He looked the car over, then looked her over, and knew it had to be a rental. "Nice car."

"It's a rental. I need to decide if I want to turn it in and buy one or keep it as long as I'm here. I've rented the place on a year's lease, but you never know.

"Right now I'm kind of at a crossroads in my life, and I haven't yet decided which way I'm going."

Garrison processed her words and his gut tightened. He hadn't gotten a chance yet to ask her about her status, living or relationship-wise. Though he couldn't imagine any man going along with her moving alone to a remote cabin for a year, if she *was* involved; at least he knew it wouldn't have settled well with him where he the one to matter.

Garrison went to the driver's side and opened her door before stepping back. Rayne smiled up at him and he knew that he'd finally done something right. He swung her door closed then went to the passenger side, glad he'd remembered to use the manners his mother had so painstakingly taught her sons.

Chapter Nine

Burt couldn't breathe as snot filled his nose and gasps clogged his throat. It wasn't only that he was being raped by his uncle, who took over once his father finished, that had him so upset this time. He was used to the pain. Had come to like it a little even, though it still terrified him and it hurt like hell each time. But this time was definitely the worst, and worse still, no one had noticed that today was his birthday. Sixteen. *Sixteen, and he knew better than to expect a cake, gifts, or even a happy birthday wish.*

And it wasn't like he had any friends who would notice or care. His father had made sure they lived out in the middle of nowhere, and the kids at school looked at him like he was an alien because he was so skinny and all his clothes came from the Salvation Army and Goodwill. But it was better to think about hating them kids, than thinking about what was being done to him.

No. He didn't hate them. He wanted to be them. With their happy lives. With their cars and girlfriends, and parents who loved them. Not like him.

No... he knew who he hated the most. The whore of a mother who had left them, left him, *and his dad who missed having sex so badly he'd turned to fifteen-year-old Burt to take care of the job she should have been doing.*

He'd become his dad's wife. He had to cook and clean and bend over when told. And now he was being shared.

This was all her fault.

"Clean yourself up, kid." His uncle said, jerking back and smacking Burt's ass at the same time.

Burt's legs buckled and his knees hit the wooden floor before he slid down to roll into as tight a ball as he could make himself. He rolled back under the table and lay there listening to his father and uncle joke about what a good whore he made, and how they should start charging their friends to come over and partake.

He couldn't move. Knew it would be many hours, if not a day or two before he could use those muscles again. He'd have to be careful. Not eat anything that would require him to shit. Which meant he'd be drinking broth.

It was no wonder he was so skinny.

"Burt! You have to wake up! You're going to be late for work!"

Burt snapped his eyes open and snatched Martha's hand before she could pull it away. He jerked her onto the bed, not caring that he was late, not caring that she had gone and prettied herself all up before waking him. He needed to feel control. To *be* in control. To erase the vivid dream that had been a repeated reality so many times in his childhood....

He loved seeing the fear in her eyes as she landed on him. He loved the smell she put off when he ripped the dress from her body. Part fear, part excitement, and definitely wet pussy. He loved that she didn't have on a bra and made short work of her panties before rolling over and flipping her so she was on her stomach beneath him.

She was so clean, always so clean, and excitement had his dick throbbing. Screaming crashed around in his head as he felt his father's dick pressing against him even though he knew his old man was long dead. His dick got even harder, angrier, whipping around like a serpent ready to strike. Ready to bite. Ready to devour.

She screamed.

He screamed, ignoring her and everything but the anger that consumed him, as he clawed into her hips and held on for the ride. It only took seconds of maniacal ramming for him to explode then several more for him to jerk himself empty inside her.

As his own ghosts subsided he could hear her sobs. He could feel her shaking and see fingernail cuts and the threat of bruising on her butt cheeks where he'd gripped her so hard while spreading her wide open. He smelled the metallic scent of blood as he pulled out.

Burt knew he hurt her this time. Had probably even

permanently damaged her in some way.

And he felt nothing.

"Clean yourself up, woman," was all he said as he backed away and left the bed. He needed to shower and get to work, or his dick of a Captain would probably fire him.

Chapter Ten

Coldness was so steeped into every inch of him and had been for so long now he didn't remember what warmth felt like. Darkness was his constant companion and no longer feared, but despair had finally taken hold and wouldn't let go. Days and nights were all the same, but he was certain several had passed since his kidnapper's last visit and the food he feared but ate anyway was nearly gone; the water disgusting.

The sounds of footsteps no longer brought much of a reaction though he was relieved, if only for a moment or two, he wouldn't be alone. He was so tired of being alone, he wished he had died with his parents. At least they were together.

It hadn't started out that way. At first he had been determined to survive, determined to escape. Determined to finish what had been started by someone so evil he knew he had suddenly become capable of murder.

But that was forever ago. And now he just wanted it all to end.

He knew the drill: The flashlight beam was so glaring it burned his eyes if he dared to look towards the kidnapper. So he kept his eyes averted. A cardboard box of several dried foods would be scooted over to his cot with the long stick that had injured him the first and only time he had tried to escape. Sometimes there was even something cooked and stored inside a plastic container inside that box, but that was rare. Once he was seated a bucket of fresh water would be delivered as well.

He knew better than to move a muscle as the act played out. Food and fresh water were withheld for days that one time, and he'd gotten the message. When the kidnapper was done delivering the new supplies he was to stand up and use the entire length of his chain to push his old water bucket and the old cardboard box filled with his trash back, or he'd be forced to live with the trash and, he feared, rats.

He'd learned about the rats the hard way.

In the early days.

When his nightmare of a life had turned into something even worse.

Finally, when those transactions were done, he was to set the slop bucket of a toilet as far from him as he could, and then return to the cot so it could be carried out and emptied by his captor.

There was no talking from or to his kidnapper so he had no idea if it was the man he had gone after, to kill, after his parents had been murdered.

He hadn't seen the hit coming. Had made the mistake of leaving his uncle's cabin in the dead of night on the motorbike he'd been given as a gift following the funeral. Only he hadn't made it to town with the gun he'd stolen from his uncle's desk.

He'd been so close to locating that murderous, sick bastard. He'd only been a few doors away from the residence he was certain belonged to the man when he'd heard the car coming up behind him. His first mistake had been to ignore it, pretending he was where he was supposed to be; hoping whoever it was would ignore a kid out riding in the middle of the night.

The pain of metal car ramming him from behind, a terrifying flight through the air, and then nothingness, was all he remembered until he'd awakened on the cot he now called home.

Maybe he deserved this. Maybe this was his punishment for wanting that man dead. But if that was so, then his family didn't really know the God they all prayed to. The God he had been taught to love and obey hadn't protected his family, and all he'd wanted was justice.

Going to the police had been a no-go as he was certain

that man had been on the police force with his dad. Telling his family had been impossible because they would go after him and there could be more deaths in the family, and he just couldn't do that to his grandparents, aunts, and uncles.

Something hit him, startling him, and Gavin felt tears sting his eyes as realization dawned. It was large and wooly and almost too wonderful to be true.

A blanket.

He had a blanket.

This was followed by what was clearly clean clothing.

That took his breath. Made the tears fall. And it took everything he had not to express his gratitude.

Without him realizing it the slop bucket had been hauled out and dumped and was being returned. Were it not for the grunts of his captor he wouldn't have even noticed. All he wanted now was for the kidnapper to leave so he could use some of the fresh water to wash several weeks' worth of stench away; he could hardly wait to put on his new clothes.

And then he was going to wrap up in that blanket, lie down on that cot, and pray for death.

Chapter Eleven

Some days just felt perfect from the moment you opened your eyes.

Rayne stretched and then stretched again as giddiness engulfed her. She smiled with the joy of nothing more than being alive. She lowered her arms and slid a glance at the bedside nightstand. The small clock radio supplied by the owner of the cabin told her she was getting lazy. But she didn't care.

The night before had been magical. Not that she and Garrison had done anything special. They'd eaten at a little diner that served good food, and plenty of it. Then they had walked up and down Main Street and he'd told her a little of the history of the town and its people.

He was related to so many people in Mystic Waters that it boggled the mind, yet at the same time those connections were what made him the confident, considerate man she was learning he was.

They had talked about the clear, star-filled night, about the phase of the moon, and about the need for a little more rain. They had laughed together over the dog running down the street and the man chasing it, cursing it, and then pleading with it to stop before he gave up and the dog returned to him on its own.

They'd looked at the elaborate displays in the shop windows, and Garrison told her that only a few years before the town nearly collapsed because the economy tanked and so many of the shops closed. Not so now. The town was neat and clean and beguiling. And she couldn't wait to go shopping from one end of Main Street to the other.

They'd talked about the coal mining that went on in

the surrounding mountains, but Garrison said for some reason the coal companies had always left Mystic Mountain untouched. Those who had come to survey decades before went away with ghost stories, and stories of mythical animals that tore up supplies and equipment used to test the area, and terrified the men bringing them in. After a few attempts no one was willing to try again. That suited the local families, especially the Native Americans, as they loved the mountain just as it was.

The night had ended back at her house with a glass of wine before Garrison rose to his feet, took her hand, and raised it to his lips. He'd smiled at her then placed the gentlest kiss on her knuckles, and the breath fled her body.

She'd wanted more. She had wanted him to pull her into his arms and kiss her like he meant business. But he'd only grinned again, and then thanked her for giving him her evening. She closed her eyes and played the kiss back in her mind again, just for the pleasure the memory gave her.

She'd never had a man kiss her hand. Had never had one treat her with the gentle small kindnesses that came so naturally to him. He had been a perfect gentleman in every way. Yet somehow Garrison relayed that he found her attractive, and desirable, and for the moment untouchable. It was as refreshing as it was frustrating.

Enough of this!

Rayne rose and made the lovely bed before heading to the kitchen. She couldn't spend what was left of the morning swooning over the man. She needed to take stock of what supplies she needed before she went on a little road trip to check out her surroundings. Had to make contact with her sisters to see how they were and what they were up to. And give them a little information on what she was up to, too, because they wouldn't allow anything else.

But she wasn't going to mention Garrison. Not yet. Not until and unless there was a reason to. One wonderful evening with a man did not a relationship make, and her sisters would badger the pants off of her if she gave even a hint of being interested in someone.

As she pulled oatmeal from the cabinet and soy milk from the refrigerator she resisted the urge to dance. While filling the teapot with water for both the oats and green tea, she pretended not to notice she was humming. While turning on the gas burner she shut down a vision of the knuckle kiss for a third time.

And by the time she settled at the table with a steaming cup of tea and milk drenched oats she had to face the truth. She was smitten and smitten bad.

****

He felt guilty as hell.

Garrison took his time making sure the table leg he was remaking matched the pattern of the others as he stewed over the evening before. He'd had a great time. They had talked and laughed, and he had even kissed her hand, and his nephew hadn't entered his mind all evening.

Not once.

Garrison turned off the lathe and stepped back to snag the cup of black coffee he'd warmed in the shop's microwave. He could have made a fresh pot, but he had learned in his youth not to be wasteful and there was plenty in the pot left over from yesterday morning's makings.

He grimaced at the bitter taste but kept on drinking until the cup was empty before pouring another, setting it in the microwave, and punching the screen to heat it.

He considered going to the small refrigerator where he kept cold drinks and getting one of the cigarettes from the pack that had been stored there since he quit smoking the day Gavin moved in with him. But he resisted the urge. They were probably as stale as the coffee was bitter. But that wasn't the reason he resisted.

It was because of her.

She was all about natural healthy living. She always smelled like honeysuckle basking in the sun. She only ate things that were organic and, other than an occasional glass of wine, drank only soy milk, green tea, or purified water.

She wouldn't like him smelling like cigarette smoke, and he wanted to get close to her. *Really* close to her.

Garrison shook his head. He had to stop thinking about her all the time. She was becoming as big an addiction as smoking had ever been. Not that he'd had such a big addiction. When Gavin came to live with him he'd put the cigs down and hadn't given it a thought. When the kid went missing he'd had an occasional urge, but nothing he couldn't ignore.

They were just something he'd picked up while in the military and had been able to put down whenever he wanted to once he was back in the world. Back in Mystic Waters. Back with those he loved.

Garrison sighed. Those he loved were reduced. Two of the people he'd loved had been killed. The town had lost some of its innocence that day. His parents had lost their children...not just their child. Because Joy had been as much their daughter as she was their daughter-in-law.

And now they'd lost Gavin. Only he couldn't allow himself to think of that as permanent. It just couldn't be.

Garrison turned his attention back to the leg and looked it over several times before accepting that is was as perfect as he could make it. He loosened the lathe's tailstock locking screw then spun the tailstock hand wheel and pulled the wood from the machine.

Glancing over it once more he allowed his thoughts to wander back to Rayne, wondering what she was up to, whether she had taken that trip up and around the mountain, sightseeing she'd spoken about, wondering if she felt the same connection he had toward her.

"Looks good, son. Nice piece of work."

Garrison didn't jump, though his father's booming voice so close to his ear quadrupled his heartbeat. Once he could, he reached over and turned down the music he always kept blaring. "Hey, Dad, I didn't know you were coming out today." He glanced past his father's shoulder. "Mom with you?"

The elder Garrison looked his son over for a long time while shaking his head. "No, Momma is at home baking like crazy. Got us a new foster child yesterday and that kid is as skinny as Mrs. Yates' rescued greyhound.

"You know Momma is gonna fatten him up or die trying. Likely will. Those kids can't resist her treats." A wry smile lifted one side of his white mustached lip as he rubbed what was still a pretty flat stomach for a man of his age. "Neither can I."

Garrison smiled at his father. The affection in his voice for his wife of forty years had nothing to do with her baking skills, great as they were. The example his parents set for their children when it came to the opposite sex was something he hoped to mirror one day. Which brought his thoughts back to Rayne.

The elder Garrison ran his hand over the lathe looking a little *too* nonchalant, before sending his son an awkward look. "Word is your spoonin' with a young lady visiting up here on the mountain."

Garrison sighed. "I guess I should have known having a meal with a woman would make it back to you before an entire day had passed." He shook his head at the situation, feeling like a teenager caught necking in the back seat of a car. "I'm a grown man, Dad. And I barely know her. We're not exactly spoonin', as you put it. We just had dinner."

Garrison Sr. shrugged. "Not saying anything about it. Glad you are getting out, actually. Was sent here by your mother. Miss Sally told her sister Miss Hester, who told her hairdresser, LidaSue, who thought your mother should know at five-thirty this morning. Darned phone woke me from a pretty interesting dream."

Garrison couldn't help the smile that tightened his cheeks. "I see the Mystic Waters grapevine isn't suffering from drought. So why did Mom send you?"

The elder Garrison looked slightly uncomfortable. "Momma was concerned that you might be...well, you haven't exactly been yourself lately, and she was concerned...."

Garrison waited. His parents hadn't inserted themselves into his personal life since he'd dated Tiffany Miller in high school and the only reason they'd stepped in then was that she had a reputation for having wild parties when her parents went on vacations. He'd been to those parties and understood his parent's concerns now that he was older and had the responsibility of a child getting to the same age.

He only wished wild parties were the worst of his concerns regarding his nephew.

"I'm fine, Dad. Sick of this whole thing with Gavin because I should have done something...."

The elder placed his hand on Garrison's shoulder in a firm grip. "Nothing you could have done. Don't know what that kid was thinking, running off like that. Has nowhere else to go. We're all sick over it." With a squeeze and a pat he removed his hand and stepped back.

"But you can't do anything more than you've been doing. And you have got to take care of yourself. No offense, son, but you look like shit."

Garrison's brows jumped and he couldn't help the bark of a laugh that escaped his lips. He'd never once, in his entire life, heard his father use profanity. "Wow. Mom would make you wash your mouth out with soap for that."

Garrison Sr. laughed, too. "Yes, she would." His expression sobered. "Still, it's the truth. You have lost too much weight. You look as old as I feel some days. Not right for a man your age. Glad to see you bothered to shave that hair off your face, finally. Guessing a pretty woman had something to do with that."

Garrison knew he'd looked like a bum lately because his appearance had been the last thing on his mind. But he hadn't realized how much it had said to the others in his family. "Guess so. And she is pretty." He grinned, picturing her. "Really pretty."

A look of concern drew his father's brows together. "That's your mom's concern. She's afraid you might let your need for something to hold onto right now push you into something too quickly. Wouldn't bother her if the woman wasn't a complete stranger, and probably just visiting. Momma's afraid you'll get attached then she'll leave, and then you'll take it hard."

Garrison studied his father knowing this wasn't just *Momma's* concern. His father was a man's man, meaning he didn't stick his nose in other men's business. So Pops coming out to express concern over Rayne stepping into his life was obviously a real concern. He hadn't thought about anyone being concerned about him, and he felt ashamed. They all had enough to worry about.

"You don't have to worry about me, Pops. It's good to have something else to think about other than Gavin. Feel darned guilty about it. But it feels good.

"And about the woman, her name is Rayne. She's nice. And sexy as hell. And makes me remember that I'm still alive, which I guess I'd forgotten. But I don't know that we'll be anything more than friends." He grinned again, this time one man to another. "But I'm not opposed to more, in whatever form it takes, and for however long it lasts."

The elder Garrison nodded; a slight grin on his lips. "Well then, enjoy, son. You deserve it." He heaved a big sigh. "And now that that is out of the way, Momma wants us all for dinner tonight. The whole gang. She wants to see her kids at the table breaking bread and wants to introduce the newest member of the family. Seems to be a good kid. Kinda scared right now as most of them are when they first go into foster care.

"Invite Rayne if you want. I'll let everyone know in advance not to pick at her."

Garrison laughed. His family could be quite a trip when they all got together although since the murders and Gavin's disappearance those family gatherings had been a lot more somber. It was time to take back a little normalcy in all their lives. And he was going to set the example.

"I'll ask her. Either way, I'll be there. Tell Mom I expect an American pie."

Garrison Sr. nearly choked on his laughter mirroring Garrison's earlier reaction to his cursing. The family joke had gone on since the movie of the same name had horrified his mother when she had taken her children to what she had believed to be a family movie. To this day, with all the baking she loved to do, she would not make an apple pie.

"I'll tell her. And she'll likely wash *your* mouth out with soap."

Chapter Twelve

The mountains were just breathtaking. And the little knick-knack shops were wonderful.

Rayne drove around and shopped for hours before realizing she needed to head back. Garrison had texted her and asked if she would be interested in having dinner with him again tonight. Which thrilled her. Then he asked if she would be interested in doing it with his family, at his parent's home. That had given her a moment's pause.

It wasn't that it had to mean anything. And she was sure it didn't. But there was something about meeting a guy's entire family over a meal that was a little intimidating. Especially since she was so attracted to the guy.

If there were no feelings on her part she wouldn't hesitate. But the last thing she wanted to do was give anyone, including herself, the wrong impression. As much as she loved the area, and as much of a free spirit as she felt in these mountains, she wasn't allowing herself to think of the possibility of staying permanently. At least not yet.

And she had no idea how his family would feel about her entering their lives at such a critical time. From what Garrison had told her the night before, they were all very close and were a part of a very large extended family that was also very close. They had all grown up in Mystic Waters, and though there had been the occasional free-spirited cousin or two who flew the coup, for the most part they were all content to stay where they began.

And after being in the area she could understand that. Where else on earth would have been as fresh and clean, and friendly? Not LA, that was for sure.

Rayne sighed. The fact was she really liked the area. And she liked the way she felt here. A *B-12 on steroids* shot couldn't compare to the surge of energy that was now getting her out of bed at the crack of dawn—well except for this morning, had her walking endless miles just for the pleasure of it, and had her heart beating with anticipation for whatever the day would bring.

Whatever it was that had pulled her down, whatever it was that had been lacking in her life in LA, was gone. Every day felt like a new adventure to be discovered, and not just because she was vacationing, but just because…well, she didn't know why and that alone was exciting.

There was something about the mountains that kept that initial boost of energy going throughout the entire day. She didn't know if it was the air that was filtered and purified by the abundance of trees. Or if it was the musical sounds of the wind blowing in the breeze as it grew at breakneck speeds. Maybe it was the birds flying overhead calling and singing to each other as fauna traipsed around the woods barking or howling while they snapped twigs and crunched leaves. Even the night sounds of crickets and frogs were symphonic.

She felt a spiritual connection to the land as if she was where she was supposed to have been all along. Mostly, she felt renewed.

I'm staying.

Rayne let the words settle around her, waiting for a sense of panic or fear. But there was nothing but peace. Assurance. Acceptance.

"Oh, my," she said, allowing all the air in her lungs to exit as she pulled into the small parking space next to the cabin. She inhaled enough to repeat, "Oh, my."

The words, *Honey, I'm home,* crossed her mind as she entered the cabin, making her smile. An almost jittery excitement carried her across the living room into the kitchen area where she placed her purchases on the counter. She rummaged through the groceries first, putting things away, leaving the apples and baking supplies out to make the pies she would take to Garrison's family home later.

She then pulled out the crystals she'd found at a roadside tourist shop and held them in her hands. The differing sizes and colors, and the fact that they had been locally mined in caves that fed the hot springs, had caught her fancy upon entering the log cabin building that seemed to be a standard in the area. But the most interesting thing about them, now that she had them home, was how warm they grew in her palms.

Not that Rayne was surprised. Her mother Celestia and her identical sisters Lune Brille and Soleli had also been gifted, and the energy of their crystals had always been used to enhance their powers.

The Celestial Divinity crystal, such as the diamond one on her mother's necklace, had played a large role in her childhood, as had the turquoise Celestial Creativity encoded crystal her Aunt Lune Brille still wore on the finger that would have held a wedding band if she had ever married. But the one Rayne found the most fascinating was the one Aunt Soleli wore as a broach. The Citrine crystal, known as a Celestial Abundance Encoded crystal, could take her aunt spiritually to ancient civilizations, and the stories she had told of those places had kept Rayne and her sisters captivated for hours at a time when they were children.

Rayne hadn't thought about any of that for a long time, and though there were some very good childhood memories associated with her mother and aunts and their powers, she didn't want to think about them now. But it was a reminder nonetheless that she had to be careful not to reveal who and what she was to people if she wanted any kind of a safe and normal life.

Putting away thoughts of how badly things had gone for the generations before, Rayne rummaged through the house looking for a place to put her booty. She studiously ignored the strong urge to put them in the living room, but finally gave up and placed them on the fireplace mantel anyway when nothing else felt right. She knew better than to force them to be somewhere they did not want to be.

The one time Rayne remembered her mother ever

taking the crystal encoded necklace off and leaving it on her bedside table, she and her sisters thought it would be a fun joke to hide it and make Celestia have to search for it. Not only had the necklace been right back where her mother left it when she went to put it back on, Rayne, Haven, and Destiny were covered in itchy measles the next morning.

Without a word their mother concocted a cure, made them drink the disgusting stuff, and then told them about the time she took her own mother's crystal. The story had made them all laugh, the spots disappeared, and they'd never touched her necklace again without her permission.

Ready to get on with her day Rayne crossed the room and turned on the state of the art stainless steel range that should have looked out of place but didn't. The oven was obviously new, as were the refrigerator and dishwasher, and she loved how roughing it wasn't rough at all. City girl she was, but adaptable too...to a point.

There was no need for a recipe as Rayne had taken baking courses years before, before she decided sugar and shortening were going to play a very small role in her life. It wasn't that she was opposed to the occasional sweet treat she just had no desire to make it a lifestyle.

Tickled to find Granny Smith apples looking so fresh so early in the year, she opened and dumped the bag onto the counter.

She sliced each large apple into thin moon shapes, placing each one in the large mixing bowl she'd found in the cabinet, then she combined sugar and cinnamon in another smaller bowl. Once mixed, she poured the cinnamon over the apples and set the bowl aside so the apple's juices could mingle with the sweetness.

She loved making the crust from scratch as hardly anyone did anymore. Whipped egg was mixed with vinegar and water. This was added to the combination of flour, butter flavored shortening, and salt she'd placed into another large mixing bowl. Everything was measured and hand-mixed together until the dough reached the right consistency: not too wet and not too dry.

She'd have given anything for a cloth covered waved pastry board, but she was content to use the heavily floured countertop surface and the wooden rolling pen she found in a large utensil drawer. A second of panic hit her and had her turning to the cabinet that held the baking ware. She sighed in relief when she found four glass pie pans. She took the three she needed and turned back to the counter.

All in all the process of putting it together, trimming the top layer of crust, and finger rolling the top and bottom edges together before cutting slits and a center hole in the top took a little over an hour and a half.

Finally she put the pies in the large oven and set the timer for an hour.

That quick glance at the oven's clock had Rayne speed cleaning the kitchen. She needed to hit the shower as fast as she could. She would have just enough time to get herself ready and get the pies out of the oven before Garrison was expected to stop by to pick her up.

It wasn't hard to admit she was excited at the prospect of spending more time with him. She just hoped his family didn't find it too hard to entertain a stranger at such a heart-aching time. Heck, truth be told, she wanted them to like her. And her pies.

****

The thrill of seeing Garrison again, all cleaned up and looking...well, *dapper*, was mixed with a slight case of nerves. It wasn't just meeting his parents and siblings; it was that she was a little overwhelmed to be so attracted to a man she barely knew. And then there was the matter of the pies.

When he'd seen them, instead of commenting on the amazing smell and beautifully designed top, he'd burst out laughing. So she'd had the sick feeling there was something wrong with bringing the pies to the family gathering.

Thankfully he was doing all the talking as they traveled a lovely country road so he had no idea how close to panicking she actually was.

"...and my sister, Kate, is a mother of three. She

teaches school at the high school. It's been especially hard on her with all the kids constantly asking about Gavin."

Rayne pulled herself together, knowing sightseeing as they sped toward his parent's house and her own jumbled thoughts had caused her to miss part of what he'd been saying. "I bet it is. Any news?"

Garrison shook his head as he turned onto a gravel driveway. Since the house wasn't visible from the road she figured the farm belonged to his family as well.

"Nothing."

"I'm really sorry. I can't imagine how this feels." Which was and wasn't entirely true, but she didn't know what else to say.

Garrison tilted his head, sending her a slight smile. "I hope you never have to find out. Anyway, we're here."

Rayne turned to look at the large house they were approaching and felt a sense of surprise. This was no old farmhouse and dilapidated barns. The house was huge and modern and the barns looked like they should be on some racehorse estate. She slid a glance at Garrison but he didn't seem to notice. Finally she understood why he'd laughed at her pies. His mother probably didn't even know where her kitchen was as there were undoubtedly cooks and maids. She cleared her throat. "So the parents are rich."

She hadn't meant to say it, or make it sound like an insult. When she was about to apologize he looked at her curiously.

"Is that a problem?"

Rayne felt foolish. Her family certainly wasn't poor. She and her sisters had inherited fortunes centuries in the making. There was no reason for any of them to work if they didn't want to, but the Cavanaugh women were not slackers. From the beginning of memory her mother had instilled a desire to pursue some type of interest, one that helped others whenever possible, though she had cautioned strongly against using the gifts they would inherit unless it was absolutely necessary.

If only Celestia had heeded her own advice, then

Rayne, Destiny and Haven wouldn't have been orphaned at the tender age of fifteen. If it hadn't been for Aunt Lune Brille and Aunt Soleil taking over their upbringing, and helping them to learn further and embrace their newly gained gifts, they would have been lost.

But she didn't want to think about that. Not right now. Not when all she wanted was to embrace a new and normal life and possibly pursue a romance with a man who she liked so much it scared her.

"No. Of course not. That came out wrong. I guess I liked that you were a...well, not a struggling artist, but a craftsman who made your own living."

Rayne felt even more foolish now. How could she tell him he liked thinking he was just the average guy living an average life? That she was seeking normal and normal people didn't come from this kind of wealth.

Garrison grinned. "No worries then. I support myself. All this," he said, indicating the massive house and manicured lawns, "won't come to me and my siblings until the parents pass on. And they are still young and healthy and our family members live a very long time. You'll get to meet my grandparents and great-grandparents, too. When Mom calls for a family dinner, she means everybody up and down the line."

"Well that isn't intimidating."

Rayne's dry comment made Garrison laugh. "Wait until you meet them. I think they will be more intimidated by you. By the way, we'll leave the pies here until after dinner. I think it will be a nice surprise."

Rayne frowned. Afraid to address the issue of the pies, she focused on what he'd said. "I'm not intimidating!"

Garrison only smiled and got out of the truck. Rayne started to open her door but he beat her to it. "My folks are looking out the windows, I'd bet on it. If my mom saw you let yourself out of a vehicle she would have my hide."

Rayne's brows shot up and she smiled. So his parents had taught manners and she wasn't one to belittle such a thing. In fact she liked it very much. "Well, I wouldn't want you to get spanked with so many people around."

The inside of the house was elegant but in such a homey relaxed way that Rayne immediately felt at home. More importantly Garrison's family was a welcoming boisterously happy group that taunted and teased each other until it was time to settle in at the table. She listened to the conversations running over top of each other, sometimes missing things when someone else's conversation bled over the one she was listening to, but she didn't care. It was nice to be included as if they had known her all their lives.

When everyone was seated, the chatter stopped and all eyes turned to the head of the table where Garrison's great-grandfather slowly rose to his feet. He lowered his head, as did everyone at the table. Rayne followed suit and listened to the praise of the Lord, the blessing of the meal, and finally the heart-tugging request for Gavin's safe return to their fold. When everyone lifted their heads following the Amen, the room was a lot more somber as one family member looked to another. Then there were smiles. And then it was as it had been before; laughing, and kidding, and so much food passed around the monstrously large table that Rayne knew she would never be able to sample it all.

She was amazed at the resilience of the family given their circumstances, but it was clear they all were leaning on their faith and each other. And she knew right then she would have to help them if there was any way she could. Even if it meant she would lose what she felt she could have in Mystic Waters. And maybe even with Garrison.

"So tell us about yourself, Rayne."

Rayne lowered her fork, deciding she didn't need another bite anyway. She had consumed more food since sitting in this seat than she'd ever consumed at one time in her life. She had expected the curiosity and the questions, and was actually surprised it had taken an entire feast for someone to ask. If Garrison had been to one of her family gatherings his bones would have been picked clean before the water was dried from his finger bowl cleansing.

"Well, I'm from LA."

The family waited and Rayne realized she didn't know what else to add.

That she had spent a good part of her adult life reading and studying, and ultimately chronicling as much of her family's history as she'd been able to, given the size and scope of the project, as well as categorizing and insuring three thousand years of acquisitions, at her aunts' requests? That she spoke to ghosts and intended to start chronicling her experiences for the next generation? That her sisters and aunts, and female ancestors all had powers that scared the begeebers out of most people?

Probably not a good idea.

So what did that leave her with? That she was an artist? She could work with that, but she had never shown her work to anyone but family so that was really only a hobby and she'd heard enough about all those gathered at the table that they would think her a lazy slacker if she said that was all she did.

"Rayne?"

Pulling herself from her desperate thoughts Rayne smiled at Garrison. He looked so concerned she hadn't said anything more, and everyone else was staring at her so intently she blurted the first thing that came to mind. "I'm a writer."

Everyone instantly relaxed and started firing questions at her.

"What do you write? Fiction? I love fiction!"

"Are you published?"

"Who's your publisher? I'd like to submit some poetry but don't know how to go about it."

"Do you write paranormal? That's my favorite! I love vampires and werewolves!"

Rayne wasn't sure who asked what, but it gave her an idea, and a goal, since she wasn't about to lie outright to all these nice, excited people. "I've only been studying the paranormal to this point and done some writing, but nothing I'm ready to have published. Actually, that is what I need time here to do. To start a book and see it through."

Instead of disappointment that she wasn't some famous author, the conversation continued to fly at her and around her. Garrison's family members were not just trying to be polite, but seemed genuinely interested about the startup of a career for someone they didn't really know. That, and the fact that she was now completely in love with the idea herself, stirred an excitement she'd felt lacking in her life for far too long.

"Well, before you all wear Rayne out, I need to run out to the truck for a moment." He jumped up and left and Rayne remembered the pies. Even though she didn't think she could eat another bite, she was glad she'd chosen apple pies as her contribution. There were all kinds of cakes and candies and pies—which nixed the possibility that they were unacceptable—but there wasn't an apple pie amongst them. She turned with the others when Garrison entered carrying a pie in each hand.

"Rayne made pies." He grinned sheepishly as several eyes turned to her with delight. "They are homemade, from scratch...and they're apple pies."

There were surprised gasps as all gazes jumped to Garrison's mother. Complete silence that lasted at least ten seconds by her estimation ended abruptly when the entire room broke into laughter.

Rayne didn't know what to do as the room became hysterical. Finally she asked quietly, "Is someone allergic to apples?"

Chapter Thirteen

"That was the best pie I've ever had, hands down."

"You could have told me."

Rayne was torn between amusement and embarrassment, but she didn't mind being the butt of his joke since her pies were immediately devoured by people who were surely as stuffed as she had been after the feast his mother spread.

"And miss out on that? Sorry, Rayne. Not in a million years. My siblings and I have been deprived for too many years."

She smiled. "Yes, you all looked terribly deprived."

Garrison laughed. "Okay, maybe not *deprived*. But we weren't allowed to even look at an apple pie much less eat one after Mom hauled us all out of that theater kicking and screaming."

Rayne allowed the pleasure she felt at being so accepted by his family to settle along with her meal. They had stayed at his family home the entire afternoon. The sun would set soon and she was still so full from the early meal that she hadn't touched the evening meal when the food was brought back out, reheated, and consumed again.

It wasn't something she'd ever even thought about before, but she knew she couldn't make eating like that a habit. There were no fat Cavanaugh women in her history as far as she knew and she didn't want to be the first. In fact, since Garrison had to leave her to take care of a delivery as soon as they got back to her cabin she decided she would take a walk before twilight. She could work some of the meal off and get some exercise after spending so much of her afternoon on her behind while visiting.

She smiled at him. "You all must have made quite a

sight."

Garrison's smiling face slowly relaxed and a pensive look entered his eyes. "Yeah. My brother, Gavin's dad, took it the worst. He was the oldest and was mad Mom still wouldn't let him stay. It wasn't until a year or so ago that he apologized to her for his behavior that day. He said having Gavin changed his perspective on a lot of things."

Silence settled in the truck's cab as they sped along the mountain. Rayne fought the urge to reach for his right hand where it rested in the seat between them. She was totally crushing on him, but she wasn't ready to let too much happen between them until she knew it was more than a crush and taking his hand could lead to…anything. But she couldn't ignore the pain that filled the cab's air, so she took his hand anyway, opting to let comforting him override her fears. She wove her fingers between his and slid her thumb over his, allowing their palms to warm each other.

Garrison didn't turn his head as he kept his gaze on the road but a subtle grin tilted his lips. Finally, he sent her a fleeting glance. "I wanted to reach over and take yours."

Pleasure mingled with surprise. "What stopped you?"

He shrugged slightly. "I don't want to rush you, or this, whatever *this* is."

The pleasure deepened. "I don't know what it is either. But I'm enjoying the slow pace."

Garrison nodded, almost as if she had said the right thing. "Slow it is then. As long as I still get to see you as often as possible."

Tingling thrills shot through Rayne's body and she nodded. "Definitely. As often as possible."

Garrison squeezed her hand before letting go to grasp the steering wheel, so his left hand was free to hit the turn signal, before turning into her long driveway. His smile stayed in place as he pulled the truck to a stop in front of her cabin. Without even thinking about it she waited for him to come and open her door. Then felt another thrill when he took her hand and walked her up the steps to settle on the porch, before her front door.

He stood looking at her for several seconds. "Slow doesn't mean I'm not going to kiss you."

Rayne smiled before setting the glass pie pans on the little drink table. She turned back, again standing before him. "Slow doesn't mean I'm not going to kiss you back."

Absolute thrill settled into her soul when Garrison placed his palms on either side of her jaw, as fingertips pushed the hair back from her face. He lifted her face then, just studied it for several seconds, finally running a work-roughened thumb across her lower lip. Her mouth fell open with a little breathless *"huh."* Garrison took that as his invitation as he slowly lowered his head and ever so gently took her mouth with his own.

Rayne felt herself melting, apparently so did Garrison as he pulled her to him, deepening the kiss, yet still keeping it gentle and searching. When he lifted his head and she opened her eyes Rayne could do nothing but stare at him. The slow smile on his still moist lips engulfed his face causing crinkled crow's feet at the corners of his eyes.

"I think I'm going to like slow very much." His head lowered again and he placed one more quick but gentle kiss on her lips before releasing her. "Good night, beautiful."

Rayne raised a hand and placed her fingers over lips that felt swollen, as she watched him walk away. She regained her senses enough to flash a goodbye wave when he waved to her as he was backing up, but she felt rooted to the spot. When a bird sent out a sharp warning of some kind she realized that he was gone and decided slow might not work for *her* at all.

She definitely needed that walk now. Not to walk off the remnants of a big meal or to exercise her legs. What she needed was a way to work off a serious case of sexual energy.

Within minutes, Rayne was up in her room and changing into sweats and tennis shoes. She glanced out of the small bedroom window at the end of the loft to gauge how much time she had until dark. As the days were getting longer, she hoped it would translate into her getting to walk at least halfway to Garrison's cabin and back although she knew going that way would be risky.

She might just want to go the rest of the way. And that would be a mistake.

So she would go in the opposite direction. Not too far as she didn't want to take a chance of getting lost with dark approaching. But just far enough to relieve some of the tension and rather erotic thoughts of Garrison touching more than her face and hands.

Despite knowing it was probably a mistake, Rayne needed to be honest. She knew it was foolish to pretend she didn't want something with Garrison. Short or long term. He was everything she wanted in a man: smart, creative, caring, compassionate, and so manly in his own way that her body was doing naughty little jumps of joy.

She set off, enjoying the coolness as the sun started its descent in the west. Since the trees were still only budding or opening fresh young leaves there was still plenty of light filtering through the canopy of branches overhead. The smells of soil, decomposing vegetation, and wintergreen from the pines that were both young and old blended together in a pleasant aroma that only came from the pristine outdoors. It was so different from the smog polluted air she had breathed her entire life that she wondered how she had kept her health. It was no wonder everyone she'd met in Mystic Waters looked so healthy.

It wasn't long before she realized she hadn't been paying attention to the lowering light and a creepy feeling crawled over her skin. She stopped and took a breath, then turned around to look back. There was nothing but trees.

Don't panic.

Okay, she wasn't panicking. That was clear. Because she hadn't actually shouted the thought but was only giving herself an order. A few more cleansing breaths and she started a determined gait back in the direction she believed she'd come from.

Of course there was nothing to help her gauge how far

she had actually walked while lost in the joy of being deliriously *in like* with a guy, his family, and his hometown. But that was okay. She would just keep walking. Which she did for another five minutes before apprehension reared its ugly head. Still, she kept walking, each step making her a little more furious with herself for being so stupid.

Irritation and a bite of anger was better than fear, and she was going to hold onto it for as long as she could because fear was trying to take hold, and everywhere she looked, was exactly like everywhere she'd been. Darkness was falling in earnest now and visibility was little more than varying shades of dark shadows big and small.

That's okay.

It will be okay.

Everything will be okay.

It didn't feel okay. It felt anything but okay. Panic was definitely taking hold and Rayne bit her bottom lip to keep from yelling.

What if there were wild animals? What if there was something worse? Gavin had disappeared after his parent's being horribly murdered. How had she forgotten that? How had she allowed herself to think that Mystic Waters and the Smoky Mountains were safer than any other place on earth?

"Rayne!"

Garrison's voice nearly took her to her knees. She tried to respond but couldn't as tears choked her throat. After she heard her name a second time she screamed and screamed and screamed until he was jerking her against him and holding onto her as if he would never let go. She felt foolish but the tears wouldn't stop as she gasped for breaths that couldn't come fast enough.

Until she felt his lips capturing hers.

At first she fought him, still trying to breathe, but he wouldn't let go. Several seconds went by with him holding her firmly, keeping his open mouth over hers, until her breathing began to slow. After a few shaky sobs into his mouth he eased back and looked into her eyes. "You were hyperventilating. Are you okay?"

Rayne nodded, understanding now that he wasn't kissing her but helping to calm her breathing. She leaned into him as her body felt too heavy to hold up. Still she couldn't speak through the shaking settling into her body.

"Let's get you home," Garrison said, holding her tight against him.

Rayne nodded, more than happy to let him take care of her. She didn't feel capable of taking care of herself, and she had no idea where home was anyway.

It only took another five minutes of him leading her before they were back at the cabin. As soon as she saw it she pulled away from him. Now that she knew she was headed in the right direction all along and was almost home, she was embarrassed. She wasn't a ninny! She didn't fall apart. And to act like the first and do the second in front of such a strong man was more than she could stand.

"What's wrong?"

Rayne shook her head but couldn't look at him. Instead she decided to study the ground. "I must look so foolish. I'm not usually."

Garrison walked around to stand in front of her. He took her jaw gently and lifted her face so that she would have had to make a ridiculous effort to avoid his gaze. He smiled. "You are the least foolish woman I've ever met."

Rayne studied him, knowing he spoke sincerely. Then a thought occurred to her. "What are you doing here? I thought you had a delivery to make."

Garrison smiled and slid his hand from her jaw to her cheek where he gently tugged her toward him. "I didn't want to leave you to deal with that, or anything for that matter. So I called my customer and begged off until tomorrow which, of course, was fine with them since they already knew I had the mysterious woman from California over to my family's home all day."

Rayne frowned. "How did they know that?"

Garrison chuckled. "You haven't yet become acquainted with the Mystic Waters grapevine. Let me just say we have lots of juice in this town. Right now me seeing the beautiful new lady in town is more fun to talk and speculate about than anything else." His smile fell away. "Especially since lately the only thing on anyone's mind or tongue has been about Gavin, and my brother and sister-in-law."

"How do you all do it?"

Garrison shrugged. "I know it probably seems strange that we can still get together and have a good time. But that's the way we were raised. My dad and mom are steeped in faith and raised us kids that way. That means although we hurt, we go on, on faith. It's been hard for me to keep the faith lately. But I'm a product of my parents and I always come back to it. I'm just hoping and praying Gavin will be back and be okay. But if not...." Garrison lowered his head then shook it before looking at her again. "I think the hardest thing is not knowing what to think, or feel. Do I worry, or is it too late for that?"

Rayne knew what Garrison was talking about. The not knowing was somehow worse than the knowing. At least then the mourning process could begin. To hang in limbo was horrible. Before they had found out her mother's fate her sisters and she had been beside themselves with worry and wondering. When Momma was found and brought back home to be buried they had all suffered greatly at the horror she must have experienced. But it was over, and all that was left was the overwhelming sense of loss, and the regret that none of them knew the whole story. The worst thing was, even with all of their gifts, none of them could have saved her.

"You've gone off somewhere."

Garrison's gently spoken comment brought her back to the realization that they were still standing outside. She found a smile and took his hand from her face and then pulled him towards the steps. "Let's go in. The air is getting a little chilly."

A flash of movement at the tree line caught her eye and she paused to stare at the ghost of the young Indian.

He was pointing back in the direction from which she and Garrison had just come. Rayne hesitated, wondering what she should do. If the brave had some more information regarding Gavin then she felt she should follow. But there was no way to explain to Garrison why she would want to go back out into the woods.

I'll come tomorrow.

She hoped the thought reached the ghost, then figured it probably had since he vanished instantly.

"What are you looking at?"

Rayne shrugged. "It doesn't look so scary now."

Garrison pulled her on to the cabin's front door and paused. "Keys?"

She shook her head. "I didn't plan to be but a few minutes, so I didn't lock it.

He glanced at her questioningly. "You didn't lock it? Knowing what is going on around here?"

Rayne shrugged. "I will next time. I guess my mind was on other things." She smiled at him.

Garrison smiled back. "Don't let it happen again. And...don't ever go out walking in the woods this late. It gets dark quickly and you could get lost. Really lost."

Rayne led him into the living room and plopped down onto the couch. He came to sit next to her. "You don't have to worry about that, I was fine. I really was. Until just before you called my name. I was starting to get a little panicky at that point because I wasn't sure I was headed in the right direction. It seemed to take so long getting back. I had expected to see the cabin already. I hadn't gone that far, at least I didn't think I had, so I started doubting myself. And then you yelled my name. The relief was so great I couldn't move."

Garrison didn't comment that a little panicky seemed an understatement and she appreciated his consideration. "I'm so glad you came back."

Garrison pulled her against him. "So am I. Now the question is are you going to send me packing?"

Rayne allowed him to take her lips, savoring the taste

and feel of him. Her mind disengaged as she delved into sensations that coursed through her body like the blood in her veins. The kiss remained gentle almost, but not quite chaste, as Garrison took his time sampling and tasting. He pulled back just enough to keep her from completely melting into the couch.

"So…you did say you made a third apple pie?"

Rayne laughed, relieved things weren't going to get too heavy, because as revved as he made her with his kisses, she was frankly exhausted. "I did. Guess lunch and that plate you had later finally wore off?"

He rubbed his flat stomach. "Yes. Especially after rescuing a damsel in distress. That takes a lot out of a guy."

Knowing he hadn't intended to remind her of her embarrassing behavior, Rayne jumped to her feet and headed to the counter separating the kitchen and sitting areas. She stopped cold when she saw the pie.

"Garrison?"

He turned his head to look back at her then stood and joined her. They stared at the tattered remainders of a nearly eaten pie. He placed his hand around her shoulder to steady her when she swayed.

Rayne looked up at him in disgust. "Do I have rats?"

Garrison released her and approached the remnants. He looked in and around the glass pan then looked back at her. "No droppings. So probably not." He studied the area a moment longer, then the pie, before looking at her with concern pulling his eyebrows together. "I think someone ate it but tried to make it look like an animal."

A chill went up Rayne's spine as she looked from him to the pie. "Should we call the police?"

Garrison chewed on his bottom lip for seconds before nodding. "Maybe so. I have a quick access contact on the force. He's the one I called before. Maybe he can get out here and check things out."

Rayne watched as Garrison searched the little cabin, then followed him outside. They took opposing seats on the porch expecting a long wait, but it was only moments before headlights indicated the arrival of the police officer.

Once Garrison introduced them, Rayne wasn't sure why, but something about the officer gave her the creeps. She knew that it wasn't fair to judge a book by its cover, but she was never one to ignore her instincts, and the guy just gave her the willies.

She wasn't sure if it was that his interest in the pie-eating culprit extended up into her bedroom area where his fat fingers touched and searched through her belongings, or if it was the way he licked his fat lips every time he glanced her way. Or it could have just been the smell of him.

Rayne glanced at Garrison as he also watched the officer look and snoop beyond what she felt necessary and was surprised he didn't seem to notice how strange the guy was. But his mind was so full of all the events weighing on him and his family that she had to let it pass.

"Well, might be a good idea to use the lock on the door from now on. Never know who might pass through," the officer said, looking at her with a strange smile.

Rayne slid another glance at Garrison only this time she could see the confusion on his face, and then something like hope entered his eyes. "Could it be Gavin? Maybe he's around somewhere close and came by and was hungry?"

Rayne's gaze jumped back to the officer only to see sudden hunger in his pig-like eyes. Something hit the lining of her stomach hard before nausea climbed up her throat. She turned away and muttered an excuse before heading to the small bathroom as quickly as possible.

Retching hit just as she leaned over the toilet. Her stomach continued to revolt until she thought she would fall over from the exhaustion of it. Finally, she felt it was over and she moved over to the sink. Cold water on her face and wrists helped a little, but she knew nothing would help more than getting the taste out of her mouth. As she brushed her teeth Rayne wondered if her sudden ill feelings had to do with the strange officer, the stress of being vandalized, or if it was simply a result of overeating.

Probably a combination of all three, she decided as she rinsed her mouth. With shaking hands she wetted a washrag and ran it over her lips then her neck. She took a minute more to calm her stomach before opening the bathroom door.

Garrison was standing there with his fisted hand up, apparently about to knock.

To her relief the officer was nowhere in sight. "Is he gone?"

Garrison nodded, immediately moving forward. He put the back of his hand on her forehead. "Yes. He just left. You don't look too good and your forehead is soaked. Are you sick?"

Rayne nodded. "I don't feel good. Can we sit down?"

Garrison led her to the couch and pulled her down against him. He held her there, cradled beneath his arm, as she laid her head against his chest. "My mother would be appalled to know her food made you sick."

Rayne figured he was joking, but just in case he wasn't... "It wasn't her cooking. But it may well have been my eating. I never eat that much. Not even close."

Rayne settled in and absorbed strength from his care and matched her breaths to his even ones as questions and concerns continued to hammer at her. There was something about that cop, and the fact he'd made it to her cabin so quickly, that kept eating at her. And his behaviors had struck her as odd, though she had no idea if it was a personality thing or if there was actually something weird about the guy. Regardless, she didn't like him, and that worried her. There were very few people she had met in her lifetime who she'd taken an instant dislike to, but those few turned out to be bad people.

She glanced up to ask Garrison about the man only to find his head lolled back and his eyes closed. The even breathing and lack of questions should have clued her in. But she'd been so content to be held while her stomach continued to settle she hadn't given a thought to how long a day it had been for him.

She knew now that he and several of his family members started their days extremely early continuing their search for Gavin, then they had full work days, and then they had family time or spent time checking with law enforcement to make sure that the search was still being taken seriously. Though, sadly, she knew from the discussions at Garrison's family home the search had changed from a rescue mission to a recovery mission.

That was the only topic during the family gathering that had turned serious, and she'd felt the frustration and anger each one felt since it seemed the police were giving up on finding Gavin alive. It was very clear they refused to give up and she was relieved. Since his spirit hadn't come to her she felt certain he was alive.

She was *pretty sure* anyway…but where was he?

Rayne slowly slipped from beneath Garrison's arm and was relieved she didn't wake him. She rose as slowly then turned to look at him. In slumber he seemed younger, the weight of the world temporarily lifted from his shoulders. She wanted to move him so that he would be more comfortable, but she feared that would only wake him up. And if there was anyone who needed rest, it was him.

She stepped away quietly and entered the kitchen area. After the cop had left she hadn't really done anything to clean up the mess. As she raked and wiped and silently dumped it all in the trash can she let her mind wander back to the young Indian. Did he know something? Was he willing to tell her?

It seemed clear he wanted her to follow him. But it was totally dark out now, and there was no way she was going into those woods until the sun lit her way and she was prepared for as long a hike as she might need to make.

It would be so much better if she could take someone with her. Garrison especially. But she couldn't explain why she was going where she was going without sounding like a fruitcake. And if it turned out to be nothing, which was the most likely scenario, she would only make matters worse.

Even if she had known how to contact him without

alerting Garrison, asking the cop to go with her was out of the question. She still felt a chill anytime she thought of him. And it scared her. She wasn't an Intuit like her sister, but such feelings were normal to an extent. Not to the extreme she was feeling, however.

Those thoughts made her realize she needed to touch base with her sisters. Something weird was happening. Even the thought gave her chills. A quick glance to check on Garrison was diverted toward the fireplace mantel and a gasp escaped her lips.

The crystals were *glowing!*

Chapter Fourteen

"A storm is coming."

Destiny nodded as she stared out into the cloudless California morning through the large glass wall of their house. She turned to Haven, noticing the dark circles under her eyes. Apparently she hadn't been getting any sleep either.

"So you feel it too?"

Haven nodded as she turned to look out to the vista they had known their entire lives. "Something is wrong with me."

Destiny exhaled heavily. "I know. Something feels…ill, I guess. I wondered if it was just me. Are we missing Rayne too much?"

Haven shrugged. "I do miss her. And I worry about her. But it's more than that. I purposely touched a kid with failing kidneys yesterday at the hospital. I just took off my gloves and placed my hands on his little tummy when his mom went to use the bathroom. I couldn't help myself. He's been waiting so long for a donor, and time is running out fast."

Destiny knew what it had cost her sister to make such a daring move. "What happened?"

"Nothing. Nothing happened."

Destiny turned to face her sister again, shocked not only by the deadpan tone but by the words. "*Nothing?*"

Haven shook her head, her gaze still going across the California landscape. "I jumped back when there was no warmth, no sizzle, no crack, no spark, then moved forward to try again." She let seconds tick by before speaking, again. "But nothing."

A chill ran down Destiny's spine to settle into her

organs. She knew it by name. *Fear.*

Chapter Fifteen

Not being able to get in touch with either sister wasn't all that unusual since both had very busy lives, but it irked Rayne more than a little not to be able to tell them about the crystals.

She was mystified by them, and so excited by the possibilities all she wanted to do was go back where she found them and investigate their origins and purposes, even though they hadn't lit up since their brief flash the night before. She didn't want to consider she may have imagined the glowing colors and, stranger still, the low hum that seemed to try to form words as they vibrated themselves an inch or so across the mantel.

But she had made a promise to a ghost. And ghost or not, a promise was a promise. So she dressed for hiking in above the knee length running shorts, a sweatshirt covering the matching tank top, long white socks, and the boots she'd found in a local store that had everything from hunting equipment to canning supplies.

Once downstairs, the kitchen yielded a large drinking container she poured bottled water into, and small plastic snack bags she filled with some of the nuts and berries she had picked up at the same shop where she found the crystals.

Her thoughts returned to them, she glanced across the cabin to the fireplace mantel, but they were sitting where she had originally left them, acting as if they'd never done a thing.

Rayne frowned. Maybe her imagination was a little too healthy.

Hoping not, she snagged the *Louis Vuitton* backpack she had brought from California and put all her hiking supplies in, adding a couple of dish towels as an afterthought, just in case she got hot and needed to wipe sweat from her brow or the back of her neck.

Thoughts of that sent her back upstairs to find a *hair pony* as she and her sisters had deemed the elastic bands as kids. Quick efficient movements had her hair up in a long ponytail, before she headed back to grab her supplies.

She snagged the cabin's keys to add to her bag and headed out the door as quickly as possible. She knew if she let herself think about what she was doing she might chicken out, and she didn't want to do that. She was no coward. And she wanted so badly to help Garrison find his nephew, if there was any chance at all.

With the door locked behind her, Rayne headed for the tree line where she last saw the Indian, hoping he wasn't too mad at her for the delay. Stepping from the sunshine to the cooler shaded trees allowed her to assess what she was about to do more calmly, so she slowed her steps and remembered to mark each tree with a snap of a young branch.

Ten minutes in, she stopped. "I'm not going any further if you don't come to me."

Silence was her answer, but she wasn't defeated yet. She pulled off her backpack and removed the water jug. Several sips later she was afraid she was wasting her time. But then the young Indian appeared before her, much closer than he had before. He solidified as much as any ghost ever had in her presence. She smiled at him but felt a little foolish when his expression didn't change.

"Good morning, Qaqeemasq. Thank you for meeting me."

He stayed where he was, though he did nod once.

Rayne waited, wondering what proper etiquette was when dealing with a ghostly native son. She bit her bottom lip before diving in. "I was wondering if you had something you wanted me to see."

Qaqeemasq nodded once, again, making Rayne wonder if that was what he had done when he was still of the Earth.

She nodded also and waited for him to lead the way. Surprisingly he did so immediately, heading in the direction she had already been taking. Rayne followed silently, deciding he must not have come to her earlier because he was satisfied with her progress until she had stopped.

A minute or so passed before she realized she hadn't been breaking limbs. She stopped abruptly and looked back, and felt instant relief that the last limb she marked was within sight. Distant, yes, but still in sight. She immediately broke the closest limb and resumed following him.

Nearly thirty minutes passed and Rayne was wondering if she had been foolish to follow him further into the heavily wooded mountain. After all, for all she knew he was just messing with her head. Ghosts did that sometimes. Probably out of boredom. And in his case it could likely be because she was a white woman and if she remembered correctly, being white and being a woman in his world, in his time, hadn't been a good thing.

Just as she was about to call it quits he stopped and pointed to the ground. Rayne moved forward and looked down. Not seeing anything but mossy vegetation, she looked back up at him. "What?"

A flash of anger twisted his lips in a face that was suddenly very clear. She was so startled at how beautiful he was that it took several seconds, and a blast of cold air, for her to realize he wanted her to pay attention.

He put his fists together, one over the other, then made an up and down motion that swept slightly to his side. It took a moment for her to realize he was making the movements of someone using a shovel. The fleeting thought that he knew about shovels was quickly pushed away by the increased speed of his movements, indicating his urgency.

Rayne held up her hand, motioning for him to stop. "Okay. I get it. You want me to dig."

Qaqeemasq just stared at her, reminding Rayne he had no idea what she was saying. She repeated his motions and pointed to the spot he had indicated. When he nodded, she did too.

Before she could allow herself to think too much about what she was doing she searched for and found a jagged rock which was slightly larger than her hand. She looked around some more and gathered a few broken branches then discarded all but the youngest looking one. Its green center would probably serve her better than those that looked about ready to disintegrate from rot.

Finally, she placed her finds beside the spot where the young Indian remained. She looked at him once more before dropping to her knees. She stared at the ground, wondering what she thought she was doing. What if she found Gavin White's remains? How could she handle that? How would she tell Garrison and others how she came across the area—and knew to dig?

She didn't know. And was afraid to think up any more questions because she wanted more than anything to stand up and run back to her cabin. But she knew she couldn't do that. If Gavin had been murdered and buried here, she needed to know. His family needed to know.

A sense of soothing warmth coursed around her, and Rayne exhaled a breath she hadn't realized she'd been holding. She glanced up to look at the young brave. "Thank you."

A slight smile lifted his lips and she realized he had understood that. She nodded again and turned herself to the task.

It didn't take long. Less than six inches of dirt was disturbed before she saw what she most dreaded. A sick feeling roiled inside her stomach as she uncovered the bones of first one finger, then another then the rest along with the hand. They were still connected to each other for the most part, and those that weren't lay as they would have had they been connected. Tears filled her eyes and she dropped her tools.

She couldn't do any more. She needed to contact the authorities and not do any more to disturb what was likely a crime scene. She didn't know she was even crying until she stood and realized she couldn't see clearly.

The young Indian was still standing there, his eyes as sad as her heart felt. She pointed to the slightly uncovered remains. "I can't do anymore. I have to go get help."

He wavered for only seconds before he disappeared and she had no idea if he understood or not. But it didn't matter. All that mattered now was she was going to have to somehow explain how she found the body. And pray it wasn't Gavin White's remains.

****

"So you are saying you just happened to be walking up the mountain, decided to use a rock and some sticks, and then just happened to dig up the remains."

Rayne knew that no one would buy the lame story she'd come up with but hadn't realized how hard it was going to be to stick to her story when the officer repeated it back to her, for the fifth time. But she nodded. "Yes. I was looking for truffles. I was told there are some in the area. And I love to cook with organic ingredients.

"Do you think it could be Gavin White?"

The officer scratched his head before shaking it. "Don't think so. Remains have decomposed too much for the length of time the White boy has been missing, in my opinion. But we won't know for sure until the coroner's office gets back with the DNA results. Hoping not, though; family will be devastated."

Rayne nodded. She was hoping not as well.

She looked up as she heard the commotion in the front of the police station. She knew immediately that Garrison had arrived. Rayne stood and headed toward the entrance but was stopped by a uniformed woman who stepped into her path.

"Not done questioning you, Ms. Cavanaugh."

Rayne looked the officer over, taking in her *I'm-in-charge* stance and nametag. Though a headache was forming at the center of her forehead, Rayne smiled at Kathy Gishwell's mistake. "That's too bad. I've told you all I know. Right now I need to talk to Garrison. He needs to know what is going on."

The male officer who had listened as Officer Gishwell asked all the questions, waved the woman back. "It's all right, Kathy. We're done for now." He looked over at Rayne. "But I may have more questions later. Not planning on leaving town anytime soon, are you?"

Rayne shook her head. "No. I am seriously thinking of moving here permanently." She smiled at the male officer then, who looked back at her with such awe that the woman officer grunted. Rayne moved past her and headed for Garrison. He was waiting for her, the stress around his eyes a clear indication of the duress he was under.

"They don't believe it's Gavin."

He seemed to deflate a little before pulling her into his arms. "What were you doing out there? What were you thinking? My God, Rayne! You were terrified only yesterday of being in those woods, only feet from your cabin. From what the officer told me of the location where you found the remains, you had to have walked at least a mile!"

Rayne nodded, hating herself for lying to him. But there was no choice. There was no way he would understand the truth, and he was under enough stress. "I was prepared this time. I packed for a hike. I broke the braches so I would know my way back. I was terrified when I saw the remains. But they don't think it is Gavin, Garrison," she repeated, as much for herself as for him.

"If not, it's still somebody's kid. Or father. Or brother. And that makes me more afraid for Gavin than I have ever been."

Rayne held on to him, not releasing him until more of his family arrived and each one wanted a chance to give him a hug in greeting. The room started shrinking as one relative after another arrived throughout the day and into the night. The room filled so the space between the front door and the windowed desk that closed off the interrogation and incarceration portion of the building were hard to maneuver.

Rayne thought about leaving more than once, not wanting to intrude, but every time she attempted to move into the background Garrison sought her out and held out a hand for her to return to him.

His family, both immediate and extended, were equally inclusive, offering to get her food and drinks when they offered to get them for Garrison and his parents. As time went on, her head told her to run while she still could, but her heart told her it was already too late. She was head over heels for him, for his family, for the community that was family whether there was a blood connection or not.

She ached for them and for the child she was coming to know, as everyone talked about memories of him from the time they found out his mother was pregnant to the day he disappeared. It felt like they were memorializing him already, but she could see the memories and the stories gave them comfort and sometimes hope.

It was well past midnight when the coroner entered the police station, seeming shocked at the number of the White relatives who were still there waiting for word. He walked past everyone until he reached the patriarch and matriarch of the family, with Garrison and her by their side. Rayne was afraid if the coroner didn't say something soon the death grip breaking her hand would find its way around his throat.

She placed her free hand over Garrison's, thankfully making him aware he had taken the circulation from her extremity. He sent her an apologetic look before turning his attention back to the coroner. "Who is it, Doc?"

There was a sad shake of the man's gray head, giving Rayne a sinking feeling.

"Not Gavin."

The collective exhale in the room could have filled a hot air balloon, but there were no shouts of joy. Somebody had lost a member of their family. And Gavin was still unaccounted for.

"Do you know who it is?"

The coroner pressed his lips together before nodding

to Garrison, then he glanced over to a woman who had been introduced to Rayne as Lucy White-Taylor, a distant cousin.

Garrison told her that his cousin had been hit particularly hard by Gavin's disappearance, as her own seventeen-year-old child had gone missing seven years before. Lucy believed he'd headed to Nashville, as it was a threat he'd made often—which had resulted in many arguments. He'd left angry and Lucy had never heard from him again, though she'd remained hopeful he would one day come to his senses and make contact with his family. Now she knew that was no longer a possibility.

The look in Lucy's eyes, the moan of denial on her lips as the coroner approached took Rayne's breath, and her own tears started falling at the same time Lucy's legs gave out. Though she couldn't take her eyes off the horrible drama being played out for this wonderfully loving family, Rayne knew there wasn't a dry eye in the room. And that hope had been further dimmed for the child they had all come to hear about.

****

Burt sat at his desk and pretended to give a shit, hoping his expression was appropriately somber. Good at acting as he was, he was confident he was carrying off concern, and not the outrage he felt at being removed as lead on the Gavin White case.

He'd gotten called into Captain Shithead's office only an hour before that woman had called in, saying she had found human remains up on the mountain, and told without preamble or regret his services were needed elsewhere within the department.

Worse than losing first notice about the kid, he'd been formally reprimanded and told he was expected to be at the station for work on time. He was to remain there for the full shift unless he was called out by the Captain for a specific purpose, and lunches were an hour and no more.

Meaning, he wouldn't be free to come and go when he wanted, wouldn't be free to see to his needs when he felt the desire for release, and wouldn't be free to make sure Martha behaved herself.

The wimpy bitch had finally grown some balls. She hadn't let him touch her for days, saying she would go to a doctor and turn him in if he didn't let her heal before punishing her again.

Hell, he knew she enjoyed it.

Damned whore begged for it, if not in words, then in the way she would get all wet and ready the meaner he got with her. Made him hard just thinking about what he would do to her next time. Threat or not, she would bow to his will, or he'd make sure she knew she wouldn't be capable of getting to a doctor. He knew that would fix everything because he'd had to make that threat before—once—when she'd mistakenly thought she might get a chance to change their relationship.

That had been at the beginning, when she had first moved to Mystic Waters in answer to his online ad for a wife. He hadn't been as rough with her then. Had been so grateful when she answered his ad, then actually went through with the wedding at the Justice of the Peace's office, even after seeing what other women had rejected all his life.

He'd tried being a good husband, overlooking all her mistakes. Until he realized she was doing stuff on purpose to anger him. That anger had fed something in him. And once he released it on her, and saw it thrilled her as much as it scared her, he'd let himself go. Now, though, he just got his jollies off and didn't care whether she enjoyed herself or not. Especially when he needed to work out the demons that invaded his dreams.

He rubbed at his pecker and balls beneath his desk, trying to ease them. There would be no going home until the Captain released him. Son of a bitch was playing politics, keeping everyone on duty long past their shifts, just so the high and mighty Whites would feel the love. Burt snorted. They could suck his dick…each and every one of them.

Chapter Sixteen

"Rayne still isn't answering. I'm getting worried."

"She tried to call us both earlier. She sounded excited about a discovery she made. She didn't sound upset at all. In fact, she sounded happier than she has for a long time. I don't think we should burden her with our problems."

Haven nodded. "You're right. Maybe we should contact Aunt Soleli. She has traveled the universe through time. She may have heard of this happening before."

"I think her last post said she's in Zimbabwe on a quest. I'm not sure. Rayne always kept up with the aunts."

"Then let's give it some time. Maybe I caught a virus or something at the hospital. It's possible." Haven tried to believe her own words, but she was sick at heart. For so many years she and Destiny and Rayne had moaned about the burdens of their gifts, but now, with the very real possibility that she had lost hers, she was terrified of losing who she was.

"I haven't been feeling so great either. Mr. Ramus came in to see me today and wanted some advice. I tried, really hard, but his aura was so weak I couldn't decide if I should tell him to move forward or hold back." Destiny grimaced. "So I told him he needed to work it out. Weigh the pros and cons.

"I felt like a fraud."

Haven bit her bottom lip. "Do you think I could have passed whatever I have on to you?"

Destiny shrugged. "Maybe. We may just need to drink more seaweed water, or get an herbal tea enema. I remember Aunt Lune Brille once said as we got older we would need to increase our internal cleansings or our gifts could become constipated."

Haven sighed. She wasn't particularly fond of enemas. Their mother had made them start what was to have been a yearly ritual from the time they were fifteen. Only she had died less than a year later. As far as Haven knew, her sisters hadn't had one since then either. Maybe that was the problem. And as a nurse she knew she should set the example and drop her panties first.

"I'll make us appointments."

Destiny made a face before nodding. "I was afraid you would say that. What about Rayne? Should we tell her she needs one, too?"

Haven thought for a minute then shook her head. "Since she's so happy she must be okay. From what she's told us she's getting lots of exercise, lots of fresh fruits and veggies—yes, she actually said veggies, and she is breathing the cleanest air imaginable. The air here can't be good for us...for anyone for that matter. We work rather than exercise and breathe air thick enough sometimes to choke a horse."

"Maybe *we* should move to West Virginia."

Destiny laughed. "Unlike our dear sister, the freest of free spirits, we have careers, men friends who might actually amount to something useful, and a monstrosity of a home with artifacts that must be maintained for the next generation. Besides, you know Rayne. She could be headed home already."

Haven nodded slowly, but the idea of change had already taken root.

Chapter Seventeen

"I'm here."

"I'm alive."

"Find me, please!"

Gavin had stopped talking to himself, to the darkness, and to God, weeks ago, so the sound of his own voice gave him pause. Had he always sounded like that? Had his voice deepened some? Even more than when he was younger and started growing hair down there and under his arms?

He didn't bother to close his eyes as there was no point. The darkness was no different either way. So he kept them open and tried to remember who he had been before all this started. What it felt like to walk freely. To run. To laugh. To be loved.

The sob startled him. Made him sit up quickly. Then made him mad when he realized the sound came out of him.

Anger had died some time ago too, so to feel it now, to feel *anything*, was wonderful and frightening in equal measure. He made himself stand, something he never did anymore unless he needed to pee or poop. He'd gotten so used to lying on the cot and reaching for the junk food and water that he knew the lean muscular body that was once his was neither lean nor muscular anymore.

He ran his hands down his stomach and felt the soft paunch that used to be rippling rock. He ran his hands up and down his arms and found nothing but fatty skin. Furious with himself he did the same with his legs, from thigh to ankle, wondering how he had allowed his captor to turn him into a willing turnip.

No more.

Gavin waited a heartbeat then slid his hands down the

sweatpants that had seemed so wonderful a week ago. He grasped his penis, held it for a moment, then dropped it before his mind could catch up to what his fingers were doing. He wouldn't think about that. Not here. Never here. The one and only bright light in the nightmare he was living was no one had ever touched him inappropriately. And he knew that was a blessing.

Count your blessings, name them one by one....

He'd heard the hymn so many times growing up. It was one of the staple songs at the church his parents had always taken him to.

A sense of overwhelming sadness threatened to pull him back down, but he refused to let it. Instead of forcing his thoughts in another direction, or refusing to think about them at all, Gavin inhaled deeply and opened his mind to the memories that made him who he was.

He closed his eyes then, and recalled his mother's smooth voice as she sang to the music from the sound system, sometimes sashaying around the kitchen with a tray of freshly baked cookies so the scent would entice him and his dad. He and his father trailing after her, pretending to try to catch her, when all they were really trying to do was make her laugh.

She'd had the best laugh.

His dad's love for her had never been a question nor was hers for him. And they both had showered so much love on Gavin's head he never knew that life could be hard. Or lonely. Or that it could end violently in seconds that would burn in his mind and heart forever, whether he escaped or died an old man in this dank dark prison.

What felt like a warm hand brushed his cheek startling him back from his daydreaming, but he was still standing so it couldn't have been a mouse or a rat. He exhaled shakily, wondering if it was possible his mother, or father, was reaching out to him from beyond the grave to comfort him.

And then, as if his father was actually in the room, as if the sound of his booming voice could actually be heard, Gavin remembered him reading: *Let not your heart be troubled.*

I am with you.

He couldn't remember the rest, but hearing it in his mind, feeling it in his chest, he knew it was enough.

He had no idea why he was being held. But he was being kept alive and he was not being harmed if he discounted what the food was doing to his body. Still Gavin knew he had no right to be lazy. His uncle was probably going crazy looking for him. His grandparents would be heartbroken to lose him, too, after already having lost so much. How could he have allowed himself to get so weak? So lazy?

Gavin opened his eyes and though he could see no difference on the outside, he felt the difference from within.

What he'd been doing ended now. He might have no choice but to eat the junk that was brought to him, but he could move and build muscle, and one day, when he felt ready, he was going to turn the tables on his kidnapper. And he would be free.

The sounds of footsteps and grunting had Gavin throwing himself back on the cot. He didn't know how much the kidnapper could see with the little flashlight, but he didn't want anything to look any different than it normally did. He'd lie there, getting up slowly as he'd done for so long now, and wait to go through the process he could literally do with his eyes shut.

Chapter Eighteen

"Can I get you anything?"

Rayne settled against Garrison on the thick comfy couch he'd undoubtedly built with his own hands, wishing she knew what to do to comfort him. He looked up from where he'd been staring into the banked fireplace and attempted to give her a smile. It was pitiful at best.

"No. Thank you for bringing me home. I know you have to be wiped out, too. If my mother knew I wasn't taking you home, but making you go on your own instead, she would have my hide."

Rayne slid even closer while turning and angling her body so she could put her arms around his neck and lay her head upon his chest. She felt his sigh of contentment and knew she was where she should be. "I'm not going home tonight. So your mother shouldn't have any reason to be upset with you."

She could tell his breath had stopped because his chest was no long rising and lowering. Rayne waited, wondering if she had overstepped bounds she hadn't expected, but his arms pulling her tighter to him was all the answer she needed.

"You're staying."

Rayne nodded, hearing the awe in his statement. It made her smile. "Unless you're strong enough to throw me out."

"I'm a very weak man, right now. I'm pretty sure you can take me."

Rayne laughed and look up at the underside of his strong jaw. Without hesitation she placed a gentle kiss on it, then another an inch to the left, then another to the right. He lowered his head and adjusted his grip on her so he could pull her back enough to kiss first her forehead, then her closed eye lids, the bridge of her nose, and the jut of both cheek bones before settling his lips softly on her hungry mouth.

If this is what it feels like to drown....

The shifting and lifting of her body disproved his claim of weakness, but there was no doubt that *she* was getting weaker by the moment. Weak with need. Weak with the knowledge that she wanted him more than she had ever wanted anything or anyone in her life. The kiss deepened, altered, eased, then deepened again, until Rayne had no thoughts beyond feeling those lips on several more parts of her body. She pulled back and placed an index finger over his lips when he tried to take hers again.

"Then let's crawl up those stairs and fall into your bed. I wouldn't want to be responsible for making you ill...seeing as you are *so* weak."

His deep chuckle vibrated through her. "I'm feeling a little stronger at the moment."

Rayne smiled at him. "I was counting on it."

Clothes somehow got lost, trailing behind them across the small living room, up the stairs, beside the bed, and finally the warmth of his bare chest met the aching hardness of her nipples while steel manhood teased her quivering abdomen. By the time they writhed in a tangle of sheets, smoldering need ignited into a blinding flame that threatened to consume.

Gasps turned to moans that sounded suspiciously like begging. The ache at her core cried out for immediate release, but it seemed Garrison wanted to prolong her agony, her need, with honey-dipped torture that stole breath and melted bones.

His mouth was everywhere, kissing, licking, and suckling. The inferno he created scorched inch after inch of willing flesh until she was delirious. Moans turned to whimpering until his mouth finally returned to hers, sealing off all sound but that of his body sliding into hers.

He filled her, then stopped, his harsh breaths an echo

of her own, his shaking biceps and quivering hard thighs between hers a testament to his restraint. He breathed hard several times as sweat pooled and slid down from his hairline, causing him to turn and wipe it away with a quickly grasped edge of sheet. He turned back to stare into her eyes, his flaring as a wicked smile lifted his lips. Then his face relaxed into a serious study of her own before he lowered himself, taking her lips, then tongue, in an erotic dance as he began a slow slide of hips. Filling and retreating, filling and retreating, until her whimpers filled the magical mouth consuming hers.

He stopped again, obviously straining for control, but she grasped his hips and slammed him hard against her. The fury of movement that followed had them both panting, his face now buried in the pillow beside her head, his groans, moans, and sounds she could not identify were an echo of ones that had never before left her mouth. He brought her to the peak, and then over, then her screams of release sent him over the edge. External movements stopped as he held her tight, his body a straining rock of muscle and flesh, as the piston inside her pounded with a life of its own.

Her legs remained locked around his hips until the strength left her and she let them fall in a lifeless mess at his sides. He slid down to lay flush against her, but kept his weight on his elbows and knees as he took her mouth again, this time is a lazy exploration.

Without the energy to do anything but accept him, she playfully allowed her tongue to dance with his until he pulled back to look at her.

"There aren't words…." was all he said, before he took her mouth again.

****

"That smells amazing."

Rayne looked to the loft while pulling the biscuits from the oven. Bacon, milk gravy, and eggs, along with grits, and fried potatoes and onions, had been her pastime since rising. She'd pulled on her panties and his shirt, then left

Garrison up in the bed, dead to the world, soundly sleeping, nearly an hour earlier. She'd rummaged around his kitchen and found the ingredients she'd needed to make him biscuits from scratch, and the accompanying items that made up a man-sized meal.

She set the cookie sheet on the mitten-covered counter and smiled at him as he hit the bottom step and entered the kitchen. "Coffee is made. Hope it isn't too strong. I'm better at tea."

He walked straight to her and took her in his arms, his mouth landing on hers with gentle pressure and a lot of teasing. He pulled back, looked at all she'd made, and shook his head. "I stand corrected. *You* are amazing."

Her giggle of delight was a little embarrassing, so Rayne turned back to the counter and grabbed the mug she had pulled from the cabinet earlier. "Black, right?"

Garrison pressed against her back, laid his hand on hers, taking the mug from her, and settled it back on the counter. He pushed aside her hair to nuzzle and nibble on her neck until she started squirming. Then he just held her. Rayne couldn't help wanting him again, but he moved back then and stepped to her side and took his cup to fill it with coffee.

"You didn't have to do all this, but I'm not going to complain. All I can do is say, 'Thank you, beautiful.' Do you have a mug? I'll get you a cup. And you should go on and sit and let me wait on you."

Rayne shook her head, knowing she was grinning like a fool. "No. I have water. And you're welcome. I can wait on myself."

He stepped to her and led her to the table, pulled out the chair, and settled her upon it. "I'm aware you can wait on yourself, but you've done all this work, which is more than I ever could have expected, so now let me wait on you."

Rayne relaxed and watched him pile two plates, wondering who he thought was going to eat everything on hers. But she simply thanked him when he put the plate in front of her and settled in his chair.

Garrison looked at her before he folded his hands and lowered his head. Rayne did the same, waiting as he silently prayed, sending one of her own for his family who had suffered another loss, for his nephew who, if alive, could be suffering untold agony, and for herself, that the food she was about to eat didn't make her sick. Or gain fifty pounds.

When he looked up again and lifted his fork, she did the same. Each bite was delicious if she did say so herself, but there was no way she could make such a meal a habit. "Enjoy this. Tomorrow we eat grains, nuts, and fruit."

Garrison slid a look that said he didn't think so, but he smiled. "So we will be having breakfast together again tomorrow?"

Rayne's fork stopped inches from her lips as she realized what she had said. She shrugged, hoping he didn't think she was being too presumptuous. "If you're lucky," she joked.

Garrison took a big bite of fluffy biscuit and studied her, his expression unreadable. Rayne swallowed what felt like sawdust before taking a drink of water that was tepid, at best. Had she misread their situation? Had their night together meant too much to her?

"I'm hoping I'm that lucky," he said, his expression serious. "I'm hoping a lot of things."

Rayne knew she couldn't avoid the discussion out of fear that she had read things wrong. "What things?"

Garrison set his fork down and folded his hands, much like he had before praying. He rested his chin on them as he leaned forward, his gaze boring into her. "I'm hoping you're not leaving Mystic Waters, ever. I'm hoping you'll want to spend a lot more time here, with me. And I'm hoping I can give you as much as you give me. And fearing I'll fall short."

Rayne exhaled, relieved, yet terrified. She didn't know what it was he needed, but her heart was his, and she would give him all she had. She just couldn't let him know how much that was. "It's only breakfast," she said, hoping to lighten the mood. But the expression on Garrison's face said he wasn't going along.

"It's more than breakfast, and you know it. You give me peace. You allow me to remember I'm alive, not just a puppet in some crazy marionette play that has spun out of control. That's what my life has been for so long, until I met you.

"You allow me to escape all the bad stuff going on and you replace it with something beautiful. You're so beautiful it takes my breath sometimes. But it isn't just your looks, which are crazy gorgeous. It's your spirit. Your ability to look to the bright side, to trust that everything is going to be okay. Your belief that Gavin is alive.

"I need that. But it's even more than that...."

Garrison frowned, looking around as if he were trying to find the right words, and failing to grasp them. Rayne rose and went to him, placing her hands on his shoulders and pushing so that he scooted his chair back. Before he could rise she straddled him and took his mouth with a kiss so deep it took her own breath away. She released his lips and pulled him closer so her head was beside his, as she held him and was held.

"I'm not going anywhere. I'm where I belong. As long as you need me."

Garrison rose while holding her against him and Rayne locked her legs around him. He took her to the couch where he allowed her to slide down him, placing her feet upon the braided rug. Without speaking he pushed her panties to the floor, went down on his knees, placed her hands on his shoulders, pushed her legs apart, then used his fingers, lips, and tongue to take her back to the edge of sanity.

Her legs began to give way. He grasped her hips, guided her collapsing body onto the couch's edge and allowed her upper body to fall back against the pillows, as he pulled her legs up and over his shoulders.

With complete access now, Garrison devoured her, sending her into waves of rapturous agony again and again until she couldn't control the wild thrashing of her hips or the sounds of desperation coming from her lips and throat.

Unable to take anymore without coming completely undone, Rayne grasped his head and pulled him up until she could capture his lips where she bit and sucked while struggling to reach the boxers he had pulled on before coming downstairs. He pushed her hands away and made short work of them then grasped her hips and pulled her to him, alternately kissing her and releasing her mouth while he maneuvered her writhing body into position.

They moaned into each other's mouths when he rammed home, lifted her hips for better access, and began the rocking motion that quickly built into a frenzy of flesh that only fed the hunger now so ravenous she thought she might pass out.

A slight alteration of his body triggered an orgasm that rushed over her like the breaking of a dam holding back a vast body of water. Unable to do anything else, she rode it out, letting the pleasure sweep her away until she slowly trickled into a puddle of sated flesh.

Her breaths eventually slowed, her mind finally engaged, and she opened eyes that had somehow closed without her being aware. Garrison had settled back on his calves, his hands resting on her thighs, as he too was struggling to breathe. Finally he took one long, deep breath, and grinned.

Rayne grinned back before holding her hands out to him. "I think we need to shower."

Garrison laughed and took her hands before pulling. "If I can get up and walk, you're on."

The ringing of Garrison's cell phone caused them both to jump. His happy expression changed as he struggled to his feet then went to the table he had left it on the night before. He glanced at it, then at her, as he hit the screen and placed it at his ear. "Garrison."

Rayne watched as he listened, knowing the reprieve was over. His expression didn't change, but it obvious it wasn't good news.

"I'll be there shortly," he said before touching the screen again. He walked over to Rayne and took her had before pulling her into a hug. "The full coroner report is in. They have asked the family to meet at Mom and Dad's, so they can let us all know at once what they found out."

"Garrison, do you want me to go home? Give you all some family time?"

He frowned and shook his head. "I want you with me. Unless you don't want to go. I know it isn't fair to pull you into all this."

Rayne hugged him tight. "I go where you go, unless you tell me you want differently."

Garrison held her as tightly. "Then you may as well give up your cabin and move in, because I want you here, with me, if that's what you want too."

Rayne pulled back as her heart pounded violently. He was perfect for her. Waking to his kisses and falling into his arms every night sounded like heaven. But the words wouldn't leave her mouth. There was so much he didn't know, and she couldn't tell him. And to accept under those conditions was grossly unfair.

Garrison frowned and then nodded in understanding. "I see I've shocked you. I know it seems too soon to ask you to move in with me. But it doesn't change how I feel about you. About us. I'll give you time to catch up, Rayne. Or walk away, if you don't feel the same in the end."

"I do," she said quickly, then wondered what to follow that up with. The truth about her feelings was all she had to offer him. Other truths would have to be revealed at some point but not now. Not before she was ready to give him up if he turned on her.

"I'm crazy about you, but we still hardly know each other. You could just feel this strongly because of the circumstances. Your life is in turmoil." When he started to protest she held up her hand. "And I have family in California who won't understand the suddenness of this.

"And...I need time. I never expected to meet you. To fall so hard for you. To want to change my entire existence for you."

Delight lit his eyes. "That's more than enough for now. And you have every right to question my feelings, given the circumstances, but you're wrong about that. Even if things were normal I would still be crazy about you."

Rayne closed her eyes, wishing she could open up and tell him everything, but he pulled her against him again and kissed her closed eyelids. When he stopped, she opened them and just held him against her with the knowledge that *wishing* never got anybody anywhere.

"Let me get my things and we will head to your place and shower. Then we'll go to my parent's house."

Rayne silently finished the sentence for him. *And deal with reality.*

Chapter Nineteen

Holding Burt off another night wasn't an option. His displeasure at life had been made clear in so many ways lately. The latest had her cleaning spaghetti off the kitchen wall and floor.

There were times she wanted to kill him. Like now. But she needed him. He not only satisfied her need for punishment, he was a buffer against the rest of the big bad world. But he was getting *too* rough. And if she didn't find a way to redirect him she was going to have to start looking for a way out.

Coming to Mystic Waters all those years before had saved her. If she hadn't answered his advertisement for a wife she would still be *there*, hiding, or running, or incarcerated.

It hadn't been her fault. Not really. But no one would believe that. And they would have locked her up and thrown away the key. That's why she allowed Burt to punish her. Because she really did deserve the punishment. Just not the kind she would have gotten if she hadn't run.

And thinking of punishment now, with Burt stomping around the other room while she cleaned up the mess, caused tingles of excitement that were as hated as much as craved.

She finished wiping off the floor and headed to the bathroom where she disrobed. From the medicine cabinet she pulled down the numbing medicine she'd purchased from the grocery store and laid it aside. Using one of the washcloths she always kept in little bathroom, and the soap she always used to make her body smell like a field of flowers, she quickly washed off, taking extra time and care with an anus that was still tender but no longer sore.

She bit her bottom lip before opening the bathroom door, grabbing the tube, and making her way to the living room. Burt had settled into his chair, his anger at life clearly visible even from this angle as he flipped through the channels on the television.

Martha swallowed hard before moving forward. She hadn't gone to him completely nude for several years as time and gravity were starting to take a toll, and she had always been proud of her body. She stopped at his side and waited for him to look over at her. When he did, his brows shot up as he slowly looked her over from the pubic hair she kept neatly trimmed to her face. She tried to smile but her lips were shaking.

"I need your help, please. I need you to numb my bottom before we make love."

Confusion, then a frown of displeasure settled on his thick lips. "What makes you think you deserve to be numbed?"

Martha lifted her head, sticking her nose in the air. She wasn't going to cower before him like she usually did. That game was starting to get a little stale. "If you don't help me, then I can't help you."

Clearly surprised, Burt rose and stood facing her. "So let me get this straight. If I don't numb you, you aren't going to bend to my will."

Hating that she was getting more excited with the threat of his violence, Martha nodded. But she had to change the dynamics before she allowed him to hurt her so badly again. "That is exactly what I'm saying."

After a slight hesitation Burt held out his hand and she placed the tube in it. He looked it over and then appeared to be reading it. When he looked up at her he looked lost.

"You realize this is for teething babies?"

Martha nodded. "It's all I could get without going to the doctor."

He grunted then really looked her over as if assessing her worth. "Your tits are starting to sag."

Knowing he'd hit her where it would hurt almost made

her turn and leave, but she wouldn't give him the satisfaction. "And your pants aren't shrinking. You're fifty pounds heavier than when I married you." Burt's mouth dropped open and she waited for him to cold cock her, but he laughed instead.

"Got a mouth on you tonight, woman. What gives?"

Feeling empowered, like she hadn't for years, Martha shrugged. "I'm tired of being treated like a dog. If you want me, you back off a little. I don't mind cuts and bruises, but you can't tear me apart like you did last time. I won't stand for it.

Burt shrugged. "Damn, woman. I didn't mean to hurt you like that. I got too excited is all. You got to give a man a break."

Not sure she was hearing right, Martha nodded then turned her back to him. "Come to the bedroom and put that on me. Then, if you're really careful, you can make love to me."

Burt followed her like a puppy and waited until she was on her knees, laying her chest upon the low bed. She waited, wondering if she was a fool to expose herself to him in such a vulnerable way since she knew he could take advantage, and hurt her again if he chose to. But he was following her lead so far, and she wanted to see what he would do.

Sounds of him settling at her side, and the gentle touch of his hand gliding around the shape of her bottom made her sigh. She knew her ass was still as solid as it had been in her youth, and his show of appreciation filled her with joy.

It galled her, but she really had come to love the jerk.

"I can't lose you," he said, not sounding like himself at all.

Now Martha was certain something was wrong with him. Burt never expressed such sentiment. But she was going to go with it. She had allowed him to make her into his slave, but for the last couple of years he seemed to have forgotten she'd willingly allowed his domination and his increasing violence towards her. Sometimes she forgot it, too, but that couldn't happen again. Not after realizing he could lose complete control of himself.

Being beaten and fucked when he was in control was one thing. Being raped until he ripped her apart was something else. He had scared her. And it hadn't been the kind of fear that turned her on.

"I don't want to lose you, either, but I can't be hurt like that again," she reiterated, wanting him to really get what she was saying. "I sent a letter to my sister telling her about all that had happened. *Everything.* She wants me to turn you in and leave you forever."

It was a lie. Plain and simple. She'd never had a sister but had used the fictitious sibling over the years when she felt she needed to restrain him some. This time *Glenda* had been more necessary than all the times she had been used before. For the first time she'd actually been afraid he would kill her with his need for violent sex. And she, as much as anyone, knew that could happen.

The fictional sister was her fail-safe since she needed him to think someone else would know if anything happened to her. Otherwise no one would know, or even care, if she suddenly disappeared.

There was silence for so long Martha was afraid she may have overplayed her hand, but to her surprise he kissed her shoulder very gently.

"I'm sorry. I've been having trouble at work and took it out on you."

Martha turned to look at him to see if he was pulling her leg, but he looked humbled and nervous. She leaned over and patted his cheek, wondering how in the world they had gotten from the furious man at dinner to the sad little puppy at her side.

Since she didn't want him completely broken, she turned back to stare out over the bed while spreading her legs as far apart as she could. "Put the gel on me. Outside and in. Deep." After a moment's hesitation, she added, "Please."

Martha closed her eyes and waited, awed when she felt

his big hand sliding over her ass again, as tenderly as before. A rustle of movement preceded her gasp when she felt his fingers spreading her labia and then felt his tongue gently lapping between those lips as his nose nudged close to her anus.

She waited, holding her breath, then was rewarded when he licked his way upward, soothing the sore flesh that he had so brutalized the last time. The touch, pressure, and then the insertion of his fingertip were all so gentle she wanted to cry. And then she did cry out when he pulled back out.

"Wait. I have your medicine."

Martha wanted to tell him he didn't need to bother but she felt the pressure of his finger again. Within seconds tears streamed from her eyes and she was bucking against the bedspread as the numbing gel burned its way into her. Instead of soothing, it was as if her rectum was consumed by fire and the flesh was being burned to dust. Her movements, and the sounds coming from her, must have excited Burt because he was lifting her and fumbling to remove his belt and open his pants.

He pushed her head down to the bed and spread her butt cheeks as she continued to writhe in pain and pleasure. Her fear that he would take her anally again was replaced with pleasure when he slid a thick cold finger in her burning ass and his dick into her vagina.

Her explosion and his made it all over too soon, and she was still burning inside, but Martha was pleased all the same. She'd discovered a new way to punish herself, and the baby teething gel would be a staple in her medicine cabinet from now on. But more importantly she'd discovered that Burt loved her back, which was something she'd never before been completely sure of.

It was something to think about.

****

Burt headed to the bathroom to wash himself, more confused by the minute. He hadn't expected to feel anything for Martha and hadn't for years. At the beginning it had been gratitude, then surprise, then he'd come to hate her before she was finally nothing more than a vessel to empty his pain into.

But she had surprised him tonight. Offering herself, but limiting him. Making demands that by all rights should have infuriated him, when in fact it made him feel wrapped in love. His situation at work was making him nervous, scaring him in fact. Everyone was acting strange around him, and he was afraid they somehow knew but didn't have enough to pin anything on him.

His stomach hurt every morning just knowing he was going to have to go in and face men and that woman, who had never treated him with proper respect but had never outright shunned him before now.

Unless he was imagining it.

That was the kicker. He wasn't sure. And because he wasn't sure he couldn't do anything but pretend everything was normal. It was just a damned shame that dead kid hadn't been the one he needed dead. If Gavin White ever turned up and told, then they would have him for sure. And his life would be over.

So he needed to kick up his investigation, but now he would have to do it without anyone in the department knowing. That made things harder but not impossible. He would look on his own time. Maybe even take Martha out with him occasionally to pretend they were simply enjoying a stroll on the mountainside.

Burt laughed. Maybe that was the answer. His wife was complaining that he had gotten fat and he would tell anyone who asked that the exercise was a means to lose weight. Then maybe, if he could lose a few pounds, he and Martha would take a vacation and go visit that sister of hers so she could see he wasn't really such a bad guy. Or knock her off, if she remained another threat to his way of life.

It was a damned shame he had to keep killing people just to have a decent life.

And, like so much of what had gone wrong in his life, this too was his mother's fault.

Chapter Twenty

The family gathering was somber to say the least, which was completely understandable given the report from the coroner. Rayne wandered away from Garrison while he and his parents spoke in low tones. The open French doors leading to the flagstone patio looked like as good an escape as any.

The fragrance of pure country air never ceased to amaze her. She hadn't realized just how bad the air she had breathed all her life was before coming to Mystic Waters. Garrison's mother had large, elaborately designed concrete planters filled with a profusion of multicolored flowers, which soothed the spirit and added their own perfume to the air.

Her spirit needed soothing.

The human remains the young brave had led her to were to be handed over to the family for burial within the hour. Garrison had volunteered to go with his cousin to take care of everything and to help her through the painful process of claiming her child's body or, sadly in this case, body parts.

The funeral date—three days hence—was set, and the entire family, the entire town more than likely, would show up to pay their respects. Rayne wandered away from the house, touching leaves and smelling blooms, wondering how anyone could survive what they now knew was a violent end to their child's life.

"I'm leaving now. Will you be okay getting home?"

Rayne turned to Garrison, seeing the pain and strain etched deeply into the lines bracketing his lips. She nodded. "I'm fine. What about you?"

He shrugged. "I'm scared. Gavin...." His voice broke

before he shook his head.

Rayne crossed to him and pulled him into a hug. "I know. But we have to hope he's okay." She searched his face. "We will *believe* he is okay."

"I'm trying. My whole family is trying, but this…."

"I know." Was all Rayne could think to say.

The coroner's report showed that his cousin had come to an extremely violent end. And he'd likely suffered unimaginable agony while being hacked to death with what the coroner believed was an ax of some sort.

"Garrison, are you ready?"

They both turned at the sound of his father's voice. Rayne stepped back as Garrison nodded. He turned back to her, attempting a smile, but the lift of his lips didn't match the pain in his eyes. She smiled back knowing it was what he needed. "Go, I'll be there when you get home."

"I'm counting on it." He pulled a set of keys from the pocket of his jeans and placed it in her palm. For several seconds he held on, cupping the keys between them. Then he let go before turning away.

Garrison walked back toward the house and followed his father in as Rayne turned to look out over the vast acreage of his parent's property. In the distance she saw movement then nothing. A chill ran up her spine, raising the hair on her arms. She strained to look harder, but there was nothing there.

"He's come to depend upon you."

Startled, Rayne turned quickly and nearly tripped as her heel caught the uneven edge of the flagstone. She felt the senior Garrison's hand steady her before he quickly stepped back.

"I'm sorry. I didn't mean to scare you."

Rayne felt heat lick her cheeks. "No, I'm sorry. I was just admiring your home. It's very peaceful here."

The elder Garrison nodded but sadness blanketed his eyes. "It was. Before all this. It was."

Rayne didn't know what to say and since no words would comfort, she simply nodded.

"I think he's in love with you."

Since the words held neither joy nor scorn, Rayne was again left speechless.

"It's a good thing. I think. Unless you're leaving to go back to California."

Seeing he was as uncomfortable as she felt, Rayne gave him the best she could offer. "I don't plan to go back. Not to live, anyway. But there are a lot of things to be worked out before I can completely commit to staying."

Nodding, the elder Garrison attempted a smile that so clearly matched his son's, if you ignored the thick white mustache.

"That's all anyone can ask." He turned his gaze to the landscape she had studied only moments before. "He's a good and decent man. A war hero. And a fine son."

Rayne couldn't help but smile. "You don't have to sell him to me. I'm already a fan."

Laughing, Garrison Sr. swung his gaze back to her. "Sorry, a father's pride."

Rayne didn't say more as the light in the older gentleman's eyes grew grave again. A flash of movement caught her peripheral vision making her look back toward the tree line in the distance. She looked to see if Garrison's father saw it too, but he was looking down, then pulling a fledgling weed from between the stones.

He stood, looking at it, then at her. "Better get out the herbicide. My wife will have a fit if she sees this.

"Stay as long as you like and make yourself at home. I better get back inside and see if I'm needed."

Rayne nodded and watched him walk away. She turned back to search for whatever it was she kept seeing out in the field but nothing moved. She turned back to enter the house, hoping against hope this day wouldn't be repeated. And that Gavin really was safe somewhere, and would soon be home.

Before she stepped over the threshold Qaqeemasq appeared before her as a solidifying vapor. Rayne's breath caught; shaking a little, she forced herself to breathe normally. She glanced through him, into the large dining room where several family members were helping themselves to the large buffet which Garrison's mother had somehow thrown together.

Even though she knew no one else could see him she stepped back away from the doors and went to the side of the house where she was out of view. He was there when she got there, still only half formed. "You can't do that."

When he simply wavered before her she tried again. "You can't appear to me in front of other people. I can't talk to you. They will think I'm crazy. And you startled me. Don't do that."

To her surprise Qaqeemasq laughed. The musical sound of it made her smile even though she knew the sound was only in her head. He seemed to get himself together after a moment before he pulled on what she had come to think of as his serious face. He pointed out towards the tree line she had been studying then he started to move that way.

Rayne stayed where she was. There was no way she could explain the sudden desire to go traipsing around the White farm without Garrison at her side, while family gathered to mourn a death.

She shook her head when he turned back to see why she hadn't followed. His irritation was clear in the cold blast of wind he sent to lift the hair off her neck. As refreshing as it was in the late afternoon heat, Rayne had to control her own irritation. Pushy ghosts aggravated her. But she owed him. He had led her to a family's heartbreak, but also to the only thing that would give them any sense of closure.

"I can't go right now."

Another cold blast, but this time weaker, as if, though displeased, he understood. Rayne looked back to make sure no one had stepped out of the house before turning back to him. "What do you want me to see this time?"

After what felt like his hesitation, Qaqeemasq pointed at the house. Rayne shook her head, perplexed. "I don't understand."

He pointed again, this time jabbing the finger angrily several times.

"It has something to do with someone in the house?"

Cold air.

Rayne thought for a moment. "It has to do with why all the people are in the house?"

The air grew warmer and Rayne's stomach tightened as she remembered the movement out close to the trees, at the edge of the clearing. She pointed in that direction. "Is the person who killed that boy out there somewhere?"

Another cold blast.

Playing hot potato, cold potato with a long deceased American Indian wasn't nearly as much fun as it should have been, and it hadn't got any more enjoyable since the last time she'd tried it. Her next thought, though, really scared her. "Is there another body out there?"

Warmth flooded her and Rayne wanted to cry out. In anger. In fear.

She made herself take calming breaths as she pondered what to do, already knowing there was nothing she could do at the moment. Someone had murdered that boy, and with another dead body yet to be discovered the last thing she wanted to do was go looking alone. And there was no way she could explain finding a second body to the White family or local law enforcement. The female officer had all but treated her like a criminal as it was.

Several minutes of studying the situation from every angle she could think of passed, before she came to a decision. "I can't go now. And I can't go alone. But I'll be back as soon as I can. If I can work it out I'll be back in a few days, right after the funeral. And, if you will come to me then, I'll try to find the body. But I won't be alone, so you will have to lead me directly there."

Warmth flooded her again as Qaqeemasq dissolved into a swirling mist before disappearing altogether. Rayne took another deep breath before returning to the house, hoping she could come up with a good reason to have Garrison give her a tour of the farm and the wooded areas, following the funeral. But for the moment, all she could do was hope Garrison and his cousin were doing okay.

****

Though the coroner diligently tried to convince Lucy not to view the remains but to remember her child as she had last seen him, she had been equally insistent that she had to say goodbye to her only child. Garrison stood with his cousin as the coroner pulled back the sheet, revealing what was left of Anthony's head and spine. His need to vomit was as instantaneous as his arms were swift to catch Lucy's collapsing body.

The sheet was quickly replaced, but the sight of the broken, barely-skin-covered skull, which still somehow had his cousin's long brown hair attached in patches, haunted him as he half carried, half dragged, Lucy to a plastic seat in the corner.

The assistant, who stood in the background while the coroner and Lucy conferred, now came forward with tissues and bottled water, but Lucy was a nearly unconscious heap Garrison was struggling to hold up in the chair, so he ignored the assistant and focused on her. "Lucy? Come on. Come on…" He patted her cheeks but she didn't respond. If anything she was going closer toward oblivion. He turned to the young woman. "Do you have smelling salts?"

Immediately the assistant set the items on the floor by his knees and took off. She returned seconds later with the small white cloth covered vial. Without hesitating she broke it and stuck it under Lucy's nose.

Lucy responded, screaming and thrashing, causing Garrison to lose his grip. He captured her again before she slid completely off the chair. He pulled her to him as he rose then swung her into his arms before making a beeline to the double doors. He turned his back to them and pushed so they swung open enough for him to turn and carry Lucy down the corridor to the exit.

Her body had settled, but the sobs coming from her nearly took the strength from his legs. When he reached her car he hesitated, not knowing how he was to open it and hold on to her too. To his relief the young assistant had followed them out and was digging in Lucy's purse for the keys.

Within minutes he had her now limp body strapped in and he was behind the wheel backing out of the parking space. He glanced over at her but she had laid her head back and was staring straight up at the car's headliner. Her cries turned to whimpering, and eventually she was silent.

"I'm taking you to Mom and Dad's."

Lucy didn't respond. Garrison wasn't even sure she had heard him, but he turned onto the road that would lead them to his childhood home, hoping his mother would know what to do. There was no way he could take Lucy to the empty house that had once housed a family of three. Raymond, her husband of nearly twenty-five years, had died of cancer a little over a year before, hurt his son and only child had never come home before he'd breathed his last breath.

Garrison made a quick call to alert his mother of their impending arrival and was relieved to see both her and his father standing out front waiting for them. His father was opening the passenger door and lifting Lucy out before he could get out and get around the car to help.

Without a word to him both his parents hurried Lucy into the house. Garrison took a deep breath, leaned back against her car, and finally allowed the horror of seeing his cousin's decomposed body to hit him. He bent over only seconds before the contents of his stomach landed on the concrete driveway.

Several minutes of violent retching was followed by dry heaving which hurt his abdomen and throat even worse. By the time his stomach had given all it had, he was weak and sweating profusely.

"Here, take this, while I get the hose."

Garrison straightened and took the wet washcloth his father offered. He leaned back against the car again as he wiped the sweat from his face and the vomit from his mouth. The bitter taste wasn't as easy to deal with, but he knew where his parents kept the extra mouthwash and he would go inside and get it as soon as he felt he could move.

When Garrison Sr. returned, unfurling the hose as he walked, Garrison held out his hand, but his father shook his head. "I'll take care of this, son. You go on up to the house and sit for a spell. Lucy told us what you all saw, and I'm sorry I sent you instead of going myself."

Garrison didn't argue about washing away the vomit but he was glad his father hadn't seen their cousin's remains. It was bad enough Lucy *had*, and he was afraid one day they might see his nephew in the same horrifying condition.

Chapter Twenty-One

"Aunt Soleli sent a post card. She's been *abiding* with monks in Bhutan for the past month and feels renewed, she says. Maybe we should take a vacation and check it out."

Haven held out her hand to take the small missive from Destiny. She glanced at the picture of snow-covered mountains before laying it on the small table at her side. She sighed. "Where is Bhutan? I've never heard of it. Probably no one has. That would appeal to Aunt Sole."

Destiny nodded as she stretched her legs out on the couch. "You're right. It would. If you'd read her postcard you would know it's in South Asia, at the eastern end of the Himalayas. It's surrounded by the Republic of India, except China is at its northern border. She said they allowed her to pitch a tent on the property, inside the monastery no less, even though they never allow anyone to do that."

Haven laughed. "So she wiggled her nose and…."

Destiny laughed, too. Aunt Soleli, or Aunt Sole as they sometimes called her, had powers of persuasion that pretty much got her anything she wanted.

As children they had compared her to Samantha Stevens, a witch character on a television sitcom which ended more than forty years before, but had been one of the few TV shows their mother had allowed them to watch in rerun.

Samantha wiggled her nose to perform the magic she was not supposed to be performing because her horribly dull, and not at all attractive human husband, disapproved.

Their mother had used the show as a learning tool. To teach them that being so blessed could be fun, to remind them bad things could happen if other people witnessed them using their gifts, and to make sure they knew that men in general were too full of themselves to consider such a gift was amazing and not something to be feared.

Celestia had even taken them to the movie of the same name. The aunts had joined them, and the three older Cavanaugh sisters ending up performing a few magic tricks of their own on the unsuspecting movie audience. It was a day filled with laughter and fun. They would remember it, and those moments with their mother forever.

Of course Celestia had disapproved of publicly using magic at first. But when the man and woman behind them wouldn't stop talking, Celestia grasped the necklace she rarely took off. Popcorn suddenly popped in his popcorn bucket and the entire cup of the soft drink his lady friend held mysteriously saturated the crotch of his pants. The noisy moviegoers left in a fit of fear and anger.

Destiny and her family had laughed so hard they'd nearly been thrown out, until Aunt Sole turned her large green eyes on the manager. She opened her mouth and sang so softly to him, no one but him, could hear.

And that had been the end of that.

The manager had left them as if in a trance, so enthralled with Aunt Sole he nearly tripped over his own feet as he returned to his office. Destiny was certain he never remembered any of it later, as Aunt Sole was a Siren and could command any man to do as she bid without ever touching their conscious thoughts. But unlike her predecessors, Aunt Soleli never led anyone to their death.

She considered that tacky.

"Remember the day Mom took us and the aunts to the movie?"

Haven smiled, nodding. "Yeah, I was just thinking about that. Aunt Sole pretended to be insulted that we called her Samantha. But she really loved it."

"Of course she did. It made her the center of attention. And you know how she loves that."

Haven adjusted her body on the large butter-soft chair so she could face Destiny. "I want my powers back."

Destiny sighed, knowing they would eventually get on

the subject they had avoided for almost two weeks since one or the other of them was always at work or sleeping. Their opposing schedules hadn't bothered her before Rayne moved out. But now she often felt lonely.

She was glad Haven brought up the subject because she didn't want to be the one to open a discussion about how awful Haven was looking lately. "Have you felt anything at all?"

Haven shrugged. "After the enema three days ago I felt energized for a while. And when I went to work that night I purposely touched a kid who had slammed his hand in a car door. He had a couple of broken fingers."

Destiny raised her brows when her sister stopped talking. "And?"

Haven sighed. "I don't know. I felt a spark. And the kid did, too, because he jumped and his gaze flew to mine. Then he smiled and said whatever I did took away the pain. I got so excited until I realized the bones were still broken. They just didn't hurt anymore." She pressed her lips together, frowning. "I don't know what to make of it."

Destiny sat up straighter, excited. "It's something! Maybe it took a while for your ability to heal, to go away. How would you have known? You never allowed yourself to touch anyone. And if it took time for your powers to diminish, maybe it will just take some time for it to return full force!

"Maybe you need more enemas. If one helped some, then more should help more. It's probably because we didn't get them every year like we were told. We may have to make up for lost time." The tilt of Haven's head told Destiny she was considering the possibility.

"Did you go in for *your* enema?"

Destiny nodded. "Yes, I did. Yesterday, actually." Her lips twisted when she thought about the experience. "By the way, the elderly, heavyset Hungarian woman you said would do it was in fact a twenty-five year old blond Adonis who loves to surf on his time off."

The horrified expression on Haven's face almost made

the humiliation Destiny had first suffered, worth it.

"Oh my, did you tell him to get lost and get Gerta?"

Laugher burst from Destiny's lips. "Gerta?"

Haven shrugged. "I'm sure that isn't actually her name, but she looks like a Gerta to me. So what did you do? Surely you didn't let a sexy man flush your bowels."

"Actually, I did."

Haven rose and paced around the room in agitation. It worried Destiny that her sister was not only looking different; older, thinner—and not in a good way—but she was acting differently too. Haven had always been the poster child for serenity, the dictionary meaning of calm, and a solid rock of composure.

Anger twisted Haven's features so ferociously that Destiny gasped at the transformation.

"What the hell! What the *bloody* hell!" Haven yelled suddenly, moving around the room as if her feet were on fire. She sputtered incoherently as her skin darkened and her irises were surrounded with a blood red that eliminated the white. The only thing missing from the angry woman standing before her was snake hair writhing around as fiery eyes turned Destiny into stone.

"After I ended up taking the first appointment I *specifically* asked that the same older woman administer your cleansing because she was so gentle! I'm going to call that rat's nest and complain, you can be sure of that! By the time I get done with them they will wish they hadn't stuck anything up my butt! I'll kill them all! I'll set them on fire!"

Destiny's mouth dropped open as she watched and listened to her normally calm and composed sister turn into a vicious and malicious alien. Her own composure shaken, she rose from the couch and cautiously approached Haven to place her hand on her sister's very tense shoulder. "You need to calm down, Sis," she said softly, hoping to break through whatever had possession of Haven.

"It actually turned out okay. In fact, I have a date with him this Friday night."

Haven looked at her in horror as the redness in her

eyes faded to pink then finally returned to normal. "You have *got* to be kidding me."

"No," Destiny said, shaking her head, trying to hide her growing fear. "It turns out he's a medical student who works there to supplement his student loans."

"Still, that doesn't make it right. The first time a man puts his hands on you it shouldn't be to pour tea into your rectum. I can't believe you are going out with him. That is so gross, to say the least."

Destiny took a relieved breath. Haven was turning back into the sister she knew. *Kind of.* "Actually, you are, too." Before Haven could express her opinion about that, Destiny continued, "We are going shopping for some pretty purple scrubs for him, *then* we are heading to other stores so we can try on outfits together. And then there is what is commonly called a *chick flick* he is dying to see."

Haven's face undergoing such extreme changes right before her eyes made Destiny a little dizzy. Fury had turned to confusion, which now transformed to delight as Haven's features smoothed out and her lips lifted into an almost childlike smile. She clapped her hands together then hugged herself.

"Aw…you found us a male girlfriend? That is so nice!"

Destiny laughed nervously. The super sugar-sweet voice coming out of her sister now was just as weird as the crazy Medusa had been. "Yes…."

Haven exhaled and smiled and looked more like herself again, but Destiny was getting seriously worried— and a little seasick.

Flying off the handle like Haven just had, looking and sounding like she was not her normal self but was several somebody elses, and the weak or diminishing ability to heal, all needed to be explored. Destiny knew the combined multiple personalities would have been enough all by itself to scare the crap out of her if she hadn't just been cleansed.

Destiny headed to the kitchen hoping the sister she knew would stick around for a while. She needed a break. "Let's start some dinner and talk about things."

Haven followed and settled herself on the stool facing the island where Destiny placed the fresh vegetables she would use to make a salad. "What kinds of things?"

Destiny tried to keep from looking or sounding too serious. "I think we need to try to get Rayne on the phone again and make sure she's okay."

Looking dejected, Haven nodded. "You mean, unlike me."

Destiny stopped chopping the first carrot, placed the knife on the marble slab that topped the island, and took Haven's hands in her own. "You are going to be fine."

Haven shook her head. "I think I'm going crazy. I can hear what I'm saying but I can't stop myself. I get so angry or so happy for no reason. I haven't seen you much lately, but I know people at work are starting to avoid me, and talking stops when I enter a room. The doctors aren't requesting me particularly, like they used to." Sadness swamped her features. "They used to argue over who got me on any given day. Now they turn the other way when I smile at them. I think I'm becoming psychotic."

Knowing now that Haven was aware of her strange behavior didn't make Destiny feel any better, but at least she wouldn't have to convince her sister that she needed help. "I'm having trouble too, reading people. It comes and goes, but it has to be temporary. I'm sure of it." *Not really*, Destiny admitted silently, but she kept the thought to herself. She didn't want Haven going off the deep end again.

Haven nodded. "You're right, of course. This is just temporary. Let's try to get Rayne on the phone. If she's having problems, too, she's probably scared to death." Haven frowned. "But don't tell her how bad I am. At least not until we know if she's having the same problems."

Destiny nodded and left the kitchen to retrieve her phone, hoping that if Rayne *was* suffering a loss of her gift it would be a mild case like her own, and not the extreme mess Haven was experiencing.

On her way back to the kitchen with her phone,

Destiny grabbed the postcard, hoping it had a contact number where her aunt was staying, as the aunts were nearly as bad as Rayne when it came to carrying cell phones.

She needed to contact Aunt Soleli, have her contact Aunt Lune Brille, and then get them both to come back to the states as quickly as possible. Having the more experienced aunts around would make her feel a lot better because she had the sinking feeling that another enema, or even a dozen of them, wasn't going to fix whatever was happening to Haven.

She stopped short when she realized Haven had turned to face her, her face an even scarier version of the Medusa of moments before. But what kept her frozen to the spot was that the knife she'd left lying on the marble slab was now being held in a tight-fisted hand.

****

"Answer your phone. Answer your phone. Answer your phone!"

Destiny sat on her bed, rocking back and forth, knowing the litany wasn't getting her anywhere, but the sound of her own voice was all that was keeping her sane. She was terrified that something had happened to Rayne too, as she'd been frantically hitting her sister's number for the last hour and a half with no results. She couldn't even leave a voice mail because, Rayne, being Rayne, had never taken the time to set one up.

She needed to hear Rayne's voice, needed to make sure she wasn't suffering like Haven was. Or that she wasn't helplessly exposing her gift to the public because she was half out of her mind.

Haven hadn't hurt her or even threatened her, really. Instead she had collapsed into a heap of uncontrollable sobbing when she realized that she held the knife and frightened Destiny nearly to death.

After getting her sister to her room and into her bed Destiny had searched Rayne's room frantically looking for a sedative of some type, as Rayne had taken something that would knock her out when her migraines wouldn't allow her to sleep. The last place she thought to look was the medicine cabinet in Rayne's private bathroom, but that's where a nearly full bottle sat.

The prescription medication clearly stated that it was only intended for the name printed on the label, but Destiny was certain her circumstances overrode any legal ramifications. So now Haven was out cold, her cell phone was on mute in case the hospital tried to reach her, and Destiny was becoming more frantic by the moment.

She made one more attempt then threw her cell phone across the room when Rayne still didn't answer. The sound of it shattering was the last straw. She rolled into the fetal position and cried in fear, in loneliness, and finally in anger, until she fell asleep.

****

Time stood still as Rayne waited for word from Garrison. She had returned to his cabin and sat waiting as minutes turned into an hour. She'd worried about him and his cousin. She'd wondered about what her Indian was up to. She'd looked at her fingernails and resisted the urge to chew on them.

Finally, nervous energy propelled Rayne to her feet. She cleaned breakfast dishes and scrubbed the kitchen, then climbed to the loft to remake his bed, dust what little there was to dust, and put the clothes he'd thrown in the corner into the hamper on the other side of the small room.

Rayne returned to the main floor and studied the craftsmanship of his furniture, then read the titles of the furniture making and woodworking books he had displayed in alphabetical order on a small bookshelf he'd probably made too. She sighed, wondering why she hadn't heard anything after so long.

Then she remembered she had left her cell phone on mute after returning from his parents' house.

Rayne pulled the high tech phone Destiny insisted she get before leaving California from her purse and slid the ring up the touch screen to wake the phone up. The thirty-two missed calls from Destiny had her completely forgetting about Garrison and Gavin. She pulled up her sister's number, hit call, and listened to the haunting Irish tune before her sister's voice told her to leave a message. She tried several more times, wishing she had taken the time to figure out how to set up her phone to receive messages.

Rayne groaned, frustrated with herself. Setting up messages had meant she would have to get a computer, go online, and somehow figure out what to do, which was a piece of cake for most people, but she was the least computer and internet savvy person on the planet.

Electronics terrified her because they made her feel stupid. There was no doubt in her mind she'd been born in the wrong century, and that her inability to grasp technology was why her sisters had always treated her like she was incapable of handling anything important on her own.

It was embarrassing.

But she was who she was, so the rest of the world could just go right on and text, instant message, engine search, and do whatever else it was they did to their heart's content. She was more than happy reading books still made from paper, and using a pencil or pen and notepad to make notes while she studied the tomes that made up her family's history.

She wasn't stupid. She just knew less about some things, and more about others.

But the things she did know about didn't do her any good now. After one more call to Destiny she pulled up Haven's number. *Her* voice mail answered immediately, which meant she was at work, so Rayne left a message with her too, as she tried not to worry over missing the repeated calls.

Seconds later Rayne smiled and shook her head at how silly she was being. Of course there was nothing to worry about. Destiny's nonstop calls had been because Rayne hadn't talked to her recently and therefore hadn't reported every little detail of her life, so Destiny decided to make a *Destiny statement* to express her irritation with her younger sibling by blowing up her phone.

The sound of a vehicle pulling up outside drew her attention from her too bossy sister and back to the man she had missed so terribly in the last couple of hours. She headed for the door as an unfamiliar truck backed away and Garrison slowly shuffled up to the porch.

Chapter Twenty-Two

It had been a long while, but hearing about them finding the kid brought back urges that hadn't stirred for some time.

That boy turned out to be a disappointment. Pure and simple. Just like the others that had followed, though by the time she chopped at the second one it had been as much about the pleasure of the act as his unacceptable behavior.

She knew it was wrong to get pleasure that way, and she blamed the Taylor kid for it. If he hadn't made her so angry she would never have known about the rush she'd get watching life drain from a human body. And she wouldn't have been anticipating the sexual release of stealing his last breath.

Anthony should have cooperated. He had been well cared for all those years ago. Shelter, food, clothing, fresh water, and his shit had been cleaned out every week, more or less. He shouldn't have wanted more. He shouldn't have wanted to remain Anthony when being Jimmy would have made them both so much happier in the end.

He shouldn't have tried to escape.

The one there now, the one they were all up in arms about, was a good kid. He didn't fight after that first time. He never asked for anything. Never cursed. Never begged. Always showed respect.

That was good.

It meant he was content. He was happy to be provided for. He wouldn't cause trouble.

But the town was more interested in this kid than all the ones that came before, and that made things harder. There were people all over the mountains at any given time now, looking everywhere. One guy had all but stumbled on the entrance. If not for quick thinking, to be sure to be in that search grid and redirect him and the other searchers when they got too close, all would have been lost.

With so many more people out hiking on the mountains rather than being the only one out there on a regular basis, it should have made getting the supplies to him easier. Just blend right in. Just act like one of those diehards who wouldn't give up and continually gave of their free time. Except hiking with a backpack on the mountains would be expected, not carrying the amount of supplies it took to feed a growing boy on a weekly basis. It would make people suspicious.

Suspicious people started asking questions and watching a person's movements. Suspicious people got you caught.

Which meant the boy would have to learn to live on less, unless opportunities arose for extra trips. But that wasn't likely. Because then there would be one person who would notice. And that would ruin everything.

The urge would be ignored. Eventually it would go away. It had to. Or another male would have to replace this one. And that was never an easy thing to accomplish.

It was a real shame she couldn't hack him up though....

Chapter Twenty-Three

Rayne opened the door with a smile that quickly fell. Garrison looked horrible. The pallor of his skin and the dullness of his eyes caused her heart to clench. She moved toward him, searching his face, hurt that he was hurting. "It was horrible, then."

Garrison pulled her to him and just held on as silent moments went by. Eventually she realized her shirt was dampening, and her heart broke even more. She allowed him his silent cry until he pulled back and turned away with a ragged breath.

Rayne tenderly placed her hand on his arm as she walked around him to look into his face. He didn't look down at her, instead looking out through eyes so heavy with unshed tears she was certain he could see nothing but a blurry landscape, if he saw anything at all. She slowly slid her hand down his arm and took his hand before gently leading him into the cabin then on to the bathroom which was so large and so nicely appointed it made the one in her cabin look like an outhouse.

She released him long enough to turn on the shower and adjust the temperature before she turned back to begin slowly undressing him. She knelt and untied then removed his boots before sitting them aside. Standing again, she fought the sting that would bring tears to her own eyes as each shirt button gave way.

He stood statue still, his breath as silent as if it didn't exist, and he allowed her to remove first his shirt, then his jeans. His boxers and socks followed before she faced him and slowly removed her own clothing.

He looked at her then. Inch by inch. Until his gaze traveled back up to lock with hers. "You are so beautiful."

Rayne pressed up against him feeling the chill of his body. She realized then that he was in shock and apparently had been since looking upon his slain cousin. Her heart twisted and the tears finally won, streaming down her face in mourning for him.

She sniffed as she took his hand again and led him into the large, elaborately tiled, walk-in shower. She settled him under the torrential spray of the largest showerhead she had ever seen then reached for the bottle of shampoo sitting within the recessed shelf.

Warm water poured from the top of his head, down the length of his body, occasionally splashing her as she squirted shampoo into her palm. Rayne returned the bottle to the shelf and turned back. "Close your eyes and face down."

Garrison instantly complied. She pulled him out from under the spray, and rubbed her hands together before lifting them to lather his hair. A shudder rippled out of him as he allowed her to massage his scalp. Rayne trembled in response as the act of running her hands through his hair ignited passion where her intent had been healing.

Her nipples pebbled so tightly they ached, and she knew it was for his touch. To distract herself from the unwanted ardor she lowered her hands to gently push him back under the spray. The deluge quickly did its work and suds changed to clear water once more.

Rayne turned her back to him and took the few steps required to reach the smaller recessed shelf that was designed to hold soap bars. Before she could grasp the soap his hands came around her and molded her breasts. Startled, she inhaled sharply, only to release the breath when she felt his hard length pressed between her lower back and his solid lower abdomen.

"Garrison…."

"Just let me feel you. Just let me love you."

Rayne opened her mouth to protest, concerned he hadn't recovered enough. She closed it to swallow the purr that threatened when Garrison lifted the weight of her hair off of one shoulder, and placed his lips on her neck to suckle.

"Garrison...." she said again, but it was surely as clear to him as it was to her that this time it was an invitation rather than a protest.

"Close your eyes, and brace your palms on the wall," he whispered, warming her ear with his breath while using his feet to gently nudge her much smaller ones apart.

Rayne's breath caught as heat built between her thighs. She leaned forward slightly and placed her palms on the tiled wall, then realized she was in a frisking stance. She smiled at the thought of playing cops and robbers with him then uttered a protest when cool air suddenly replaced the warmth of his body.

Before she could make another sound he was back, his heavy erection teasing her from behind as his soapy fingers returned to her breasts where he shaped and reshaped the globes, yet was careful to avoid where they ached to be touched most.

He leaned into her back, cloaking her, and ran his hands up and down her front from collarbone to tummy. With each pass he made over her breasts, her nipples tilted in whichever direction his hands were going until they were so tight she wanted to scream.

Rayne kept her elbows locked, though the rest of her trembled as she rose on tiptoes when he increased the upward friction, then her heels lowered onto the wet tile when his magical fingers slid down her abdomen, each time getting closer to, but not touching, her mound.

Not sure her quavering legs would hold her much longer, Rayne was relieved when he spun her around and lifted her up so that her thighs were at his waist. She opened her eyes and wound her legs around him, locking her ankles, as her arms automatically encircled his neck.

Garrison slid his hands beneath her bottom, holding her securely, and moved forward until the heat of her back met the coolness of the tiles that hadn't been warmed by the spray. Rayne locked gazes with him, her excitement evident by quivering nostrils and the rapid rise and fall of her chest, his by the hot throbbing girth poised at the juncture of her thighs.

"I need you," preceded a smooth entry that stretched, filled, and scorched her, and the only response she could manage was to tighten around his heat and hold his shoulders as securely as the strength left in her arms allowed.

He closed his eyes and his head fell back as he rocked his hips in a motion that stripped her of all thought. Rayne's lips parted to release a moan with each smooth thrust, to inhale sharply as she anticipated the next. The strength that had wavered rebounded and every muscle in her body strained to absorb the increasing speed and fullness of him.

As her leg muscles clenched his hips she eased her grip on his shoulders to slide her hands upward until her fingers were locked at the base of his skull. Secure in his ability to hold her she leaned back to rest her shoulders on the wall, and let go, allowing herself to drown in the power he held over her body.

Friction became tension that built and burned until her body was so tightly wound that the only thing left was the explosion that shook her to the core and tore a scream from her throat. Her release ignited his, and the gargled sounds coming from between his clenched teeth echoed the final hard thrusts, before he stumbled forward enough to pin her hips between his and the shower wall.

Garrison curled into her, laying his head on her shoulder as he continued to empty himself into her. His harsh breaths warmed the skin covering Rayne's collarbone and mirrored the rapid rise and fall of the hard chest smashing hers. Straining to catch her own breath, Rayne held tightly to him, resting her chin on his strong shoulder. Eventually their breathing eased and Garrison raised his head, loosened his grip so her legs could slide down his, and held her steady as her feet gained purchase on the tile floor.

She looked up at him, so crazy in love she was afraid to speak. But she needn't have worried that he needed words because he sealed her lips with a kiss so deep, so passionate, so loving, that her legs nearly gave out.

Rayne allowed Garrison to pull her back under the spray that was now considerably cooler. She didn't mind. Her body had known fire.

****

Garrison knew he was in deep. No woman had ever meant as much to him as Rayne did.

He held her to him as she slept, wondering why he had never known how great it was to snuggle after sex. His former lovers had been everything from sweet and tentative to bold and adventurous, but once they finished making love, he hadn't given snuggling a thought.

It wasn't that he'd been cold. He always made sure the women knew he appreciated their time and talents, and that no matter the shape of their bodies or the level of their education he respected women in general. He could do no less having been raised by his parents.

Garrison glanced down at Rayne when she made a funny little noise. He gently slid out from under her to keep from disturbing her rest. There was no way he could relax and sleep, so he needed to leave her in peace.

He walked down the stairs to the living room then headed straight to Gavin's room. Garrison entered what had once been his office and felt the pang that always hit these days. He'd painted and decorated the room just for the kid, while he'd still been under hospital care following Grey and Joy's deaths.

Garrison had used the wood he'd had on hand that was meant for another project to make a bed especially for Gavin, as his brother's house had been taped up, and nothing could be moved for almost two weeks after the assassinations. Garrison shook his head, looking at the thickness of the pillow topped mattress he'd purchased in the hopes it would give Gavin comfort, though he'd known it would never replace a mother's arms. Once he was able,

Garrison had retrieved the highboy and another dresser, and the things Gavin said he needed to have from the house. But the furniture, the blue paint, and even the new carpet meant absolutely nothing, if his nephew never had a chance to use the room again.

He crossed to the bed and sat on it, wishing he could somehow convey a message to his nephew, hoping Gavin was still alive to hear it. Even knowing it was foolish, he lowered his head. "Gavin. Please be okay. Please stay alive until I can find you. I'm trying. And I'll try harder. But I need you to help me. I need a sign. Something...anything...."

Of course there was no response. He hadn't expected one. So he rose to his feet and looked at the room again, only this time with a more critical eye. A chill ran through him when he realized he hadn't been smart. He could have wasted precious time by not searching his nephew's things instead of making the room into a shrine. What if there was something his nephew had been involved in that led to his disappearance? What if he had left something behind that could lead to his rescue?

Of course the police had looked the room over, but even they hadn't believed the boy would leave behind any relevant evidence in such a neat room. Many of them had known him since his birth, being close friends and coworkers of his father's, so they hadn't even questioned if drugs or other illegal actions could have played a part in the mystery.

And maybe, just maybe, they had looked for the wrong thing. The question was: what was the right thing?

Garrison started at the chest of drawers, pulling his nephew's neatly folded clothes out and stacking them just as neatly on the bed. He emptied them all before pulling the drawers completely out and inspecting each one from every angle. When that yielded nothing he got on his knees and ran his hands along the tops, sides, bottoms and backs of each opening.

Trying not to get discouraged that it wasn't going to be

easy, he replaced the drawers and then the clothes just as he had found them. Next, Garrison turned to the highboy, and his breath caught on a sob. The dresser had been his first attempt at making furniture and had led him to dream of making more.

He'd built and presented the tall dresser with the little closet as a baby shower gift to his brother and sister-in-law only a few weeks before Gavin's birth. Grey had hugged him hard while Joy broke into tears. She finally pushed her husband off of Garrison to hug him too, her large belly pressed between them. Their exuberant delight and overwhelming gratitude had embarrassed him at the time, especially since all the other family members gushed over it too. Embarrassment eventually turned to pride, though he'd kept that to himself.

Since the gathering hadn't been about or for him, but rather for the lovely lady who had blessed his brother with a happy marriage and was about to give him the son he had wanted so badly, Garrison had stepped into the background as soon as he could manage it.

Now he ran his hands over the smooth surface allowing the feeling of fine wood to soothe him. He silently reminisced about walking his parent's property for days, looking for just the right oak tree. Once chosen, he and his father had gone out and cut it down together. And together they cut it into long logs that eventually became boards.

As he hadn't yet begun his own business, only taking a well-deserved lengthy leave between deployments, Garrison had borrowed the equipment Garrison Sr. has set up in one of his barns years before and used childhood memories of fatherly instructions to guide him through the process.

Working on the baby gift had been a pleasure on so many levels. The stripping of bark, the sawing of logs into varying sized boards, and then painstakingly shaping and dovetailing each component, so he could assemble it without the use of nails, had turned a labor of love into a personal passion.

The sanding and staining took days as he had wanted it

so smooth a child would never catch a splinter, and the depth of color had to be as warm and inviting as his sister-in-law had made their home. By the time he'd finished it, he'd known what he wanted to do once he left the military. And he'd never once regretted making that dream become a reality.

Afraid he would break down again if he allowed himself to think too much about how he'd loved the people he'd made the dresser for, Garrison forced his thoughts to the present.

He opened the five narrower drawers to the left of the highboy's closet and removed more clothing before repeating the search he had done in and around the drawers and within the frame of the other dresser. He replaced those and opened the top longer drawer that ran the width of the dresser and stopped, then lifted one item out at a time. Baseballs nestled in mitts; a newer yet heavily used smaller one, and a well-worn, much larger one Garrison knew had belonged to his brother.

He set them aside making sure the balls didn't roll out before lifting the autographed football his brother had earned his senior year of college, as the most valuable player for the game that sent his school into the bowl season. Every member of the team and the coaching staff had signed it, and his brother had beamed for days after that victory.

Reverently he also sat it aside. Not sure he could continue, but knowing Gavin's life could depend on it, he lifted a shoebox and removed the lid. His breath caught on a sob and he had to fight for control before examining the stack of banded ticket stubs from the various professional sporting events Gavin and his dad had attended together.

Garrison placed them back in the corner and lifted a nickel-plated whistle and chain. He could only surmise Grey had used it while first coaching the Little League games his young son played, and then again for the municipal leagues as Gavin grew. Once Gavin made it to high school and was a star of the team, Grey finally got to sit in the stands and cheer his son on. To Garrison's knowledge, his brother had never missed a game.

Like their own father, Grey had loved his child well.

The loss Gavin had suffered was so much worse than any of them knew, Garrison was sure. He only hoped his nephew was still alive and doing anything he had to do to survive until they found him, because all the rest of the family wanted was to shower him with love.

Garrison set the whistle back in the box and lifted and then flipped through a stack of photographs. Some of them were very old, some of them very new, and some somewhere in between. Memories swamped him as he looked at the top picture of himself and Grey, both dressed like little gentlemen in their Easter suits. Grey was a few inches taller at seven than he had been at four years old, but their features and expressions had been nearly identical.

Even with the age difference they had been best friends, and though he was sure now he had been a pest then, Grey had never pushed him away or excluded him when they got older and he got to do things with friends that Garrison was still too young to be a part of. Thankfully their father had enough sense to force Garrison to stay home sometimes when Grey was old enough to start spreading his wings.

But it never altered their relationship and he ached anew at the loss.

He took a moment to look at some of the others. A snapshot filled with happiness of Grey and Joy; Grey dressed in a tux, Joy in a simple, elegant wedding gown. The next was a picture of Joy standing sideways, one hand on her bulging stomach, the other holding her summer dress tight below it so they could capture just how large their son was making her belly grow. She was making a face at the camera, and Garrison could only imagine what Grey was saying to her as he snapped the photo.

Most that followed were of one or both of them with their infant, then toddler, then Gavin as he looked the last time Garrison saw him. He stared at the picture, absorbing the natural smile that had always lit Gavin's face. Until the day he lost his parents.

Garrison couldn't help but wonder if he would ever see Gavin's smile again.

He replaced the photos and closed the box then sat it next to the sports equipment. What remained in the drawer, too neatly organized for a teenage boy, were a variety of toys that had meant something to him, or perhaps to his parents, from infancy on. The brown Teddy Bear that had his birth year embroidered on its right foot, a model airplane he had built at some point, possibly with the help one parent or the other. There were a few video game cartridges, but Garrison knew Gavin had been too active to sit in front of a television for long. A variety of smaller toys took up the rest of the drawer; they were the only things that hadn't been stored uniformly. Though the toy soldiers, yoyo, and other small items were still neater than one would expect from a child. Garrison inspected the drawer and the opening it belonged in before replacing everything, *again*, just as Gavin had left them.

The last drawer was a surprise. Although it held more of the same; toys, photographs, and a couple dozen baseball caps that seemed to match the teams on the ticket stubs, with the exception of the hats, it was a mess.

He just looked at it for a moment, wondering if it meant anything. Although he was finally tired, both physically and emotionally, and wanted nothing more to climb back into the bed with Rayne, he gathered and lifted out a handful of photographs. Sharp pain caused him to drop them again.

The shard of glass embedded into his middle finger wasn't that large, but he rose and headed to the bathroom as blood started seeping from around it. At the sink he turned on the cold tap, stuck his fingers under it, and pulled the glass out.

The water ran red for a moment, pooling in the basin before flowing down the drain. He applied pressure on the wound for a couple of minutes more before pulling a washcloth from the linen closet. He reapplied pressure with the cloth before turning back to rinse the sink.

Garrison left the bathroom and reentered Gavin's room. While holding one hand with the other, he stared at the haphazard mess of photographs now seeing that there was more broken glass covering nearly the entire drawer.

Throbbing pain started at the wounded finger, increasing with each heartbeat. He held his arms up to get the finger above his heart while trying keep the pressure on it. Knowing there was no way he could pick through the broken glass without at least one free hand he left the room and returned to the bathroom.

Bandages, in several shapes and sizes, were a staple for a woodworker so he had no trouble finding gauze and tape to wrap his finger. But every time he took pressure off the wound it started bleeding again, so it took three tries, six large gauze pads, and half the roll of tape before he finally had it securely covered and not soaked with blood.

Garrison left the bathroom and headed for the loft. He was just too tired to do any more without rest. As soon as the funeral was over tomorrow afternoon he would resume searching Gavin's room.

Chapter Twenty-Four

The air was thick with heartbreak as the Mystic Waters community gathered to bury one of their own. The White family and those related to them either by birth or marriage made up a large portion of the hundreds gathered. As Garrison introduced her to one after another, Rayne noticed that they seemed to fill the church and settle in a pew depending on how closely they were related to the deceased.

Of course Garrison's grandparents and parents were in the front pews, as were Lucy, her parents, and her late husband's parents.

Though the service was set to begin at two, the number of people filing in and going to the front to say a word or two to Lucy and her in-laws, or to the elderly matriarch and patriarch of the White family, meant the funeral was delayed for another forty-five minutes. Once everyone was settled, the minister walked to the front of the church and opened the service with a prayer.

Rayne, Garrison, his remaining brother, Gary, his sister Kate, and her husband, Judd, shared the pew directly behind their parents and grandparents, just as the closest members of the Taylor clan sat behind the grieving mother, and the poor child's grandparents on the opposite pew.

The minister, having personally known Anthony White-Taylor since birth, and his family for nearly as many years, as well as many of those in attendance who regularly attended his church, struggled to maintain his composure throughout much of the service. Rayne heard the quiver in his voice as he told of being a youth pastor before taking over the pulpit when the last pastor retired the year before. He spoke of the sadness he felt for Lucy and the family when Tony suddenly disappeared. And about his hope that she would hear from him after he'd fulfilled his desire to become a country music star. He expounded on what a wonderful voice Tony had as he had always sung, and often soloed, in the youth choir, and how delightfully it would blend with the angels' voices in Heaven.

Lucy cried quietly through the entire service as she leaned into her father's shoulder. Only crying out loudly once, when the minister spoke of how horrible it was that Tony had been so close all this time, and no one had known.

The service ended with a woman Rayne hadn't been introduced to singing a hymn that was familiar to those gathered, as many joined in with hushed voices. She glanced around, realizing rivers of tears were being shed not only for the loss of life, but for the loss of innocence as well. Now they knew their children were no longer safe in the home they had always known.

She turned to Garrison, knowing he and his immediate family had already learned that lesson in the harshest way. He had his eyes closed and his head was down, and she knew he was still reeling from seeing Anthony White-Taylor's remains, as well as being filled with fear for the nephew he adored.

Her heart broke for him all over again. And she had no idea how she could put him through the trauma of finding another body.

It took a considerable amount of time for everyone, starting with those closest to the front of the church, to file past the closed casket then load into the cars already lined up outside. Rayne was relieved Garrison chose to drive his truck rather than ride in one of the limos the local funeral parlor provided the families. They waited beside it silently until the pallbearers carried the casket to the awaiting hearse.

Rayne looked at Garrison as he stared at the vehicle that symbolized death. She touched his arms and he flinched. "Please let me drive."

Garrison opened his mouth with what she knew was a protest, but he closed it again and handed her the keys. "I'm sorry."

"Don't you dare apologize, but let's get in the truck before they leave us."

He nodded as she went around and opened the driver's door and got in before he had even moved. He entered the passenger side and repeated, "I'm sorry."

Rayne let it go this time, knowing he was barely with her, and arguing that he didn't owe her an apology for anything would be a waste of her breath. She followed the limo in front of her, occasionally glancing back through the mirror at the endless line of cars and trucks following behind.

The cemetery only took ten minutes to get to, but it took another forty before the mourners from the last cars arriving made their way to the burial site. The funeral home set up enough draped folding chairs to accommodate all those who sat in the first two rows of both aisles of the church, so Rayne settled beside Garrison, glad he was getting to sit down.

As the minister began the graveside service, she could think of nothing but the man beside her. Garrison was in bad shape and had been since returning from the coroner's the day before. Even their lovemaking in the shower last night hadn't completely wiped the horror from his eyes. She had tried so hard to stay awake with him once they went to bed, but eventually she fell asleep. She had no idea when, or even if, he had slept.

When she awoke that morning he was already up and showering. When he came from the bathroom dressed for the service and ready to take her to her cabin so she could get dressed, she noticed the bandage on his finger. When she asked him about it he brushed it aside, and there was something in his eyes that told her to drop it.

So she did. But at some point, once he was himself again, she would ask him to share his pain with her and allow her to carry some of his burdens.

The night before he had claimed to love her, and if he meant it, then he had to let her in, even when, no, *especially when*, the pain cut so deeply he could barely function.

The service ended, and Lucy, knowing she would never again be this physically close to the child she brought into the world, let go and cried in great gulping sobs that caused those around her to join in. Tears flowed freely from Rayne's own eyes as she stood to leave, but Garrison stopped her.

"Give me a moment."

Rayne nodded and stood where she was as Garrison knelt before Lucy. He touched her hand and she turned to him before leaning into him. They held each other for timeless moments and Rayne realized he had needed it as much as Lucy did. When their embrace ended he rose and leaned down to whisper in her ear.

Rayne had no idea if she would ever be privy to what he was saying to his cousin, but she knew she would do anything she could to help him never have to repeat this experience with the child he so loved.

Even if it meant ignoring a ghost.

****

The White farm was covered with parked cars and the large home filled with people when Rayne and Garrison arrived at his parents' house. It struck her as strange that so many people had already made themselves at home since the owners of the house hadn't yet arrived. She watched as several women set massive amounts of food on the huge dining room table along with paper plates and plastic utensils.

Five large glass containers with spouts were being lined up on the countertop. A couple of men opened large bags of ice and half-filled each one before carrying in large vats and filling each container with lemonade, sweet tea, unsweetened tea, cherry Kool-Aid, and fruit punch. Rayne only knew which was which because someone had the forethought to make little signs to sit in front of each one.

Garrison Sr. and Mary White arrived and went right to

work helping put together the post-funeral feast. Apparently, when anything of importance happened in Mystic Waters, it was the White's' home that everyone migrated to. Which made sense, she realized, given the size of the house and property. There was no way this many people could invade a normal home.

"Can I get you something to eat?"

Rayne turned, realizing she had done nothing but gawk since entering the house. She shook her head, relieved to see, that now Garrison was in his childhood home, he seemed more himself. "No. Thanks. Can I get you anything?"

Garrison shook his head. "Can we talk?"

Rayne's heart skipped a beat and she didn't know if it was from fear or excitement. As much as she would love to be in his confidences, she also knew something as traumatic as the events filling his life could make a person step back and reassess their life. She didn't want to be something he reassessed.

"Of course."

"Come on," he said, taking her hand and leading her to the large winding staircase. They took the steps side by side. At the top he turned to the left and walked down a long hall where he opened a door and entered a room. It didn't take a genius to realize that this had once been his room, or that his parents were perfectly content to leave it as he had the day he moved out. Yet there wasn't a speck of dust anywhere.

She smiled at him, hoping he didn't break her heart. "Your room."

Garrison nodded, but he didn't return her smile. She bit her bottom lip and went to sit on the queen size bed. If he was about to dump her she needed to be sitting down. "So, what do you want to talk about?"

Garrison settled at her side, clasped his hands together, and focused on them. "I want to apologize for today. I'm just in a bad place over all this. Until you found Tony's body I don't think I ever really believed something *horrible* could have happened to Gavin. Now I know it's possible, but even worse, probable."

Rayne reached over and clasped his hands and squeezed, relieved he unclasped his to take hers. "We don't know that. Don't give up hope unless we find there is none."

The thought of Qaqeemasq waiting for her somewhere out in the woods caused her insides to twist with guilt. If she ignored him then someone was going to continue to go undiscovered, but if it turned out to be Gavin she knew it would kill Garrison. Right now, even his wavering hope, was still hope. She couldn't take it from him, and selfishly, she couldn't let it take him from her.

"I love you."

The words slipped out, but she couldn't regret it as a spark returned to his eyes and his lips lifted in the first real smile she'd seen in days. Garrison reached up and ran a finger over her cheek as if he was testing the softness of her skin, then down her jaw. He slid it under her chin and pulled her towards him as he leaned closer to her.

The touch of his lips wasn't filled with passion, but was a gentle seal that meant more at that moment than all the passionate kisses in the world. He pulled back only a little, gazing into her eyes. "Will you marry me, then?"

Perhaps it was the unexpectedness of the proposal. Perhaps it was the fact that her heart was about to burst with happiness. Regardless, Rayne had never thought she was one of those women who cried at being proposed to. But she knew now she had been wrong.

She nodded, laughing with joy as the tears coursed down her cheeks.

"Say the word," he said, his mouth inches from her lips.

Rayne pulled herself together and nodded again. "Yes. Yes, I'll marry you."

Garrison pulled her to him and they fell back upon the mattress. He kissed her forehead, then her eyelids, and finally her lips. He didn't linger, but gave her another quick peck before sitting up abruptly. He held out his hand and she took it before sitting up too. "I hate this, but we need to get back downstairs. Kissing you will make me not want to leave this room for a very long time. And I'm sure my parents are wondering where I am."

Realizing that for a few precious moments she had forgotten the horror and sorrow that had filled the day, Rayne nodded. "Okay. I guess if I'm going to join the family I had better get down there and get to know everyone. But I don't think we should say anything about being engaged today. Today is about Tony. We can have tomorrow."

Garrison rose and pulled her up as well, only he didn't let go. He pulled her into his arms, this time for a very proper, very deep kiss. When he lifted his head he rested his lips against her forehead. "Thank you."

Rayne snuggled into him, loving that he was going to belong to her forever. "For what?"

"For being you."

The joyous flight her heart was on took a dive as she remembered that Garrison loved the woman she was, but he didn't know the whole of her. Now she understood why her mother had let her and her sisters watch that television show all those years ago. Samantha Stevens had been willing to hide her powers for the love of a man. And it hadn't worked out very well for either of them.

****

Rayne decided to stop making herself crazy over something she couldn't change. There really was no choice to make. She loved Garrison and didn't want to consider a life without him in it; she would marry him and build a happy life with him, and she would never in a million years tell him she could see and talk to ghosts.

That taken care of she made herself useful, which seemed to delight Mary White. After asking what her future mother-in-law needed help with, Rayne kept an eye on the more elderly guest to make sure no one needed anything, and she took care of removing used paper plates and plastic cups and utensils when someone forgot to clean up after themselves.

Fortunately, those incidences were few and far between. Even most of the children roaming the house and playing out in the yard had manners and knew boundaries, and Rayne understood why Mary and her husband hadn't freaked out at finding so many people in their home following the funeral. The Whites were highly respected, and they treated everyone with respect in return.

She glanced around, looking for something more to do, and noticed one of the large garbage cans was full. Though the men had done a stellar job of keeping the trash carried away, she was never one to leave something for someone else when she was available to do the job herself. She pulled the liner out and tied it off then looked up to make sure she wouldn't bump into one of the many children who had returned to snag more food. But children underfoot were not her problem, the vision of an irritated Indian wavering only a couple of feet away had the potential of being a big one.

"Here, let me take that."

Rayne hardly glanced his way as she released the bag to one of Garrison's distant male cousins. Barely moving her head, she glanced around the room, for some reason always surprised no one ever saw what she saw. Certain no one was paying attention to her, she mouthed, *"Go away."*

A cold blast of air hit her. She pressed her lips together and shook her head.

"I can't go right now."

Not able to deal with him at the moment, Rayne mentally began shutting a door in her mind but only got it half closed before she was suddenly blinded, and her mind flooded with scenes and narratives that only made sense because of her years studying her family's history.

After losing their mother on the long rough voyage, Clara, Esmay, and Cassandra Cavanaugh arrived in the New World in the year of sixteen hundred and twenty-nine on a vessel owned by the Massachusetts Bay Company. Having been raised with an education few of that time had access to, they were able to chronicle their voyage and several of the subsequent events they witnessed firsthand, just as their ancestors had throughout history.

Aggrieved already by the loss of a beloved mother, Cassandra Cavanaugh wrote of her sorrow that the native peoples, who had accepted the newcomers so readily, and had treated them with such kindness, were now being treated so badly by the Europeans, they were rebelling.

She hadn't blamed them and, with the innocence of youth, had spoken out on their behalf. Her protest, and that of her sisters, had put them in danger, as the early settlers were a pious and hatefully suspicious bunch, especially when it came to the three identical redheaded sisters.

Though they had traveled the vast ocean together, and the pilgrims ran to one sister or another when they were sick or injured and in need of help, the fourteen year-old Cavanaugh triplets knew they too were always only one step away from persecution.

That their beauty outshone every other woman's in the river settlement didn't help, either, as the women resented them, and the men desired them. After three years of living in fear of both, they had earned enough by growing herbs for medicines, and tending the ill and injured, that they were able to have an enclosed wagon built.

The three became nomads and were called gypsies by most of the Christian folk, as if the word were a curse. They quickly became close friends and sometimes students of the native peoples they came across in their travels.

The peoples of the differing Wampanoag Tribes treated them with the respect given their elderly men and women, who were healers and spiritual leaders, and who sought the help of the spirit world, including the Great Spirit, for the good of their communities. The Europeans called them Medicine Elders, or Medicine Men or Women, but like the term gypsy, each was always said with contempt and suspicion.

For nearly sixteen years the Cavanaugh sisters camped in the untamed wilderness from spring to autumn growing their own vegetables and herbs, as well as collecting plants that held a natural chemistry for healing--or killing. They captured, killed, and bottled the secretions of poisonous reptiles and used both the lessons chronicled by their ancestors, and the lessons learned from their new friends, to create useful concoctions that could do everything from eliminating pain to taking life.

They spent the winters traveling from burgeoning town to burgeoning town where they sold their potions, always making sure their customers knew which were for healing family members, and which were for eliminating the growing number of rats and other pests in each town.

Sometimes they considered settling down in one spot and would try living amongst the townsfolk, always hoping for acceptance, eventually having to move on.

Sometime around their thirty-second year, Esmay fell in love and, though the details about the timing and the man were a little sketchy, the results were triplets of her own at the age of thirty-three.

The women tried to continue living as they had for a few more years, but with growing children to care for, and the violence between the white men and the native peoples increasing, they finally accepted they would have to hide who they were and pretend to be like everyone else.

They eventually settled on the outer fringes of a town called Salem and worked diligently to conform even though the people there were as pious as any they had met before. But now there were children to care for, so they dressed in binding clothing and acted like life was meant to be lived without any joy at all, as smiling and laughing in public resulted in mean stares and wagging tongues.

One year turned into the next and they were careful to keep to themselves and follow the customs dictated by the local minister, at least publicly. Secretly, they continued to make their potions and taught the growing children about their individual gifts, and how and when to use them.

Fawntain, Leaffe and Romae grew into beautiful young women, and like their mother and aunts before them, were considered the fairest of face and figure. They had mastered the family trade of healing and potions and continued to hone their gifts in the privacy of their still heavily wooded home.

Although they desired families of their own, the women had grown up with constant warnings of how dangerous it would be to marry and become intimate with the local men. Their only protection, they had been taught, was to maintain the private lives they had always known.

Fawntain and Leaffe headed the warnings, but at thirty and three years, Romae grew tired of the constraints. She secretly began meeting with a man ten years her junior, while her mother believed her to be hunting and gathering the plants they used to ply their trade.

During one of their passionate couplings, her beloved jumped to his feet unexpectedly and ran away. Romae, having no idea he was married, worried over his strange behavior as she picked the required variety of plants before returning home.

As the law of the day dictated that adultery was punishable by death, and her lover's wife didn't want to lose the one who kept her housed and fed, she ran to the minister and declared Romae a witch, saying she had witnessed the gypsy woman dancing with the devil.

Within a week, all three of Esmay's daughters were accused of witchcraft, as were many other young women who had no gifts at all. Never expecting the chaos that immediately followed the arrests, the sisters were horrified to learn that Romae had been tried and hanged without them being informed, and her body had been burned in a pit with the rest who had been condemned in a farce of a trial held in the middle of the night.

Subsequent trials, which lasted until a little over a year later, were held by the town's leaders and the minister who led them all. But the now elderly Cavanaugh sisters didn't wait for a justice they knew wouldn't come soon enough.

The night following Romae's murder they packed their wagon with as much as they could carry, threw off the cloaks of proper society, and snuck into town where they used forbidden magic to rescue Fawntain and Leaffe, before they too were falsely convicted and executed. The brokenhearted family fled Salem that night, and never looked back, their only hope to run to their native friends.

As the onslaught of narrated images faded and her mind cleared, Rayne once again saw Qaqeemasq before her. Dazed by the experience, she was torn between sympathy and anger, but as her thoughts once again became her own, anger grew.

She *also* knew firsthand the results of persecution and lies, and remembered reading Cassandra Cavanaugh's last contribution to their family's history, word for word: *During the early years of the country's conception the native people were lied to and tricked and learned to hate those with white skin because of the broken promises they had made. We were treated no better, because people fear what they do not understand.*

Rayne understood his point. He felt she had also lied to him, but that still did not give the dead Indian a right to take over her mind.

"Don't *ever* do *that* again!"

"Don't do what, again?"

Rayne swung around at the sound of Garrison's voice. The rapid rise and fall of her chest and the distress swamping her stomach must have been reflected on her face because Garrison immediately pulled her into his arms.

"Hey, what's wrong? Has someone upset you?"

Rayne exhaled the air rattling her lungs. She shook her head and pulled back, aware the noisy room had grown silent. Heat flooded her cheeks and she shook her head again before stepping away and heading to the French doors. Thankfully no one was between her and them so she made a rapid escape.

Garrison followed her and grasped her arm once they were standing on the flagstone patio. "Rayne, what happened?"

What could she say? That a ghost had temporarily taken possession of her mind and not only reminded her of the plight of *his* people, but made her relive the horrors of her own ancestors? That the only way to avoid it happening again was to follow the Indian, and lead Garrison to the remains of another dead body? That marrying him was the same impossible dream that kept killing the women of her family? And that she was reconsidering? Not one of those would make his day any better, and his day had already been hell.

She forced her breathing to calm before turning to him. "I'm sorry." She glanced back and to her horror several people were looking out at them from the inside the house. "I need a walk." She pivoted and took off at as fast a pace as she could manage without actually breaking into a run.

Garrison was right behind her. He didn't say anything but just followed until they reached the barn at the far end of the property. "Okay, stop!"

Rayne kept going. If she stopped he would want to talk and there was nothing she could say. But now she was trapped. If she didn't stop they were headed straight for the woods. And bless his no longer beating heart, her mean little Indian chose that moment to appear.

Rayne stopped so abruptly Garrison ran into her. He immediately turned her to face him and lifted her chin, forcing her to look into his eyes. "What the hell is going on?"

Okay, it's now or never. But no matter how hard she tried, she couldn't open her mouth and tell him the truth. She hated lying to him, but there was no choice. "I'm sorry. I feel like an idiot. It was nothing."

Garrison's brows lifted and he shook his head. "Not buying it. Did someone hurt you in some way?"

Rayne sighed, because she was going to have make up some stupid lie that would make her look like an idiot. But it was better than the alternative. "I thought I saw a rat."

Garrison's pulled back slightly, the surprise in his eyes turning to amusement. "You think you saw a rat? In *my parent's house?*"

Rayne nodded, hated herself, but hating her little Indian friend more. "Yes. But I was wrong. It was one of the kids playing a trick on me."

Garrison's brows furrowed. "You yelled at one of the kids?"

Oh crap! "Yes. It was a reaction that I'm not proud of, but I was so startled I didn't stop to think. And then I was so embarrassed I couldn't look at anyone. So I had to get out of the house."

"I missed the kid somehow. Which one was it? I may have to soothe some ruffled parental feathers."

Double crap! Rayne looked at him, wishing she could

just come clean, but she had dug this hole and she was going to have to play in it for a while. "By the time I reacted the kid had already run from the room laughing. I don't think he even knew I yelled at him."

Garrison seemed to relax a little and it killed her that he thought she would be hateful to a child. Maybe she wouldn't have to worry about telling him her deep, dark, secret. Maybe he would be the one to rethink marriage and save her the trouble.

"Well, don't worry about it. My family members are too polite to ask any questions."

Which made Rayne feel about as big as a slug.

She stepped back then and forced herself to say what had to be said, figuring since she had already ruined his day....

"Can we walk a while?"

Garrison smiled at her and pulled her in for a kiss, seeming relieved that everything had turned out to be okay. "We can do anything you want."

Rayne closed her eyes and leaned into him, knowing she was going straight to Hell.

Chapter Twenty-Five

Haven strolled through the large home, touching an item here and an item there, wondering why the things that had always been a part of her life no longer felt like they belonged in her home. She walked to the three-story high glass wall, which displayed the endless miles of the city and ocean she had always called home, and felt claustrophobic. The most personal of her things, stored in both her bedroom, and bathroom, felt as if they belonged to someone else. But worse than all that, so much worse, was when she looked in the mirror and hardly recognized the woman reflected back at her.

Haven knew she was losing herself, and she had no idea how to stop it.

She couldn't tell Destiny.

She couldn't tell Rayne.

She couldn't tell anyone. All she could do was try to hide what was happening and hope she wasn't somehow disappearing altogether. That's what it felt like. Like she was slowly fading into nothingness.

"I'm so scared."

Haven closed her eyes and allowed the tears to fall. Admitting what was happening made it more real. She continued to stand there helplessly as afternoon turned to evening. The little strength she'd had left flowed from her body as she watched the sun being swallowed by the sea.

Chapter Twenty-Six

Rayne allowed Garrison to hold her hand as she chose the path they took. He didn't question her when she would abruptly turn to head in a different direction, he just kept up a running dialogue about the flora they passed or would pull her to stop so he could examine a mature tree he felt would make a particular piece of furniture.

That he saw what the finished product would be by the size and shape of a tree impressed Rayne, and reminded her that people's gifts came in differing packages, and came out in different ways. She tried to ignore Qaqeemasq and pay attention to Garrison each time he would stop to show her his passion, but her fear that Qaqeemasq would take over her mind again, and that she couldn't shut him out, got her moving again as quickly as possible.

Garrison didn't seem to notice, or if he did he didn't act like he minded, but it made Rayne angry she couldn't give him the time and respect he deserved.

As they continued on, the shade of the trees darkened, and Rayne was afraid Garrison would suggest they turn back before the sun completely set. While she was trying to figure a way to say it herself, so her Indian guide would understand and not blast her, she tripped over some large roots and was glad Garrison was there to catch her.

Rayne turned to thank him but stopped short at the expression of horror on his face as he stared at the ground where she'd tripped. Even before looking she knew they had found the body. Qaqeemasq dissolved, leaving her to clean up the mess he had led them to.

"Don't move," Garrison said, his voice tight.

She nodded, and glanced down, then felt the lurch in her stomach. Not wanting to desecrate the remains and the crime scene any more than she already had, she quickly moved away and fought down nausea, and tried to stop the trembling that had taken hold.

Garrison was at her side immediately, pulling her into his arms and holding her tightly to his chest. "Don't look."

"I'm sorry. I'm so sorry," she said, fighting the tears, as the shaking increased.

"It's okay. It was better for you to move away. I shouldn't have asked you stay there." He pulled her further from the remains and took out his cell phone.

Garrison's voice shook uncontrollably as he called in the report that they had stumbled over another body in the woods on his parent's property. Rayne continued to cry softly because she couldn't stop. She hated herself and was heartbroken for him. And she was absolutely furious that someone was putting them all through another round of questions, pain, and loss.

It was best Garrison believed her apology was for moving when he had told her not to, but it still left her feeling like a creep and a liar. And not worthy of his love.

"We need to wait here until they come. It's going to be another long night."

He held her in shaking arms as he repeatedly looked towards the base of the tree where the body lay. Rayne knew there was a part of him that wanted to go and take a closer look, and a part that was afraid to look too close, so she was relieved when a half dozen flashlights and several voices were seen and heard coming toward them. It was nearly completely dark now and she had little doubt that those coming were family members who'd lingered at Garrison Sr. and Mary White's house following the funeral. Garrison was right. They were all in for a very long night.

****

A sense of déjà vu had Rayne ignoring the suspicious glares of the female police officer. Only this time she wondered if it was because Officer Kathy Gishwell suspected her of having something to do with the murders, or if it was because the officer was sweet on Garrison. If the woman hovered over him any closer she could give him a lap dance.

Since he seemed oblivious to the attention or chose to ignore it, Rayne too ignored the woman and repeated what she had already told the officer in charge once before. As bad as she felt about putting Garrison through finding the body she was glad she hadn't put herself in a position of suspicion a second time.

She hadn't been national news, *thank goodness*, but if the Mystic Waters police department started investigating her past she was afraid that their LA counterparts would be more than happy to share what they knew of her abilities, or *antics,* depending on who they spoke with.

"Well, I guess that's all we have. It will be morning before Doctor Parson gets with us. He said it would take a bit more time to identify the body this time with so little to go on. Unless, they find more of the remains after sunrise. We have officers that will be there all night to make sure no one disturbs the area."

Rayne glanced at Garrison to see how he was taking the officer's words. It turned out that the remains had been incomplete. And the initial word from the coroner was that it looked like the victim had been dismembered. But it was too dark, and the forest too dense, to do any more than they had already done until they got more light and personnel to search the area.

Garrison looked ill, which wasn't surprising. He tried to smile at her but it didn't quite gel. She slid her hand across the tabletop toward him, and he took it before they rose together. She stepped to his side and thanked the officer before turning to find the female officer staring at her again. A chill ran up Rayne's spine, but before she could mull it over Garrison placed his arm around her shoulder and led her out of the interrogation room.

Bone tired, and more than a little ill with the events of the day, Rayne didn't question it when Garrison drove her to his cabin without asking if that was where she wanted to go. She understood his assumption had to do with the fact that they were now engaged. But her lack of protest had nothing to do with that. Something wicked was going on in Mystic Waters and for the first time in her life she was truly afraid to be left alone.

****

Two full days and the better part of the third were spent waiting for word while his parents' farm was combed by not only the local law enforcement, but the local FBI as well. With two murders and possibly another—if the deceased wasn't the missing White child—the possibility of a serial killer in Mystic Waters was more than the local police wanted to handle alone.

Garrison couldn't work, was barely eating, and Rayne was worried sick about him. By the middle of the second day she wanted to suggest they go for a walk just to get out of the cabin, but her last request for a walk was what had put him in the condition he was currently in, so she'd kept the thought to herself.

Members of the family came and went, and she and Garrison finally returned to the farm to visit with his parents and grandparents the afternoon of the third day, which turned out to be handy when the police chief arrived two hours into their visit with the news they had all awaited.

Garrison grabbed her hand, keeping his gaze lowered to the floor.

"It's not Gavin."

The collective sighs were followed by many tears of relief. Rayne closed her eyes and held tightly to Garrison's hand, thankful that yet again the family had been spared that.

"Do you know who it is?" the senior Garrison asked, while holding his wife closely.

The officer nodded. "It's the Hanson boy. Don and Jenna's youngest."

Mary White gasped as Garrison's head lifted quickly. His eyes were haunted as he stared at the officer. "Logan's little brother?"

Nodding again, the officer answered a few more questions then took his leave. Garrison continued to sit there, his mind somewhere else. Rayne released his hand and patted his knee to bring his attention back to her. "Who is Logan?"

Something of a sad smile briefly touched Garrison's lips. "He was my best friend when we were growing up. We did everything together, including getting in trouble."

At that his mother laughed lightly, though there was a sob mixed in.

"We even applied and were accepted at the same college. I enlisted after we graduated together, but he was pre-med so he went on and went to medical school for another four years. I ended up in the thick of combat from the get go, did my six years then came home. He had moved away by then. I haven't seen him for years."

Rayne processed the information as Garrison stared straight ahead. She knew he was lost in thought again. Whether it was about his youth, the young murdered man, or the friend who would surely now return to Mystic Waters to deal with the tragedy, she didn't know.

"He hasn't been home for a long time." Mary sighed. "But he sends Don and Jenna airline tickets to go visit him a couple of times every year. They are in West Palm Beach, now, as a matter of fact." Mary shook her head, her eyes misting over, again. "My heart just breaks for them. Donny was a late in life surprise, but a joyful surprise for that poor woman.

"We all thought Donny had gone deep into the Amazon to study the indigenous tribes that still live without contact from the outside world about a year ago. Jenna had worried about not hearing from him after the first few months, but Don had assured her he was fine, and to remember what Donny said about the trip." Mary looked at her husband, and he nodded, his handsome features lined with stress.

"What was that?" Rayne asked, figuring she was the only one in the dark. Garrison took her hand, rubbing his thumb along her knuckles as his mother continued.

"Donny told them before he left that the area along the Amazon River Basin was still pretty remote, that his cell phone would be useless, and they shouldn't expect to hear from him until they heard from him." Mary shook her head, sadly, her voice quivering. "They are going to be just heartbroken."

Garrison rose then and walked to his parents, taking his mother into his arms. As he held her, his father's arms wrapped around them both, then one after the other of Garrison and Mary's remaining children followed suit. Rayne hesitated, but then Garrison's younger brother, Gary, turned back to her and held out his hand. Rayne smiled and joined them, and was enfolded in the family hug.

Rayne closed her eyes and absorbed the love, the heartbreak, and the strength that the White family had for each other, for their extended family, and for their friends. She felt blessed to know them, and her heart broke for them all over again.

****

The Hansons arrived back in Mystic Waters the next day and Rayne rode with Garrison to the farm adjacent to his parents' land. Garrison was quiet the entire way, his features reflecting the conflicting emotions rolling around in his head. "Are you okay?"

Garrison slid a glance her way, then reached over and took her hand and squeezed. "I'm okay. I was just thinking. I'm sorry I haven't had a chance to go look for a ring yet. Would you like to help me pick it out?"

Rayne couldn't help the grin. "*That's* what you've been thinking about?"

Garrison nodded. "Yep. See, I've got this incredibly beautiful woman who has agreed to take me on at the worst time in my life, and I haven't even bought her an engagement ring."

Rayne shook her head. "Garrison...really, I don't care about that. You have so many things going on. We can deal with all that when things settle down."

With his gaze still focused on the curving country road, he lifted her hand and kissed her knuckles, then held them against his mouth for another moment before kissing them again. "You are something special." He looked at her briefly before returning his attention to his driving.

He released her hand and turned onto a gravel driveway. Rayne studied the two-story white clapboard house with its black shutters. "That's an old house."

"It was built in1860, in the Carpenter style." At her look of surprise, Garrison grinned. "Logan and I did a paper on it in the fifth grade. We were supposed to do a paper on the history of our own houses, but since ours was under construction at the time, my teacher said I could partner with Logan and do my paper on his house, too." He shook his head at the memory.

"I didn't think your parents' house was all that old, where did you live before?"

Garrison pulled to a stop behind a sleek sports car, which sat behind a nice pickup truck, parked behind a couple of cars. "We still lived there, only in the doublewide trailer that my parents put on my grandfather's property when they first married. After the land was deeded to my dad and the big house was built they had it removed."

He glanced at her. "I never told the teacher that my grandparents had this really neat old house sitting way back in the woods, past where we...."

He stopped talking for a moment, and Rayne knew he was thinking of the place they found Donny Hansen. She waited, giving him time to get whatever it was he needed to get under control.

He cleared his throat. "It's on back there, deep in the woods. It's a really little house that has the property's original log cabin attached to it. No running water inside but there is a well that's filled by a natural spring off to the side. The house isn't fit for anyone to live in anymore, and hasn't been for a long time, but Dad and I have been reluctant to do anything with it as long as my grandfather is alive. Once he passes, we plan to take down everything but the original structure.

"Dad finally got my grandparents to move out of it and in with them when they built the house they live in now. That was one of the reasons they built so big. There were eight of us at home at the time; Dad and Mom, Granny and Grandpa, and us four kids.

The sound of a door slamming turned their attention to the tall, dark, and very handsome man walking toward them. Garrison got out of the truck and went to open her door, then he turned to the approaching man. Rayne stepped out of the truck to stand by Garrison's side. She looked from one man to the other and could see joy in both of their eyes.

"Hi, Dog Face."

"Hi, Donkey Dung."

Both men's laughter was strained as they threw their arms around each other, and Rayne watched silently as they took a moment to absorb each other's pain. They stepped apart.

"Man, I'm so sorry about your brother," Garrison said quietly.

Logan nodded, "Me too, about Gavin. Is there anything new?"

Shaking his head, Garrison turned to look at her but addressed his answer to Logan. "Nothing at all, but on a lighter note, I'd like to introduce you to my fiancé." The sadness in his eyes lifted with the smile on his lips. "Logan, Donkey Dung Hansen, this beautiful creature has proven dumb enough to take me on. Rayne Cavanaugh from California, Logan Hansen, lifelong friend and pain in the ass. But mostly, another brother, from a different mother."

Rayne moved forward, ready to shake his hand, but Logan pulled her into a hug and kissed her dead on the lips before grinning up at Garrison. Garrison shook his head, the amusement in his eyes refreshing after so many days of heartbreak and worry. So she slid one arm around Logan's waist, and he kept one around her shoulder as they turned fully to face Garrison.

One brow slid upward. "Gotch'er hands on my woman, dude."

Logan nodded. "Now that she's seen me, and tasted a *real man's* lips…it's all over for you, I'm afraid, my friend."

Garrison burst out laughing and stepped to them. "Don't think so, but we can—"

"Are you boys coming in the house?"

Logan looked back and nodded. "Coming, Dad." He placed a quick kiss on the top of Rayne's head then released her. Keeping a slight grin on his lips, he moved forward to sling his arm around Garrison's neck and started for the house. "Lucky dog, my dad saved you from me again!"

"Don't be so smug, city boy, those lily soft doctor's hands don't satisfy a woman like these rough, hard, manly hands do. And I can assure you, she likes these lips just fine, as well as the rest of the equipment."

They stopped abruptly and looked at each other for a moment, as the laughter fell from their eyes. Garrison's filled with moisture. "Damn, man. I'm so glad you're here."

Logan nodded, looked up towards his parent's house, then back at Garrison. "I'm glad you're here, too. I don't know if I can do this again."

Rayne watched as something passed between them while she wondered at Logan's choice of words. Whatever he'd meant wasn't lost on Garrison, as understanding filled his eyes before he slowly nodded his head. She pondered their sudden mood swing as she followed them to the house, thinking something more than a young man's death was involved. Deciding whatever it was, wasn't any of her business, Rayne was just thankful Garrison's friend had come home. Though she hated the circumstances, at least they had each other to ease what they both were going through.

Chapter Twenty-Seven

"Garrison!"

Garrison awoke from a sound sleep and nearly tripped and fell as he hurried down from the loft. The sound of his name was repeated, Rayne's voice anxious, her tone high. He hit the floor and glanced in the kitchen, then headed back to peek into the bathroom, when he didn't find her there he turned to Gavin's room, noticing the opened door.

He placed his hand over his chest to still his pounding heart. She had scared him to death!

So much had happened since he had started searching the room days before that he hadn't returned to finish the job. He stepped into it to find her stooping down, looking in horror at the mess he'd left.

She looked up at him, clearly fearful. "We need to call the police. Someone broke in and went through Gavin's things!"

He pulled her up and into his arms. "No. It was me. I was looking for something...a*nything* that would give me a clue as to what could have happened to him. And then the first body was found, and then the second. And I forgot to come back. I'm sorry it scared you. Not that I mind, but what were you doing in here anyway?"

She blew out a long breath. "The same thing. I thought if there was something that would indicate what had happened...I don't know...I probably wouldn't have even known it if I saw something useful."

Garrison nodded. "I know. I was thinking the same thing when I was going through his things. Until I cut my fingers on the broken glass in the bottom drawer. I need to get back in here and look."

She turned into him and slid her arms around his waist.

"Do you need any help? Or would you rather I go make you one of those cardiac attack breakfasts you love so much?"

Garrison smiled, inhaling the scent of her hair. "Cardiac. Definitely cardiac."

Rayne look up and kissed him before releasing him to head to the kitchen. He smiled as he watched her swinging hair going in the opposite direction of her swinging behind, wondering if she was swinging it a little more than usual for his pleasure. He shook his head and chuckled, then his smile melted as he looked back at the mess he had to deal with.

He jumped right in, carefully lifting the pictures that were covered in glass dust, and placing them in a pile he could take to the bathroom and wipe off with a cloth. Those that had larger shards he tilted to make the glass pieces land back in the drawer. Eventually he'd have to take it out of the room and clean it, but for now, just keeping the glass off the floor was a big enough goal.

He was three quarters of the way through the pile of pictures when he saw the culprit. Garrison lifted the broken eight by ten presentation frame that still had a couple of large pieces of broken glass in it. The picture was one he vaguely remembered seeing somewhere. Figuring he'd seen it in his brother's house, he glanced at the picture, and looked at the frame and remaining glass closely.

The group photo of the members of the Mystic Waters Police Department had been taken the year before, Garrison was pretty sure, as his brother had complained about having to sit for one every year. The larger pieces of remaining glass were triangularly shaped. Since the break looked like something had hit it where those shards met, Garrison studied the officers closest to the sharp tips of glass, wondering if the break was significant. Or of it had been broken by accident and he was making something out of nothing.

Most of the officers he knew and had known most of his life. The few he didn't know consisted of a woman officer with short dark hair, the overweight officer who had originally led the search, another woman who sported a salt and pepper crew-cut, and a tall redheaded guy with a handlebar mustache.

Knowing it was probably a waste of time, Garrison mentally filed the information away until he could talk to his deceased brother's best friend on the force. He seriously doubted that anyone on the police force would have anything to do with kidnapping a child. But he didn't have anything else to go on.

Garrison bit his bottom lip, chewing on the knowledge he'd have to use tact. These people were the same ones who had spent weeks and months looking for his nephew. He didn't want to insult any of them if he could help it. But, as remote as the possibility of them being involved was, he would leave no rock unturned if it meant getting his nephew back alive.

He continued cleaning up the glass until Rayne called him in for breakfast. As he began to leave the room a thought popped in and out of his head so quickly it stopped him. Frowning, he glanced back into the room and looked around, wondering if something triggered whatever it was that now ate at him, but he couldn't put his finger on what it might have been.

****

The second funeral was as sad as the first had been, and like the first, the Whites opened their home for the mourners to gather following the graveside service. But, unlike the first time, most people only stayed a short while before heading back to their own homes.

It wasn't that the Hansens were unloved. People were just worn out with all the tragedy, and the fear it wasn't over yet. The last to exit from the post-funeral gathering were Garrison's brother, his sister, and her husband and children.

Since it was now only Rayne, Garrison, his parents, and the three remaining members of the Hansen family, everyone settled in the living room with coffee or tea.

Rayne sat in the middle of Garrison and Logan, facing their parents. Garrison's grandparents had excused themselves and headed to their suite earlier, worn out from the emotional events of the day.

Mary reached over and took Jenna's hand and held it on the couch between them. Rayne tried not to stare at the grieving mother, but she was amazed by the woman's composure. By everyone's composure really.

"I'm so sorry for your loss." Rayne knew the words were inadequate, but she didn't know what else to say.

Jenna Hansen sent her a sad smile. "Thank you, dear. And I'm sorry I haven't had a chance to congratulate you and Garrison on your engagement. Have you set a date?"

Garrison's father and mother turned their way, their faces masks of delighted surprise. She heard Garrison clear his throat before his fisted shot behind her to land on Logan's shoulder. "You could have given us a chance to tell my parents," he said, looking around her now.

Logan sent him a cheesy smile. "Not my fault."

Garrison turned back to his parents. "Sorry. We were going to tell you once we got a chance to get to the jewelers. Been kinda busy lately."

A collective sigh went through the room while they all thought about what had kept them busy. Then Mary stood and walked to Rayne. Rayne stood and went into the open arms. "Welcome to our family, Rayne. I knew you were the woman my son would marry the day I met you."

Rayne didn't know what to say in response to that, so she just smiled and thanked her future mother-in-law before Mary returned to her spot on the couch. She took Jenna's hand again. "What can I do for you?"

Jenna's composure slipped and her eyes filled with unshed tears. "Just find Gavin before it's too late. The coroner says whoever is doing this doesn't kill them right away. The difference between the time they were last heard from and the approximate time they were...killed, is significant."

"Yes," her husband added, "he said your cousin had to

have been held somewhere for around three years or so, and Donny, just a few months." He looked down then, his eyes filled also when he looked back up. "He said the way they died, and Donny was...dismembered, was a sign of rage. That these boys were killed because they made their captor angry."

Rayne closed her eyes, sickened for these nice people. To know someone had chopped up their son, to know it had to have been done less than a mile from their own home.

She felt Garrison's arm come around her before he pulled her close, only then realizing tears were running down her cheeks. She looked through them at the other women, as they too were being held and comforted. Rayne turned to Garrison, knowing he should be the one being comforted, rather than the one doing the comforting, but his eyes were dry, his mouth set in a grim line, and she knew that *his* pain had solidified into a ball of anger.

She placed her hand on his clamped jaw, pulling his gaze to her. His body relaxed immediately, though a shudder went through him. Knowing she needed to get him away, and give him time to deal with his demons, she turned back to the others. "We should be going now. It's been a long day." She turned her gaze on Don and Jenna Hansen, "If there's anything we can do, please don't hesitate to call."

Garrison stood then and so did she. Together they walked to his parents who also rose to their feet. He hugged each one then as the Hansen's stood, he hugged them as well. They also hugged Rayne before she turned for the door. Garrison nodded to each, and then he turned to Logan. "Got a minute?"

"I'll be right back," Logan said to his parents, before following them out.

At Garrison's truck they stopped and Garrison and Logan pulled each other into a manly handshake hug before Logan stepped back.

"When will you be heading back to Florida?"

Logan sighed. "I don't know. I've taken a leave of absence and have a couple other surgeons handling my cases for the next month. I guess I need to be here right now. I know she doesn't show it, but my mom is about to lose it. She's barely slept since we got the call. And when she does she wakes up screaming, and then cries for hours. I can't believe she held it together all day today. I wasn't sure she would, so I gave her a sedative. But I still wasn't sure she could make it through the funeral."

"What about *you*?"

Rayne looked at Garrison, mystified by his tone.

"I'm doing okay. You know…."

Garrison nodded. "Yeah, I do. That's why I asked."

Logan shrugged, making Rayne more confused by the minute. Whatever they were talking about, it was obvious neither was happy about it. And this time she was certain it had nothing to do with the loss of his brother's life.

Rayne moved to Logan and gave him a hug, then Garrison joined them and they stood there for a while. Finally they all stepped back, and Logan waited as Garrison opened the door and waited for Rayne to enter the truck. He looked back at Logan. "Where are you staying?"

Logan slid an uncomfortable glance at Rayne, then shrugged as he looked back at Garrison. "I'm staying at Mom and 'Dad's house right now, but I think I'll rent a place for however long I end up staying. I need to do it as soon as possible." He looked pointedly at Garrison. "I need my own space, and I need some time to process all this, too."

He shook his head and stared at the ground for so long Rayne left the truck and she headed Logan's way. Garrison followed and returned to Logan's side. She gently laid her hand on Logan's arm, bringing his attention to her. She smiled at him, hoping kindness would ease his hurt. "I have a fully furnished cabin you can use. I rented it on a twelve month lease, and I'm moving in with Garrison so it will be vacant."

Garrison smiled at her in surprise before turning back

to his friend. "We'll have her things out by this evening if you need us to."

"And if you want to go by and check it out before moving in, I hid the spare key on the porch rafter directly above the top steps. You'll have to feel around up there. I hid it pretty well."

Logan looked at Rayne, his relief obvious.

"Thanks. I appreciate it. But tomorrow is soon enough. I think. I should stick around to see how my mother does tonight. If she can cope, I'll head over there sometime before dark tomorrow evening."

They hugged again before Rayne and Garrison headed back to his cabin. On the drive Garrison took her hand and kissed each finger. "I'm glad you're officially moving in."

Rayne turned from watching the countryside go by to look at her fiancé, the love she felt filling her heart. "Other than to go and get clothes, I haven't even been there since we made love the first time. In essence, I already moved in. I barely have anything left there now."

She tilted her head. "I guess I should have said something to you first, though."

Garrison shook his head. "Nope. I already told you, I want you with me. Until I'm so old I don't have any teeth left in my head, in fact."

"And I want to be with you, too. Though keeping your teeth would be nice. I'm thinking toothless probably won't be a great look for you." Rayne smiled to herself as she turned back to watch again as the trees sped by. A flash of something running caught her eye and she turned to look back as far as she could without taking off her seatbelt, but they had moved past it so quickly she couldn't tell what it was. It was probably nothing more than a deer, anyway.

"So marry me."

Smiling, the shadowy figure instantly forgotten, Rayne once again turned to him as he pulled into his parking spot at the cabin. "You make me so happy…it seems wrong to be so happy right now."

Garrison took her hand, and as was his habit, kissed

her knuckles. "I need happy. My family needs happy. This town needs happy."

They left the truck and walked hand in hand up the path and then onto the steps that led to the front porch. He stopped before opening the cabin's front door and pulled her into his arms and kissed her soundly.

"I've been sick in love with you from the moment you caught me peeking in your window." Garrison grinned at her. "That love has compounded every day since. I couldn't have survived these last weeks without you. And I know the only way I'll be able to survive what comes is with you by my side. I want you to have my name. You already have my heart."

Rayne knew it wasn't fair to be so delighted with her life, but she was so filled with love for him that it even spilled from her tear ducts. "I love you. More than I ever thought it possible to love any man. And I want your name. It's an honorable name.

"I'll need to call my sisters and let them know I won't be going back to Los Angeles to live, and to invite them to come here to meet you, and your family. Although I imagine they're furious with me right now. I lost my cell phone in the woods that night we found Donny, and I have no desire to go back out there and find it." She searched his face as his thumbs dried her tears.

"You should have said something. What's mine is yours. We'll get you a new phone tomorrow but call them tonight with mine."

Rayne sighed. "Something you haven't had a chance to learn about me yet is that I am nontechnical. And I don't know their numbers. They're stored under their names in the phone I no longer have. I'll see what I can do about that tomorrow too.

"But back to the wedding. I think we should wait just a little while before arranging one. I'm not sure how long it will be before both sisters can arrange vacations at the same time, but more importantly, if Gavin comes home soon you don't want him to think that you just moved on."

Garrison nodded, his eyes haunted. "I know. I thought about that, too. But I'm losing hope." He pressed his lips together then sighed. "What if he never comes home? How long do we wait? I want to honor you with marriage, not just shacking up. I'm a little archaic sometimes."

Rayne snuggled into him. "I'm quite fond of your old-fashioned thinking. And you honor me just by loving me. Don't ever give up. Not yet anyway. I..."Rayne couldn't finish the sentence. She wasn't sure of anything anymore except that she loved and adored the man holding her. She couldn't stand seeing the pain in his eyes another second, so she pulled his face down to her own and took his lips in a kiss that teased, taunted, then deepened with a passion that left them both gasping for breath when their lips parted.

Garrison playfully slammed her against him in a one armed hug as he unlocked the front door. "I can't think of honor when all the blood has drained from my head."

Rayne laughed at his playfulness as she rested her chin on his shoulder. The sight of the Indian brave wavering along the tree line in the distance knocked the smile from her lips. Unaware, Garrison lifted her off her feet and carried her backwards in through the doorway and pushed the door closed behind him.

"Until you say differently, the wedding can wait. But I'm a man in love, so my heart and body work in tandem. I'm willing to give you all the time you need, and in the meantime, until we *are* married, I'll take comfort in your arms, and give you the comfort of mine." A gleam entered his eyes. "And just to be sure we are really ready for the nuptials...."

Epilogue

Haven followed the mountain road until she found the mailbox with the numbers indicating she had finally reached her destination and glanced at her silenced cell phone as it was buzzing again.

Destiny was mad at her for leaving California without a word to anyone and was burning up her phone with voice mails and text messages. But she would have to get over it. Haven needed time away from her. And time away from everything in a life that had fallen apart in every imaginable way.

She'd left a note and was an adult. Destiny would have to accept it was all she was getting until Haven felt like talking. Right now all she wanted to do was get to Rayne's cabin, climb in a bed, and sleep until her mind and body were renewed enough to function again.

The driveway was quite long and the cabin remote, which was a little disturbing, but Rayne had lived there for a couple of months now, and if her youngest sister could handle it, then she could too.

Since there was no car out front when she pulled up, Haven figured Rayne was out, probably shopping if she knew her younger sister at all. She left the rental car and approached the cabin thinking it was quite charming in a Daniel Boone sort of way.

Haven tiredly climbed the porch steps and tried the front door. Of course it was locked. She glanced around to see if there was anything that might hide a key. After trying under the rug at the door, and the potted plants on little side tables, she looked up, studying the rafters under the porch roof.

She smiled to herself as she recalled how Rayne always

hid the key to her diary when they were teens. Haven pulled herself up using the eight by eight piece of lumber that supported the roof and railing on the left side of the porch. She stood on the railing and felt along the top of a couple of the rafters before she felt the thin metal she was searching for.

Delighted with her success, she opened the door of the cabin and carried her bags in. Knowing she would love to snoop if she had more energy, Haven dropped her bags behind the couch and began stripping off her clothes. She wandered the small area only long enough to locate the tiny bathroom with its barely adequate shower.

But she didn't care how small everything was. All she wanted to do was get naked, shower away the long day, and fall into the bed she could only guess was at the top of the ladder type stairs leading to the loft.

She would worry about the energy required to climb the stairs when she was done showering.

Since Rayne had everything she needed to shower, Haven didn't bother to go back for her own bath supplies. She made quick work of washing her hair and body, then moisturizing everything, enjoying the products her sister had obviously bought locally.

Certain she smelled like honeysuckle, and maybe even a hint of verbena, Haven padded her way out of the bathroom. She loved being naked and freshly moisturized, having the place all to herself allowed her the freedom to indulge. She seriously thought about going outside and dancing nude in the yard, but that would have to wait. Right now all she wanted was to lie down and relax.

And if she just happened to fall asleep it was no big deal. Rayne had seen her naked just as she had seen Rayne naked, just as they had both seen Destiny naked all their lives. Celestia had raised them with a love of all things natural and a lack of inhibition when it came to the human body, and though her mother had been gone for far too long now, Haven had always embraced those particular teachings.

Confident Rayne would be home soon she climbed up to the loft and threw the comforter off the bed before plopping down on top of the sheets. It wasn't until she rolled over onto her back and stared up at the pitched roof that she realized she felt better and more at peace than she had for a very long time.

Smiling, she closed her eyes and relaxed, ignoring the sounds of the house settling...or was that the sound of a door opening and closing...?

THE END

The Cavanaugh Series Books Now Available!

(The Cavanaugh Sisters Trilogy)

#1 **Mystic Thunder**
#2 **Touch of Lightning**
#3 **Tempest's Embrace**

(The Cavanaugh Series continues!)
#4 **Jewel of the Nile**
#5 **Sapphire Blues**
#6 **Diamond in the Rough**
#7 **Luna's Landing**
#8 **Celestial Liaison**
#9 **Zeus:** *Unbound!*
#10 **Apollo:** *Unleashed!*

The Cavanaugh Series Books to come!
Heracles: Undone
Soleli's Secret
Gavin's Ghosts

The Blood Moon Chronicles
Blood Moon Rising

Visit my website: **www.jcwardon.com,** my Facebook pages: **www.facebook.com/jc.wardon** and **https://www.facebook.com/JCWardonNovelist** and tweet me: @jc_wardon. Thanks for sharing my world. I'd love to hear from you!

And… if you'd like a little taste of the Second Book of the *Cavanaugh Sisters Trilogy,* read on!

Touch of Lightning

Prologue

Blood chilled in his veins as his tension strained body shook uncontrollably from both the cold and fear.

Gavin White knew what he was going to do was risky. He needed more time but was afraid time was fleeing as quickly as sand pouring through the cinched center of an hourglass. It killed him that he'd worked as hard as he had trying to rebuild muscle tone and had so little to show for his effort, especially since he'd pushed himself as far as he'd been able given his restraints and weakening condition. He knew he was galaxies away from the shape he'd once been in, and hadn't expected to get back there before trying to break free, but he'd hoped for better than the skeletal frame he feared he appeared to be.

Feeling his arms with their tiny knots of muscle nearly made him sick. His legs were even worse, the sinewy muscle now nothing but soft flesh that barely covered bone. For once he was thankful for the constant darkness he lived in, knowing he had to look as bad as he felt.

Once upon a time he'd played sports; all kinds, but baseball had been his life, his love, and he'd planned to make it his profession. His parents had supported that dream, had provided everything including their time to help him achieve it. But they were gone forever. And he was too unless he succeeded in escaping.

If only he was still that kid who thought life was wonderful, and fun, and the world was filled with loving, good people. If only he was still strong and muscular and healthy.

That was a lifetime ago, if it had ever really been....

The weekly provisions he'd come to expect since first being kidnapped and imprisoned now came less frequently, and worse, with less food both in quantity and quality. Now his captor only brought boxes of cereal, candy bars, bags of chips, and beef jerky that made his teeth hurt when he tried to bite into it. Occasionally there were other things like little cups of pudding or custard he was forced to dig out with his fingers, and though he hated custard he ate it anyway; beggars couldn't be choosers.

Until he'd landed in Hell he hadn't really understood that saying.

His seemingly stellar plan to take the time to get stronger before attempting an escape had backfired from the get-go. It was as if the kidnapper read his mind and knew exactly when he'd decided to quit accepting his fate and fight for his freedom. It killed him now to know that the self-pity and fear he'd wallowed in after being imprisoned had allowed his once toned body to turn into nothing but flabby fat beneath increasingly sore skin.

The flabby fat was gone now....

The muscle tone he'd once rocked was gone as well, not only from the lack of any exercise, but from the lack of nutrition his mother had always provided. Now, with only junk-food as his staple he belatedly appreciated being forced to eat all those green vegetables when his life was normal, and he wished he could let his mother know that he was sorry for the times he'd turned his nose up at peas and Brussels sprouts.

How he'd hated Brussels sprouts; he'd give anything now to have some.

But she would never know, and he could never express his regret as she and his father were dead; murdered before his eyes almost two months before he'd been captured and imprisoned in the hellhole he now called home. He wasn't sure, had no idea really, if the one holding him was the same one who had fired bullets into the dining room window killing his father instantly before breaking into the house to kill and then attempt to molest his poor mother's corpse.

The man had seen him, but hadn't killed him, and Gavin knew it was only because others had rushed the house, and that cop decided to escape rather than finish the job. It sickened him remembering it all, but he needed the anger to give him the strength to do what must be done.

Gavin's biggest regret was waiting so long to get his head together.

He heard the sounds—the muffled footsteps, the grunts, the occasional thuds—that always preceded the arrival of whomever it was that hit him with the car that night so long ago. Gavin had no idea how long he'd been in the hellhole; he only knew it seemed like he'd lived in dank darkness for all of his sixteen years.

Like a choreographed dance, their routine began with him lying back on the cot and remaining completely still until the person responsible for his present predicament shined the light in, as they made their way toward him. He never heard a door opening or closing; never saw beyond the spot where the beam of the flashlight fell. Once the kidnapper was satisfied Gavin was blinded by the light a box was placed on the dirt floor then pushed his way with a stick. His captor had known from the first just how far away from him to leave it, as he'd know exactly how long the chain was that was attached to metal cuff encircling Gavin's wrist.

Gavin's body vibrated even more now as fear and anticipation raised the hair on his arms. He averted his gaze as the bright beam of the flashlight was directed his way, knowing he couldn't allow it to burn his eyes if he was to have any chance at all. He was so over whatever game this person was playing, but he knew he had to be careful. In the beginning, when he still hadn't known what was happening and tried to fight back, it had taken him weeks to recover from the beating.

Since he couldn't look directly into the light he attempted to determine the distance between himself and his captor by looking at the space of packed dirt that separated them. But the endless darkness in which he lived, and the brief amount of time he had to accomplish his goal, on top of nerves that had gone from fearful to panicked, made it impossible to focus his thoughts, much less his vision.

Gavin silently cursed himself for a fool. Somehow he'd convinced himself he'd have a chance to reach his captor; somehow he'd allowed himself to forget that no matter his planning, nothing would change unless the kidnapper moved closer to him than ever before. Anger took too much energy and he was getting weaker by the minute, so Gavin forced himself from the cot and to his feet. He wondered if the devil in the darkness noticed how badly he swayed, and wondered too, if he was now being slowly starved to death for its amusement.

Hesitating until he was certain of his balance, then straightening even more until he was completely erect, Gavin tried to hold back the nausea that didn't quite hurt his stomach, but did made him feel seven shades of green. He forced his shoulders back and held his chin up, determined to let the kidnapper know he had his pride, even if he had nothing else.

He moved forward with rigid steps, determined not to stumble, afraid any sign of weakness would result in more than he could withstand. When he reached the box he didn't immediately bend over and lift it as he always had, instead he stared straight ahead, knowing his bravado could cost him his life. His captor said nothing, nor made any sound which indicated movement, and Gavin was certain he was being silently laughed at. Feeling defeated, and figuring he looked ridiculous, tears threatened. With no other choice available to him, he gave in and retrieved the box then return to his bed.

As expected it was light in weight and he feared held even less food than the last delivery. Instead of following protocol, Gavin sat the box down and turned back. He held his hands over his eyes to shade them from the light, knowing it was now or never. He'd never dared speak after that first time, but it was obvious he wasn't going to make it out alive if something didn't change immediately.

Pulling on the strength of his upbringing, and remembering that his mother taught him that you caught more flies with honey than with vinegar, he made sure his rusty voice was as conciliatory as possible. "Please. It isn't enough. I'm starving. You have taken such good care of me. But I'm starving now. Is that what you want?"

The flashlight instantly went dark and Gavin's knees nearly gave. He bowed his head and closed his eyes as he fought hard, but the tears fell anyway. It was clear he'd done the wrong thing, and wished now he'd waited to get fresh water and to have his slop bucket emptied before he'd wagered it all. He took a ragged breath and wiped at his face as he waited for his captor to simply leave him to his misery.

"I'll try to bring more. But let us finish with this now. I need your buckets."

Gavin's head jerked up at the sound of the woman's voice. It had never occurred to him that a woman held him captive. The women he had always known were kind of heart. Mother's aunts, teachers.... With a clicking sound the flashlight was back on and the burning ray that followed stung eyes he hadn't realized he'd opened.

He looked away quickly, but halos of white floated before him anyway. He tried to ignore the results of being so blinded by the light and to clear his mind so he could do what he needed to do, but his thoughts were reeling with shock over the new information about his kidnapper. Nearly dizzy with so much physical and mental overload, Gavin tried to find his water bucket until he realized he was going in circles when the chain tightened around his legs. Once he forced himself to calm down he untangled himself and made his way to the cot to retrieve the bucket that held the remaining stagnant water he'd been drinking.

Still blinking rapidly, he carried it across the floor until he reached the end of his chain. He left it there and went back toward his cot then veered off to the right and walked the length of his chain again since he kept the slop bucket as far away from his bed as possible. Holding it out the length of his arms, Gavin retraced his steps back to the cot and then turned in the direction of his kidnapper. He'd walked around in the darkness for so long, using only his memory as a guidance system, it didn't occur to him to look toward the small circle of light the woman shined on the ground, until he sat the bucket down and noticed, for the very first time, that it gave him a glimpse of her shoes.

Not sure if she was aware she'd finally allowed him to see a part of her, or wondering if she figured it didn't matter now that he knew she was a woman, Gavin returned to his cot and sat down to try and process all the new information.

When she returned Gavin continued to wait at the cot, as he always had, until she pushed the first bucket to the spot that would allow him to reach it. Once she was gone again he retrieved it, realizing it was the fresh water, knowing the next bucket would be emptied and cleaned. He sighed, wondering why he hadn't realized before how significant that was. If a man had held him captive he probably would have just dumped the waste and not bothered to clean it, if he had even bothered to do that.

Gavin bit his bottom lip, wondering what to do next. Talk to her? Beg her to release him? Not say anything more and hope she carried out her promise to try to bring more food so he could get some strength back before thinking again of escape?

When movement of the light beam indicated that she was back, and then it was getting further and further away indicating that she was leaving, Gavin ran forward until the chain jerked him to a stop, though his heart raced on. He grabbed the light weight bucket that now smelled of bleach as tears threatened again. Unable to let her go without saying or doing anything to help his plight, Gavin struggled with allowing the words that needed to be said to pass his lips. "Thank you!"

The movement of the light stopped then circled around until it blinded him again. Gavin didn't look away this time although the pain made his eyes water as he squinted. He held his breath, hoping she would say something. Hoping she expressed regret. Hoping for anything that would keep him from being all alone for however long she'd be gone this time.

Disappointment nearly took him to his knees when the light swung back down to the dirt. It was clear she was done with him for now as the circle of light she held off to the side kept getting further away, and smaller, until he was once again in total darkness.

Gavin's entire body shook as he took the course back to where the slop bucket needed to go before returning to the cot where his legs gave out and he plopped down. He stared blindly ahead, wondering if knowing that she was a woman would make any difference to him.... Wondering if she ever planned to let him go....

ABOUT THE AUTHOR

JC Wardon loves writing fantasy and spends her days weaving stories for those who love it as well. Though she has great appreciation for romances, a juicy and complicated plot is what she holds most dear. Danger, mystery, and magic are the life's blood for her Mystic Waters Books. She hopes you are captivated and stimulated, and your hearts become engaged.

If you enjoyed *Mystic Thunder* by JC Wardon, consider telling others, and writing a review.

A special thanks to Sherri Sutherland!

Here is Ms. Sutherland's Homemade Apple Pie
(Printed with the permission of Ms. S. Sutherland)

Pie Filling
8-10 Granny Smith apples
1 1/2 - 2 cups sugar (to taste)
3+ teaspoons cinnamon (to taste)
1/2 cup flour

Peel and thinly slice apples. Place in large bowl. Add
sugar, cinnamon, and flour, mix together before setting
aside to marinate while making the crust.

Double Pastry Crust
3 1/2 cups flour
1 1/2 teaspoon salt
1 1/2 cup shortening
1 egg
1 tablespoon vinegar
5 tablespoons cold water

Combine flour and salt. Add shortening. Mix with fork
until dough is size of small peas.
    In separate small bowl, whip together egg, vinegar, and
cold water. Add all at once to flour mixture.
    Mix just until blended.
    Roll out half of the dough at a time onto a floured
pastry board (preferably), or heavily floured surface, and
place in pie pan. Fill this with the pie filling. (At this point it
will have liquefied some).
    Place the second half of the rolled out dough on top
and curl/press bottom and top dough together so that they
are sealed. (Can make a design while doing this)

Cut slits into the crust on the top, with a cross cut at the center, then brush top with egg-white followed by sprinkling on desired amount of sugar and cinnamon.

Place in preheated 350 degree oven for one hour, to one hour and fifteen minutes.

Available now in ebook at Amazon!

BLOOD MOON RISING
JC Wardon

In the beginning, before the time of man, there was a great battle between those angels who believed in One True God, and those who did not. At the battle's end, those who did not believe were damned by the Creator, destined to a life in the pits of despair with the leader of the revolt, the master of vanity, Satan.

But there were those angels who realized their mistake immediately. Filled with regret and repentance, they begged an audience with the Creator, prostrating themselves as they asked His forgiveness, even if they remained damned for all eternity.

The Creator looked upon those who had followed what was once His most beautiful angel into ruin. A God of mercy, as their repentance was sincere, He forgave all. As a God of justice, He knew a price was still required. But instead of damning the repentant, God gave them a sentence of eternal life in service to Him, cleaning up the wreckage He knew Satan would design.

Those few angels who had repented would be known as The Brethren, sheathed in physical form, commissioned to reproduce, and capable of magic. They were to become an elite army of guardians who would watch over and protect the Creator's newest creation. *Man.*

Now, many generations later, Satan's son has risen to a power so deviant even Satan fears him. Natas, the ultimate spawn of evil, is master-mining the cataclysmic destruction of mankind to prove he is greater than his own father, and of God Himself.

With the battle for all mankind rapidly approaching, The Brethren are desperately seeking the destined mates the Creator designed just for them. These women, once the mating ritual has occurred, enhance The Brethren's powers and become the vessels to reproduce the Creator's future warriors.

But the prophesied blood moons approach, the mates have all but disappeared, and evil is gaining ground on the earth. With so much at stake The Brethren know they must prevail with all haste, as time is rapidly running out for all.

Prologue

Riagan Absalom flew low over the ocean as fast as his large wings would carry him. His heart beat at dangerous levels, not because of his always heightened need for haste in the sleek hawk's body he preferred for solo flight, but because she was calling to him in a panic that terrified him.

For centuries, no, *forever*, he had waited for her, looking for her on every continent, in every time period, until finally, only a decade or so before he had come to the conclusion that he, the hereditary Prince of his people, was meant to spend an eternity alone, without his destined mate.

It was happening too often now. The Brethren never knew who their mate was, or what her gift was, they only knew that a life with that one special female was their required destiny. Together they were both stronger than apart. Their individual gifts, once harnesses and sharpened, not only doubled in strength, their lives were almost always instantly enriched with offspring which would bear one or both of the talents of their parents.

The lack of mates and offspring for centuries had seriously depleted the army. An army needed to protect those to whom the Creator gave the earth. With reports that Natas was raising his own army for a major onslaught against all humankind, and with the majority of his own brothers-in-arms still without their mates, he feared the world in gravest danger.

Riagan didn't know what had happened. His father, the first of the original fallen who had repented, had been promised by the Creator that mates would be created, one each for every one of the brethren. Since he didn't doubt the Creator for a moment, it meant that Natas and his *vamphere* were getting to the mates first.

It made him sick to think of it. The mates were pure. Females who would instinctively know that to lose their purity before mating with their destined master would cost them their place in paradise. Such degradation would be worse than death to these women. And the loss of them would be worse than death to each male.

Age held no meaning to the brethren except it was a burden to spend century after century in limbo while risking their very lives. Waiting and wanting that which they were designed to crave. Alone and lonely. With nothing more than an entire existence filled with nothing to look forward to; with only pursuing evil to pass the time. These burdens, after centuries, would destroy the spirit, slowly, until one after another of his brothers had sought the only escape available to them. They would seek that which they were sworn to destroy, and allow themselves to be slain.

Until recently.

Natas was as wicked as his father, or perhaps even more wicked as he'd been the spawn of two evil souls. Satan had once been God's beloved servant, and though he had done a stellar job of tempting man to sin, even he hadn't gone to the lengths Natas had to destroy that which the Creator made into flesh.

Now, somehow, Natas found a way to destroy the reprieve of death for the disheartened brethren by keeping them barely alive until continual exchanges of blood from those demons known as vamphere would turn his brother's silver blood, black. The brethren would then turn into creatures that needed human blood to exist. To deny the need would mean certain death and an eternity in Hell, with all the other forever damned.

Accepting that he would never give in to such a fate, thus accepting that he would spend eternity alone had been a bitter pill to swallow for Riagan. He, as Prince to his people had a duty to perpetuating his breed. To create a successor should he fall in battle. To help his brothers find their own mates even if he could not find his. And he had done his best to do his duty. To be obedient. To remain humble. To ignore that need that sometimes made him forget that his first and only real purpose was servitude, first to God Almighty, then to mankind.

The irony that the Creator had made him and all his kind with a physical need that was as strong as it was powerful sometimes felt like a mean joke. The need to breed, to share his seed, was absolutely necessary for his, and the brethren's happiness, he knew, and for all their well beings. Sure, he was capable of dalliances with human women if he felt so inclined, but none of those encounters would ever produce offspring, as children could only result with a true mate. And those encounters would not satisfy in any way that mattered. Only his destined mate could satisfy his needs, as he would be the only one ever able to satisfy hers.

But after thousands of years, she'd failed to appear. She'd never sought him. Had never even given him a hint that she existed. And now, after he had all but given up she summoned him. Not with the subtle scent he'd expected, but with so many pheromones filling his senses, as well as the universe, he feared that Vamphere would find her, too. Which meant he had to hurry.

Now that he'd found his way to her, there was no way he'd lose her.

Not to man.

Not to beast.

Not to the devil, himself.